"I'm going to steal that crown— whether you help me or not."

Noah wondered what he'd done wrong in his life to get mixed up with a woman like Sara Madison.

"You're crazy," he told her. But he knew that if he didn't go along with her featherbrained scheme, she'd probably end up at the bottom of one of Arizona's desert lakes.

"All right," he agreed. "You've got yourself a partner. But I call all the plays. And *I* get possession of the crown."

Sara realized she'd have to pretend to accept his terms. Later she would figure out how to extricate herself from the sticky web in which she'd become entangled....

ABOUT THE AUTHOR

JoAnn Ross wrote her first romance when she was in the second grade—a tragic love story about two mallard ducks. Since then, she has broadened both her subject matter and her audience by writing more than a dozen romance novels that have been published under her own name as well as under the pseudonyms JoAnn Robb and JoAnn Robbins. She lives in Glendale, Arizona, with her husband and teenage son, both of whom she fell in love with at first sight.

Books by JoAnn Ross

HARLEQUIN INTRIGUE
27–RISKY PLEASURE

HARLEQUIN TEMPTATION
42–STORMY COURTSHIP
67–LOVE THY NEIGHBOR
77–DUSKFIRE
96–WITHOUT PRECEDENT

These books may be available at your local bookseller.

Don't miss any of our special offers. Write to us at the following address for information on our newest releases.

Harlequin Reader Service
901 Fuhrmann Blvd., P.O. Box 1397, Buffalo, NY   14240
Canadian address: P.O. Box 2800, Postal Station A,
5170 Yonge St., Willowdale, Ont.   M2N 6J3

BAIT AND SWITCH

JoAnn Ross

Harlequin Books

TORONTO • NEW YORK • LONDON
AMSTERDAM • PARIS • SYDNEY • HAMBURG
STOCKHOLM • ATHENS • TOKYO • MILAN

Harlequin Intrigue edition published February 1986

ISBN 0-373-22036-7

Chapter One

There was definitely something to be said for a life of crime, Sara Madison considered as she dressed for work.

While she had never given the matter a great deal of thought, if asked, Sara would have guessed that criminal activities turned a person into a shifty-eyed, grim-lipped individual who spent every waking moment looking back over his shoulder. But that image certainly hadn't materialized in her case. On the contrary, Sara decided, since she'd begun her unorthodox association with Malcolm Brand six weeks ago, she'd never felt better.

Even Jennifer had noticed the change, commenting on it last evening as they shared a frugal dinner of macaroni and cheese. It had been all Sara could do not to let her sister in on the secret that very soon they'd be dining on filet mignon. But Jennifer had never been known for her discretion. Let one word slip and before they knew it, the FBI would be pounding on their door.

"One more week," she murmured, flicking a brush through her straight blond hair. "Seven short days." At this moment, it seemed like an eternity. She could hardly wait.

THE TALL, DARK-HAIRED MAN forged his way through the throng of peddlers, beggars and pickpockets filling the twisting dirt lane that cut through the shanties. An elderly woman who could have come from another time made her way from house to house, selling water from cans strapped onto her donkey's sagging back. Shabbily dressed men called out from doorways, inviting the American stranger into their shops to peruse their cache of French perfume, Japanese radios and American jeans.

Despite the abundance of smuggled goods, the sprawling Altindag slum on the outskirts of Ankara, Turkey, did not appear to be a place where multimillion-dollar deals were struck. But Noah Winfield had learned years ago that things were seldom what they seemed.

He felt a tug on his jacket and turned around, confronted by wide, dark eyes that were unnervingly knowing for such a young boy. Noah shrugged, reached into his pocket and extracted a handful of coins. The youngster grabbed at them, thin, dark fingers curling around the silver like claws. He ran off into the swarm of people without a backward glance.

"A few more years and he won't bother to ask," Noah muttered fatalistically, remembering the last time he'd ventured into these narrow streets. He still had the knife scar as a souvenir.

Although it hadn't been his first brush with death, it had been the most senseless. Noah still grew angry when he thought about having almost given his life for a pocketful of Turkish lira worth less than two hundred dollars. He had always known his way of life carried risks, but at least in all those other instances the stakes had been higher.

After leaving the hospital, he had wrapped up his business in Ankara swiftly and decisively. Then he had disappeared. Only a select few individuals knew of his rambling home deep in the San Juan mountains of Colorado. To the rest of the world, it appeared that Noah Winfield had stepped off the edge of the earth. He had his own reasons for wanting it that way.

"So what are you doing here, pal?" Noah asked himself as he ducked his head to enter the dilapidated coffeehouse.

When he'd first been approached to do this job, Noah had considered the outrageous scheme extremely dangerous and ultimately impossible. Nothing had changed. He still did.

But as he viewed his contact sitting in the back of the smoke-filled room, Noah felt his adrenaline surge. If there was one thing Noah Winfield thrived on, it was a challenge. And this caper represented the zenith of his career.

Mehmet Kahveci did not bother to rise as Noah joined him at the table. Nor did he look at the newcomer directly. His gaze continued to be directed at the billiard contest going on across the room.

Noah did not waste time on preliminaries. He slid a package of cigarettes containing a folded bill across the table. "When do I get to meet with Yavuzoglu?"

Kahveci pocketed the pack with the same swift dexterity displayed by the street urchin. "He's dead," he said in Turkish. "They found him this morning."

Noah muttered a short, harsh oath. "And the package?"

Black eyes briefly skimmed the coffeehouse, never once stopping to light on Noah. He refocused his attention on the billiard table. "That's difficult to say."

Noah reached into his jacket, pulling out a box of matches containing an identical amount of money, which he placed on the table. It immediately disappeared.

"His murderers do not have it."

"How do you know?"

When the man remained as stubbornly silent as the Sphinx, Noah reached into his pocket once again. A small Turkish/English phrase book immediately joined the cigarette pack and matchbox. Then, for the first time since Noah's arrival, Kahveci met his gaze.

"Because, my friend, it has already left the country."

"Damn," Noah ground out. His mind whirled as he debated what to do now.

The air in the small, windowless building was stale, ripe with the odors of onions, sweat and smoke. It was a far cry from the clean, crisp Colorado air Noah had left behind. And for what? A wild-goose chase.

Kahveci calmly poured two cups of tea. "It is not so bad," he advised Noah. "You Americans are always in too much of a hurry." He held out a heavy earthenware bowl filled with plump raisins. "Here—eat, drink. Then I will tell you where you can find your package."

Noah's cup stopped on the way to his lips. As he slowly lowered it to the table, he felt his hand begin to tremble and forced himself to relax. He didn't want Kahveci to realize how important his information was. If that happened, the wily Turk might decide to auction what he knew.

"How much?" Noah asked bluntly.

Kahveci popped a raisin into his mouth and appeared to be mulling the question over. "My daughter returned home from Istanbul last month. Her husband is out of work, so they are living with my wife and me. Did I tell you that I am now a grandfather?"

"Congratulations."

Sly black eyes twinkled, and Noah could practically see the calculator clicking away in Mehmet Kahveci's head. They'd done business several times over the years, and while Kahveci was expensive, he'd always proved himself trustworthy. In this business, in which lives were simply another commodity to be sold to the highest bidder, that counted for something.

"Little Vedat is a delightful child," Kahveci continued. Then he shrugged. "But who could imagine such an appetite belonging to one so young? I used to buy two kilos of meat each week. That was enough for my wife and me. Now, with my humble home filled to the rafters with hungry relatives, I am required to buy six kilos."

"How much?" Noah repeated.

"Ten thousand dollars."

Noah was not about to reveal that he had been prepared to spend several times that figure. "That's a lot of meat," he responded easily.

"I'm certain that if knowledge of the package got out, the buyers would be lined up at the door," Kahveci countered.

"Be careful," Noah warned, suddenly serious. "I wouldn't want Vedat to grow up without a grandfather."

Kahveci's smile flashed under his shaggy black mustache. "That's what I have always loved about you, my friend. You are so sentimental."

"Yeah," Noah grunted, reaching into an inner lining in the jacket. "That's me. Mr. Bleeding Heart."

The crisp thousand-dollar bills were clipped together in bundles of five. Noah carefully extracted two, keeping the remainder hidden. After plucking a raisin from the bowl, he slid the bills under the fruit.

Kahveci wasted no time in taking a handful of raisins for himself. Noah knew the man had been an expert pickpocket in his youth. That skill was exhibited by how quickly the money vanished.

"Your package is in America," Kahveci revealed. "Or will be very soon."

Noah's eyes narrowed. "Are you sure of that?"

The Turk rose from the table. "Very. By this time next week it will be in the possession of an Arizona collector."

"His name?" Noah demanded before Kahveci could leave.

"Brand. Malcolm Brand."

DEEPLY ENGROSSED IN WORK, Sara did not hear the door of the sun-filled studio open. She first realized she was not alone when a whiff of tobacco reached her nostrils.

"What do you think?" she asked. "Will it pass?"

Upon first meeting Malcolm Brand, Sara had found it difficult to believe the man controlled such a far-flung financial empire. Of average height, slender, with thinning white hair and an almost-frail appearance, he did not exude an aura of power. Then she had noticed his eyes. They were constantly alert, missing nothing—and hard. They had reminded her of two gray stones. Sara had decided that in Malcolm's case those steely eyes were indeed windows to a dark soul.

Malcolm chewed thoughtfully on the cigar as his sharp gaze moved back and forth between the two canvases. "You've done an amazing job. No one could ever tell which is the original."

"I like Rousseau," Sara replied, leaning forward to put a few touches on some overscaled water lilies. "He paints as if it's always Sunday. The light is magnificent, radiating from no apparent source, dreamlike. And the way he invented laws of perspective..." Her voice trailed off as she stepped back to eye her creation.

"Did you know," Sara continued conversationally, "that Picasso was quite taken with Rousseau? The fact that he discovered Rousseau's totally invented world in his passage from poetic realism to cubism was terribly important."

Malcolm laughed. "Ah, Sara," he teased. "Always the teacher."

A soft, embarrassed flush colored her cheeks. "Guilty," she admitted. "I do tend to run on from time to time. I'll try not to submit you to a lecture every time you come into the studio."

His eyes returned to the two canvases standing side by side. "Sara, dear," he said with husky enthusiasm, "so long as you continue to paint like the angel you are, you may lecture me all you like." He shook his head as if unable to believe his eyes. "You've accomplished a lot today," he noted, turning toward the door. "Why don't you knock off early? Surely there's some young man who hasn't been receiving enough attention from you the past six weeks."

Sara shook her head. "I'm not involved with anyone. But if you're certain it's all right, I *did* promise my nephew I'd take him to the movies tonight."

Malcolm waved away her concern. "Go, go," he agreed ebulliently. "Have a good time."

She began cleaning her brushes. "Thank you, I think I will," she said with a smile. Once Malcolm Brand had left the studio, Sara's blue eyes hardened. "Bastard," she muttered, glaring at the closed door.

Sara wondered who, exactly, they thought they were kidding. She had been amused when Peter Taylor had shown up at the university a few weeks ago, offering her a summer job. That amusement had given way to uneasiness when he related his knowledge of Jennifer's financial straits and offered to ease the situation with a salary double what Sara could make teaching the summer session at a local community college. She couldn't understand why this stranger had gone to the trouble of having her investigated.

Sara had begun to understand when Peter told her a tall tale about his employer, who possessed a valuable art collection. Apparently the man did a great deal of entertaining and was looking for an expert copyist to duplicate his paintings. Peter had asserted that the copies would be hung in the place of the originals at such times. A security precaution, he'd called it.

Sara had grown annoyed at the idea that this suave, sophisticated man considered her so naive. He had obviously bought the stereotype of the absentminded professor, assuming that since Sara dwelt in that ivory-tower world of academia, she was too dense to understand what was going on under her very nose. They wanted her to paint forgeries. For what purpose, she didn't know, but she certainly wasn't about to do it.

She had opened her mouth to tell him exactly what he could do with his checkbook when he revealed the name of his employer: Malcolm Brand, the man who had treated her father so ruthlessly many years ago. When he'd stolen the patent rights to an invention designed by Walter Madison.

Sara had immediately accepted Peter Taylor's offer. She had no idea what these two crooks were up to, but she was going to make damned certain that she would be the one to pull the rug out from under them.

It was after she had begun work that Sara discovered the existence of a basement vault filled with stolen works of art that Malcolm had been acquiring for years. Last week she had overheard Peter and Malcolm discussing the treasure that would be the crowning glory of Malcolm Brand's illegal collection. That information had proved to be the icing on the cake.

Ten minutes later, Sara was standing outside the library, unabashedly eavesdropping. Every nerve in her body was on edge, but it was imperative that she know exactly how much time she had to finish formulating her admittedly haphazard plan.

Malcolm Brand's voice displayed his impatience. "What's the latest on our recent acquisition?"

Sara recognized the voice of Peter Taylor, Malcolm's longtime assistant. "We've passed the second hurdle. It's out of the country."

"So we're still on schedule?"

"A week, ten days at most," Peter Taylor confirmed. "We expected trouble, so we're moving it through a circuitous route. That was an odd thing, really."

"What do you mean? I thought you said the job went off without a hitch."

Even without seeing him, Sara could tell that Malcolm had grown instantly alert. She imagined she could feel the electricity radiating through the thick mahogany door.

"It did," Peter allowed. "It's just that the item in question wasn't reported stolen."

There was a long moment of thoughtful silence. "It wasn't?" Malcolm asked finally. "Are you certain?"

"Positive. We've been monitoring that part of the world carefully. The only thing we've heard that might be of the slightest interest is that the dealer's dead."

"Did we do it?"

"No, he was alive when our men picked up the package. I wouldn't be concerned if I were you. It turns out that the idiot was also into growing flowers."

"He had a hand in the poppy trade?"

"It appears he did; dangerous business, heroin trafficking."

"Damn dangerous," Malcolm agreed. His voice cracked on a brittle laugh. "That's why I've always stayed away from drugs. Besides, you can't hang the stuff on the wall or display it under glass."

As Peter Taylor joined in the laughter, Sara tiptoed away from the door, her adrenaline racing. As she drove down the twisting roadway, heading toward the apartment she had been sharing for the past six months with her sister, Sara didn't know what excited her more: the knowledge that very soon she would be in possession of one of the world's greatest art treasures or that she was going to steal that treasure right out from under Malcolm Brand's nose.

In the past, Sara's dinner hour had been a quiet, calm time of reflection. Admittedly a creature of habit, she would return home from teaching art history at the university every evening at seven o'clock. She would open her mail and leaf through the advertisements while she sipped on a glass of dry California wine. After that, she'd change into something comfortable, then, humming along to the music from the Valley's FM jazz station, prepare a light, simple dinner. An omelet, perhaps. Or if she was feeling ambitious, a spinach salad with homemade croutons.

On the evenings she felt particularly lazy, she'd simply settle down with a peanut-butter-and-jelly sandwich and watch an old movie. She preferred period films from the thirties and forties—screwball comedies that were light, entertaining and gleaming with sparkling repartee. She also secretly adored thrillers, often setting her alarm to wake in the middle of the night to experience vicariously the heroes' spine-tingling adventures.

Her colleagues at the university would have been stunned to realize that quiet, scholarly Sara Madison would gladly forgo sleep to watch Alfred Hitchcock's spy thriller *Foreign Correspondent* one more time. Nor would they have suspected that she had seen *Casablanca* and *The African Queen* so many times she had lost count. Secretly, Sara didn't believe they were making men as they used to. After all, how could any man compare with Cary Grant and his debonair charm or Humphrey Bogart and his cynical machismo?

All that had changed six months ago when Jennifer had moved in with her seven-year-old son. While Sara loved her sister and nephew dearly, they had definitely disrupted her peaceful existence. As she entered the house with the box of pizza, she tripped over a baseball bat lying on the floor just inside the door. The pizza flew into the air.

"Kevin, I told you to put your things away when you come in from playing," Jennifer scolded, reaching out just in time to catch the cardboard box before it hit the floor. "Aunt Sara's apartment isn't as large as our house."

"Sorry," the young boy apologized absently, his attention glued to the television screen. The noise level in the room rivaled that of the Concorde.

Jennifer piled the thick slabs of Gino's take-out pizza onto paper plates. "It's really sweet of you to watch Kevin tonight, Sara. I know this will be the third night in a row you're stuck with him, but I promise to make it all up to you."

"That's what sisters are for," Sara assured her, turning down the television. Kevin looked inclined to complain, but he caught the sharp glance from his mother and smiled benignly at his aunt.

"Hi, Aunt Sara. I picked out a movie for us to go to."

"Oh? Which one?" Sara had fond memories of gentle Disney pictures but knew instinctively that was not what her nephew had in mind.

"The Ghoulies from Outer Space," he announced.

"Ghoulies?"

"You're going to love it. A bunch of extraterrestrials come down and take over Kansas!"

"Delightful," Sara declared. "I can't wait." She took a tentative sip of the wine Jennifer had just opened. It wasn't bad for something that came in a bottle with a screw top.

Jennifer initiated the long-running argument. "I still think I should have gone to work. It can't be easy for you, supporting all three of us."

Sara shook her head, wishing she could tell her sister that in seven short days—ten at the most—all their financial problems would be solved.

"You've only got one more year until you graduate," she pointed out. "Then you won't have to worry about supporting Kevin yourself."

It wasn't fair, Sara thought sadly, looking at the young boy who seemed enthralled by the sight of so many cars being wrecked only ten minutes into the television program. A year ago, Jennifer's life had appeared so idealistic. Paul Harrison, her husband, had been a successful young attorney; the three of them had lived in a lovely split-level house in Paradise Valley. Who could have suspected that he'd be killed on that rain-slicked highway? And if that blow hadn't been enough, who ever would have guessed that he'd cashed in his life insurance to enter into a land-investment deal that had ground to an abrupt halt when excavation crews uncovered an ancient Indian burial site?

Of the two sisters, only Sara had grown up with a need for independence. Jennifer had been the baby of the Madison family. Tiny and dark haired, she reminded one of a fragile porcelain doll. Everyone had always taken care of Jennifer. She had never had to cope on her own.

She was doing remarkably well now, however, Sara mused. Six months after Paul's death, Jennifer sold her home to settle her husband's debts. At Sara's insistence, she had gone back to school to finish the education that had been interrupted by marriage and motherhood. By this time next year she would have her degree in counseling and could begin to earn her own living. It might not be the luxurious life she had been accustomed to, but at least she would have the satisfaction of standing on her own two feet. In that respect, Sara considered, perhaps some good would come out of tragedy, after all.

"Wow!" Kevin's shout shattered Sara's introspection. "Did you see that, Mom? Two police cars just ran into each other!"

"I don't know what I'm going to do with him," Jennifer complained good-naturedly. "What ever happened to Captain Kangaroo or Mr. Rogers?"

"Obviously they can't compete with Mr. T." Sara cringed as she watched a Toyota bite the dust. The *A Team* might be terrific at solving crimes, but she couldn't say a lot for their driving habits.

"It's amazing how he's grown up this past year," Jennifer observed, lifting a wedge of pizza toward her son. The seven-year-old obediently opened his mouth, biting into the gooey cheese without taking his eyes from the riveting car chase. "I wish..."

Sara reached out, covering her sister's hand with her own. "I know," she said quietly.

Jennifer rose abruptly from the table. "Come into the bedroom and talk to me while I change."

Sara looked longingly at the pizza. Then, deciding that the last thing she needed was more calories, she followed her sister into the bedroom they had been taking turns occupying since Jennifer's arrival. They had worked out a schedule: Sara slept on the living room couch on the even days of the month; Jennifer, on the odd.

"I've got a confession to make," Jennifer blurted out the moment they were alone.

"You cheated on last week's exam."

Jennifer's lovely heart-shaped face was etched with worry lines. "Don't tease me, Sara. This is serious."

Sara sat down on the bed. "I can see that. Is it about Kevin?"

Jennifer began pacing the room. "No... Yes... Well, not exactly."

"Want to try that question again?"

Jennifer stared out the window. "You know that I was having trouble in my clinical-psych class," she said softly.

"I thought that was going better."

She nodded. "I went to the department tutorial service. They assigned me a wonderful tutor."

Sara still had not discerned the problem. "So?"

Jennifer turned, her eyes glistening with tears, her face crumpling in anguished folds. "So he told me last night that he's in love with me!" she wailed.

Personally, Sara thought it was about time. Jennifer was not the type of woman to be happy living by herself. "How do you feel about him?"

"I don't know." Jennifer sat on the bed beside Sara. "Brian is a wonderful man. He'd probably make a terrific husband. And he's marvelous with children—his field is child psychology. But I feel so guilty!"

"It's been a year," Sara reminded her sister needlessly. "No one could ever criticize you for getting on with your life." She offered an encouraging smile. "Besides, you haven't agreed to run off to Las Vegas with him or anything, have you?"

Jennifer's answering smile wobbled slightly. "Of course not. We're only going to study. Then perhaps go out for coffee afterward."

"I think that sounds marvelous," Sara pronounced firmly. "It's time you started seeing men again. Especially ones who can get you a passing grade in clinical psychology."

Jennifer laughed. "At this point in my life, that's even more important than looking like Tom Selleck."

Sara groaned. "Don't tell me..."

Jennifer grinned, looking younger than she had in months. "A dead ringer," she professed.

As SARA SAT in the darkened movie theater with Kevin, absently watching the aliens on the huge screen attacking Kansas City, her mind returned to her earlier conversation with her sister. If Jennifer married, she would no longer need the money Sara had planned to surprise her with.

It didn't matter, Sara told herself firmly. There was far more involved here than mere money. This was a question of honor—her father's honor. Malcolm Brand had cheated Walter Madison and ruined his career. Now, after all these years, the chance to turn the tables had dropped right into her lap.

When one particularly nasty alien began to devour a corn silo, Sara smiled, her mind projecting to Malcolm's expression after he discovered his precious treasure missing.

Chapter Two

The air in the apartment was rife with anticipation. It was always this way in the planning stages, Noah remembered. He had forgotten how danger could make his blood race a little faster, how much he enjoyed the thrill of the hunt.

As he leaned back in the chair, the damaged muscle covering his rib cage pulled, and he reminded himself that there were always two sides to everything. Danger had its way of demanding a high price. Nevertheless, he remained where he was, formulating strategy.

The two men could speak openly; the place had already been swept for bugs. Not that Noah had expected to discover any hidden listening devices. Thus far, it appeared that they had been successful in their efforts to keep the news of the theft from leaking out. In that respect, he considered, the death of the dishonest art dealer had been an unexpected plus.

"Here's your papers." A tall man sporting an iron-gray crew cut handed Noah a sheaf of documents. Daniel Garrett was an ex-military man who had refused to allow time to make inroads on his rock-hard physique. "You'll be posing as a reporter from *Art Digest* magazine. It goes without saying that you're well covered."

Noah wasn't surprised. After all, his uncle was the publisher of the prestigious monthly. While his family had never approved of his unorthodox career, neither would they do anything that might jeopardize one of their own. Blood was thicker than water. Or money.

"What makes you think Brand will even let me in the door?" he questioned skeptically. "I wouldn't think he'd want anyone nosing around right now. Especially a reporter."

"Brand possesses a fatal flaw; despite his fame and fortune, there's one thing his money has never been able to buy."

"Respectability."

"Exactly. It's always irritated him that the world he wants to gain entrance to so badly considers him nothing but a gangster."

"Which he is."

Dan nodded his agreement. "Of course. The man has been involved in every racketeering scheme ever invented; one of these days it's going to catch up with him."

"In the meantime, we're going to make his life a little more uncomfortable."

"That's the plan."

Noah leafed through the sheets of paper, studying his new identity. Noah Lancaster. At least they'd let him keep his own first name this time. That always made it easier.

"Provided you're right and these get me into Brand's fortress, where do we go from there? He isn't going to have the package sitting around in plain view."

"You've always been an inventive man, Noah. I trust you to come up with something."

Noah merely grunted a reply. Some things never change.

SARA SIGHED as she examined the morning's production. It was definitely not her best work. She was tired, out of sorts and had a blinding headache. It had been after two in the morning when Jennifer had arrived home, flying higher than a kite. Sara had dutifully listened to the ecstatic recital of her sister's evening, trying to respond with encouraging statements at the appropriate times. She was truly happy for Jennifer, but what she needed was a few hours of relaxation.

"Something wrong?" a deep voice inquired from the doorway.

Sara turned, managing a weak, welcoming smile for Peter Taylor. Although she knew him to be up to his tanned neck in Malcolm Brand's unscrupulous dealings, it was hard to hate a man who possessed Cary Grant's suave sophistication.

"I should have stayed home for all I've accomplished this morning," Sara complained.

Peter crossed the room to look down into her face. "You look a little pale," he replied sympathetically. "Perhaps you're coming down with something."

"I've just got a headache; I didn't get much sleep last night. With Jennifer and Kevin staying with me, it's like living in Grand Central Station."

"I've got a solution to that." He flashed Sara a smile so beautiful she almost forgot this man was the enemy.

She put down her paintbrush. "I'm all ears."

"Stay here."

Sara's eyes widened. "Here? In this house?"

He shrugged, the shoulders of his superbly tailored gray suit lifting with the gesture. "Why not? It's a huge house; there are plenty of empty bedrooms upstairs." Again, that encouraging smile. "I don't know why I didn't think of it sooner."

It was too easy, Sara reflected, seeking the trap. She had been trying to figure out a way to break back into the house after dark so she could determine how to carry out her plan. Now Peter was handing her the answer on a silver platter.

"I wouldn't want to put you out," she demurred, feeling that she should offer some token resistance.

He waved away her words, the gold cuff links at the wrists of his pristine white shirt sparkling in the bright morning sun. "Nonsense. Besides, I'm thinking of myself as well as you. I can't imagine anything nicer than seeing your smiling face across a breakfast table every morning."

"But what about Malcolm?"

"He'll be all for the idea."

"Are you sure?" If Sara were Malcolm Brand, she wouldn't want any invited guests hanging around the house for the next week.

"Sara, Sara," Peter said with a slight sigh, "surely you've noticed that Malcolm enjoys beauty. After all, he's spent his life surrounding himself with beautiful works of art." His look could have melted butter. "And if you won't think me too forward for saying so, you're far lovelier than any of his other acquisitions."

While Sara was undeniably flattered to receive such a smooth compliment from a man who undoubtedly had women falling at his feet, Peter's words tolled a warning bell inside her head.

"Peter, I wouldn't want you to think—I mean, I wouldn't want Malcolm to believe..." Her words trailed off as she felt the color rise to her cheeks.

Peter laughed heartily. "Darling Sara," he joked, his cultured voice shaking with laughter, "I promise no one will corner you in the upstairs hallway and demand you relinquish your virtue. You're perfectly safe.

"Look at it from Malcolm's point of view," he suggested. "You'll be able to accomplish much more if you're well rested. There's also the fact that you won't be locked into working a strict nine-to-five day. You can paint when the spirit moves you. At any time, day or night."

Night. He'd just said the magic word. She could search out her treasure while the rest of the house was asleep. What did professional thieves call it? Casing the joint. The entire scenario was absolutely, wonderfully perfect.

"I'll go right home and pack."

Peter rubbed his hands together, obviously pleased with the way things had turned out. "Terrific. Oh, and Sara?"

She turned in the doorway. "Yes?"

"Don't forget to toss in your swimsuit. There's nothing like swimming a few laps to work off stress."

Stress. Now *that* was a word she was all too familiar with these days. "That's a good idea," she agreed. "I think I will."

LATER THAT SAME AFTERNOON, Noah stood in the doorway of the studio, silently watching as the painter covered the canvas with swift, bold strokes. She was definitely something, he mused, his gaze leaving the painting in progress to skim over lush curves the terry-cloth jacket she had thrown on over her swimsuit could not hide. She was blond, ripe and delicious. She was also a damn good forger.

"Hi," he greeted her, curious what her reaction would be to an interloper watching her illegal task.

Sara spun around, dropping her brush in surprise. As usual, she'd been caught up in her work, oblivious to anyone and anything. Although how she could have missed this man's appearance in her studio, she didn't know.

He was, in a word, huge. Tall and broad, with muscles straining at the seams of his sport coat. His dark hair was thick, and although she suspected he'd recently run a comb through it, those unruly waves appeared to have a mind of their own. His eyes, in the golden afternoon sun, gleamed a brilliant topaz.

"Who are you? And what are you doing here?"

He did not appear at all put off by her challenging tone. "Noah Lancaster. I'm here to see Malcolm Brand."

"Well, he's not here."

"I can see that for myself," Noah answered reasonably.

While Sara couldn't define the feeling, this man made her incredibly nervous. "He doesn't allow just anyone to roam around the house," she replied briskly, inviting him to leave.

"Ah, but I'm not just anyone."

"Oh?" Her blond brow arched challengingly.

Noah couldn't miss the question in her tone but chose not to answer. "You dropped your brush," he informed her helpfully.

Sara's eyes dropped to the Mexican tile floor. She wasn't about to bend over and pick it up. Not dressed as scantily as she was, with this stranger's bold eyes focused on her.

"I've got others." She pulled the edges of the terry-cloth jacket together. When he moved toward her, the unbidden image of a lion stalking his prey came to mind, and she backed up a few inches.

When he was far too close for comfort, he suddenly bent down, retrieving her fallen paintbrush. "Here."

Sara hesitated, then realized she was behaving ridiculously. "Thank you."

Her tone was cool, polite, controlled—totally at odds with how unsettled she was feeling. It was as if, after keeping her feet firmly placed on the ground for thirty-one years, gravity had suddenly failed her. If she wasn't careful to hold on to something solid, she'd probably go floating off into space.

Noah didn't answer; nor did he make a move to leave. Instead, he just kept looking at her, his eyes probing as if to delve into secrets from her very soul.

"You'd better leave," Sara suggested finally. "If you'd like to wait for Mr. Brand out on the terrace, the view is lovely this time of day. The sun sets right into the mountains."

His eyes remained riveted on hers. "Thanks, but the scenery's fine right here."

This man was definitely no Cary Grant, Sara decided. While his tone was light and teasing, the message his eyes were giving her was something else altogether. He looked perfectly prepared to seduce her, right here and now, if given the chance. On the other hand, something else flickered in those tawny depths that appeared to be anger. What in the world could she have done to deserve that response?

She turned away, forgetting for the moment that she should not allow this man to view the copy she was making of Max Beckmann's *Acrobats*. Since Noah Lancaster's sudden appearance in her studio, Sara found herself identifying with the colorful allusions to sexual struggle and approaching war filling the chaotic painting.

"Do you have an appointment with Mr. Brand?"

She was tense, Noah determined, viewing her stiff shoulders as she turned her back to him, pretending to clean her brush. Too tense.

"I have a five o'clock appointment," he answered. "I assured the guardian at the door that I could find my own way to Mr. Brand's office, but it turns out I overestimated my pathfinding ability. I got lost and ended up here."

Sara glanced back over her shoulder, studying him carefully. His expression was absolutely guileless, but she knew he was lying. This was a man who always knew exactly where he was going. He might not be Cary Grant, she mused, but she'd bet Noah Lancaster could give Bogie a run for his money.

"It's a big house," Sara agreed nonchalantly. She returned to cleaning the brush.

As a thick silence swirled between them, Sara belatedly recalled the painting. She debated turning the easel to the wall but decided it was too late. She sought an excuse, any excuse, knowing it had to be better than the one Peter had given her when offering her this position. Whoever this stranger was, Sara knew he wouldn't buy Peter's thinly veiled story any more than she had.

"I teach art history at the university. Malcolm was kind enough to allow me to copy some of his paintings so I could demonstrate varying styles to my classes." Sara extended to him a false, sweetly innocent smile. "These are a much better visual aid than photos in textbooks."

She was a liar, Noah determined. But a lovely one. "You're quite talented."

Sara shook her head. "It's not a talent," she corrected. "Actually, it's more of a skill. Or a knack." This time the smile was genuine. "I adore art, but I discovered in my undergraduate days that I'm a totally unimaginative painter. I can, however, do a reasonable facsimile."

"It's more than reasonable," he argued, approaching the canvas. "In fact, it's downright uncanny. If you ever decide to turn to a life of crime, you could probably make a fortune selling your own forgeries."

His words hit a little too close to home for comfort, and Sara paled. Before she could come up with an answer, they were joined by Malcolm Brand.

"Mr. Lancaster?" Malcolm inquired as he entered the studio.

"That's me," Noah agreed cheerfully. "I'm sorry I was late for our meeting, Mr. Brand. I'm afraid I got lost in the labyrinth of hallways."

Malcolm's eyes narrowed as they moved from Noah to Sara and finally to the dual canvases standing side by side on their easels. A muscle jerked along his cheekbone.

Sara rushed in to dispel Malcolm's irritation. "I was just telling Mr. Lancaster how kind you were to let me copy your paintings for my classes." She didn't know which of them she was protecting—Noah Lancaster or herself—but she had to make the effort.

Malcolm relaxed visibly. "I wanted to send the paintings over to the university so that Sara's students could see the originals, but unhappily my insurance company vetoed the idea. It's fortunate that Sara is a superb copyist."

"She's amazing, all right," Noah agreed. He had not missed Malcolm's reaction and couldn't resist tugging the lion's tail. "I was just telling her that if she ever wanted to delve into the murky world of the art underground, she could make a fortune selling her stuff as originals."

The friendly atmosphere that had begun to be established disappeared like puffs of misty fog under a blazing sun. "Yes," Malcolm retorted brusquely, "I suppose that would be a possibility. Speaking as a collector, however, I'm grateful that Sara doesn't have a deceitful bone in her body."

Sara refused to acknowledge Noah's swift, mocking glance. He hadn't bought a word of that story, but who could blame him? It was nearly as flimsy as the one Malcolm and Peter had concocted to get her here in the first place.

"I'd better get back to work," she said.

"You do that, my dear," Malcolm agreed. "This gentleman and I have a lot to discuss." His eyes gleamed. "Mr.

Lancaster is a reporter for *Art Digest* magazine. My collection is going to be featured in an upcoming issue," Malcolm revealed with undisguised pride. He suddenly reminded Sara of a pigeon, his breast feathers puffed out to enormous proportions.

"Oh, really?" Sara inquired, meeting Noah's bland gaze. If this man was a reporter from *Art Digest*, she was Rembrandt.

A grin quirked at the corners of Noah's mouth as he noted Sara's disbelief. Suddenly, they were on even ground. Two liars caught up in an intrigue that was only just beginning. Noah found himself looking forward to the impending battle of wits.

As Noah drove back down the twisting roadway after his interview with Malcolm Brand, he carefully took in all the security precautions the man had employed to protect himself from intruders.

The house itself was situated atop a slight knoll—Noah refused to call it either a mountain, as Sara had done, or even a hill—and was completely surrounded by a block fence. As far as he could tell, electric wiring was unnecessary; an enormous pair of rottweilers had been let out at dusk to patrol the grounds. The two guard dogs would make anyone think twice before trespassing.

In addition, guardhouses sat at both the east and west gates. Anyone seeking entrance would be immediately stopped and questioned. There was one thing working in his favor. Once again, Malcolm had sacrificed caution for vanity. Instead of blazing mercury vapor lights to illuminate the property, he had opted for soft, muted landscape lighting in shades of blue and green. If someone was intent on hiding in the shadows, those lights would prove an enormous asset.

Noah pulled over to the side of the road and got out of the rental car. He stood looking up at the house for a long, silent time. It wasn't impenetrable, but it was riskier than need be. The moment he'd entered the grounds, Noah had entertained the notion that this job would have to be pulled in the daytime. While it still wouldn't be a picnic, at least he'd enjoy the element of surprise. With the package due in a matter of days, Noah was certain security would be increased. If Brand feared a theft, he'd be expecting it to happen under the cover of darkness. Daytime, Noah decided now. It was his best chance.

He climbed back into the car, grateful for the blast of icy air-conditioning as he started the engine. Although the sun had set, the temperature was still in the low hundreds. Misty mirages glistened on the black asphalt, remaining steadfastly out of reach, and he was forced to brake suddenly as a roadrunner raced across the highway, disappearing among the creosote and paloverde on the other side.

Noah glanced up into the rearview mirror for the third time since leaving the estate. The bronze Mercedes was definitely following him. Noah decided to allow it to continue. After all, reporters from *Art Digest* magazine did not go around ducking tails. He didn't want to blow his cover before he managed to hatch his plan.

As usual, Dan had been right on the nose when he had predicted Brand would gladly open his doors to a reporter from *Art Digest* magazine. The entire interview had been a piece of cake. The collector had informed the staff that Noah would be working around the house for the next few days, setting up camera shots, taking notes, getting a "feel for the place."

Noah smiled at the memory. He had told Brand that *Art Digest* magazine wanted more than mere pictures of famous paintings. They wanted to dig out the "essence" of the collector. That entailed understanding the man, learning how he lived, talking to his friends, as well as his employees. Brand had bought it—hook, line and sinker.

"You're right, Dan," Noah murmured to his absent partner. "The man definitely has one gigantic flaw."

He cast a surreptitious glance at the mirror again. The Mercedes was still behind him, but he couldn't view the driver through the heavily tinted windshield. He made a mental note of the license-plate number and vowed to call Dan as soon as he got back to the hotel. If Brand was going to start playing games, Noah wanted to make damned certain that he knew the names of all the players.

THIS DEFINITELY BEATS the socks off jug wine and take-out pizza, Sara considered as she savored the delicious lobster salad. The accompanying chardonnay was smooth and dry, and she knew it to be a good year. Malcolm Brand might be a crook, but he sure knew how to live.

"What did you think of Mr. Lancaster?" Malcolm asked, passing Sara a basket of fragrant, fresh-baked rolls.

I could gain ten pounds in a week living here, Sara thought, eyeing the tempting bread. She accepted, vowing to swim extra laps after dinner.

"I really couldn't say," she hedged. "He seemed nice enough, I suppose. He's different from what I'd always pictured a reporter from *Art Digest* to be."

"And how is that?" Peter asked curiously.

Sara shrugged as she buttered a pumpernickel roll. "I don't know exactly. I suppose some pale, skinny little guy with stringy blond hair and a sallow complexion."

Peter laughed. "Wearing a pair of wire-framed spectacles, no doubt."

"Precisely." Sara gave him an answering smile. Then a puzzled frown worked its way between her brows. "But Mr. Lancaster isn't anything like that at all. He's so big."

"Rather like a California redwood," Peter agreed. "However, he seems harmless enough."

Sara feigned sudden interest in her roll, layering on additional butter in an attempt to keep Peter from viewing the astonishment on her face. Good heavens, was the man blind? Noah Lancaster, whoever he was, was a great many things. But never, in a million years, would Sara ever be foolish enough to describe him as harmless.

"I've given him full run of the house," Malcolm surprised them both by announcing.

"Really?" Sara asked.

Peter frowned. "Do you think that's wise?"

Malcolm's jaw firmed. "I wouldn't have done it if I thought it unwise, Peter," he remarked smoothly, reminding everyone in the room exactly who was the employer, who the employee.

A dark flush rose up from Peter's white collar. "Of course," he agreed immediately. "I didn't mean to question your judgment."

"Good," Malcolm stated abruptly. "You know I don't like it when you do that."

Peter dropped his eyes to his plate, suitably chastised. Sara found herself almost feeling sorry for him. There had been no need to treat him like a rebellious child. Besides, Sara considered Peter's caution extremely sensible. How could they be certain Noah Lancaster was really who he said he was? She, for one, certainly didn't believe it.

"Did Mr. Lancaster show you an ID?" she asked casually.

Malcolm was appearing more annoyed by the moment. "Of course he did. What do you take me for, a fool?"

"Of course not," Sara replied. Peter flashed her a sympathetic smile. She had the feeling that at any moment both she and Peter would be sent to their rooms without dessert. "I was just wondering what type of press cards *Art Digest* reporters carried. I do hope it was gilt edged, with his name done in calligraphy."

"Actually," Malcolm revealed, "it was decidedly plain. White pasteboard and raised black lettering."

Sara sighed dramatically. "How disappointing. Another fantasy bites the dust." She made a vow to call *Art Digest* first thing in the morning and check out Mr. Lancaster's credentials. At this point, she wasn't interested in any more surprises.

Both men laughed appreciatively, and the mood changed to one more cordial as they began to discuss Sara's progress on the paintings.

After dinner, Sara burrowed into a leather chair in the library as she waited for the house to settle down for the night. Once everyone was asleep, she planned to study the alarm system hooked up to the secret vault.

Fortunately, Malcolm's library collection was as extensive as his art collection, and it had not taken her long to locate a book on early Christian art. As an art historian, Sara knew early Christian art was divided into two periods. The first preceded the Edict of Milan, in 313, by which Constantine the Great decreed official tolerance of the open practice of Christianity. The second period, and the one she was now studying, came after the year 313, by which time Constantine had converted to Christianity himself.

She was familiar with the Hellenistic origin of the art of that time, just as she knew of the Church of the Holy Apostles. Construction of the church had begun under Constantine's reign and had been completed by Constantius II, in what had been first known as Byzantium, then

Constantinople, and finally, Istanbul. The building had been more a mausoleum to honor the first Christian emperor than it was a church; the sarcophagus of Constantine had stood in the center, surrounded by memorials to the twelve apostles. The display unabashedly invited worshipers to believe their late emperor was the thirteenth apostle, which had probably been the intention of the emperor in planning the church.

Unfortunately, all scholars knew about the Church of the Holy Apostles was from a description by Eusebius of Caesarea; the church itself had been destroyed by invading forces several years later. At the time, no mention had been made of a crown installed in a special niche in one of the walls. Sara had read rumors, of course. What art historian or treasure hunter hadn't heard the stories over the years? But that's all they had been. Rumors. Until now.

Now she had proof. After overhearing the conversation last week between Peter and Malcolm, Sara knew, without a single shred of doubt, that the rumors that had persisted for over sixteen hundred years were indeed true. There *had* been a crown in the Church of the Holy Apostles. A glorious golden crown encrusted with precious jewels. And in one week's time that fabled crown would be hers!

Chapter Three

When he arrived at his hotel, Noah went directly into the cocktail lounge. He sat down at a table by the window, which gave him a clear view of both the parking lot and the lobby. Then he waited.

Less than three minutes later, the Mercedes arrived. A blond woman exited the car, flashing a brilliant smile at the parking attendant. Somewhere in her early fifties, she wore a silk dress, veiled hat, gloves and despite outdoor temperatures in the low hundreds, a chinchilla stole. Whoever the woman was, she was definitely not what Noah had been expecting.

He watched her enter the lobby, moving purposefully on shapely legs straight to the desk. In answer to her question, the clerk pointed in the direction of the cocktail lounge. The woman rewarded the clerk with another dazzling smile; then, wrapping the stole more securely around her shoulders, she headed toward the lounge.

She hesitated for a moment in the doorway, allowing her eyes to adjust to the dimly lit room. Easily spotting Noah, she proceeded to hone in on him with all the accuracy of a heat-seeking missile.

"Mr. Lancaster," she gushed, holding out a gloved hand, "you've no idea how absolutely thrilled I am to meet you."

Noah decided she must possess an endless supply of those smiles, for he had become the third recipient in as many minutes.

He rose, unable to refuse the offered hand. When he would have let go, her gloved fingers continued to hold his with a remarkably steely strength. He glanced down, eyeing the rings worn over the black silk gloves. An emerald the size of Vermont covered two knuckles.

"I'm afraid you have me at a loss," he apologized.

She laughed, a silvery musical sound that must have taken years to perfect. "Darling, you are so right." Her lush voice carried an Eastern European accent. "I've been horribly remiss. I am Baroness Gizella Levinzski."

She waited as if expecting the name to ring a bell. When Noah didn't respond, she glanced down at the table significantly. "May I join you?"

Noah decided that it would be difficult to turn the woman down while she was still in possession of his hand. Besides, he was undeniably curious.

"Be my guest."

There was a bit of awkward maneuvering as they settled into chairs across the table from each other, their linked hands almost knocking over his mug of draft beer. A grouping of marquise-cut sapphires was digging into his finger, and Noah tugged ineffectually. For such a lushly feminine woman, the baroness had the grip of a Russian weight lifter.

"Would you like a drink?" Noah offered, giving up for the moment.

Thick lashes that couldn't possibly be all her own fluttered their appreciation. "That would be delightful, darlink," she agreed throatily.

Noah found himself staring. This woman couldn't be real; she had to be Dan's idea of a practical joke. "What would you like to drink?" he asked finally.

The baroness stared at Noah as if he'd just committed a cardinal sin. "Why, champagne of course," she announced imperially. "What else is there?"

"What else, indeed?" Noah murmured. He gave the order to the waitress, who informed him that they didn't serve sparkling wine by the glass. Vowing to get his money back from Dan, Noah ordered a bottle of domestic champagne.

"Is something wrong?" he asked, noticing the way those full red lips had suddenly formed themselves into a small pout.

Immediately, the smile returned, and she patted his arm with the beringed fingers of her free hand. "Not at all. I'm certain that I'll absolutely *adore* California champagne."

You'll have to, lady, Noah responded mentally. He was damned if he'd let Garrett con him into springing for imported.

As she squeezed Noah's fingers reassuringly, the sapphires cut even more deeply into his skin. "Excuse me," he said, "but my hand is going to sleep."

"Oh, dear!" She immediately released him, but before Noah could return his hand to his side of the small, intimate table, the baroness began to briskly rub his fingertips. "Let me help restore the circulation," she offered helpfully.

Noah was never so relieved to see anyone as he was the waitress returning with the bottle of champagne. The diversion allowed him to yank his hand under the table, where he flexed his fingers, easing out the stiffness. Once the ceremony of opening the bottle was completed, Noah handed the tulip-shaped glass across the table.

"Bottoms up." No one was going to convince him this wasn't a ruse.

The baroness lifted the glass warily to her well-shaped lips and tasted the wine tentatively, as if she expected it to be laced with arsenic. One penciled brow lifted in surprise.

"Why darlink, this is not so bad, after all."

"You don't know how relieved I am that you approve," Noah stated dryly. He leaned back in his chair, taking a drink of his own beer. "Okay, lady," he asked abruptly, "why don't you tell me how much Dan paid you for this little scene?"

"Dan?"

"Yeah. You know, tall guy, gray crew cut. Looks like something out of a nineteen forties war movie. Garrett."

She shook her blond head. "I don't believe I know this Garrett. Does he look anything like Jeff Chandler? I adore those old movies, don't you? If I was an American, I would have voted for Ronnie because he made such a dashing naval officer." Her smile flashed attractively.

Damning himself for even going along with this farce, Noah couldn't resist asking. "Ronnie?"

Those huge green eyes widened. "Why, your president, of course, darlink."

What was Dan up to, anyway? "I suppose you knew *Ronnie* in Hollywood," Noah stated dryly.

Her lips curved into a reminiscent smile. "Of course."

"Of course... Lady, what are you doing here?"

She suddenly leaned across the table, her voice low and urgent. "I must see you. Alone."

This thing was getting wilder by the moment. Dan's sense of humor had definitely taken a weird turn. Noah decided the man must have been working too hard.

"Sure. You wouldn't want to hand over the microdot in plain view of those KGB agents sitting in the corner."

To his surprise, Dan's "baroness" paled visibly. Her eyes darted nervously about the room. "KGB?" she whispered, an unmistakable tremor to her voice. "Here? In Arizona? Are you sure?"

Something wasn't ringing quite true. A minute ago, Noah had been convinced that she was a twenty-four-carat phony. But he'd viewed that fear in individuals' eyes before. It was too unforgettable to be feigned.

"Hey, I was just kidding," he said quickly.

Her lips firmed, and she tugged her stole more tightly around her. "That is nothing to kid about, Mr. Lancaster."

He felt duly chastised. "I realize that. I'm sorry."

The smile returned like the warm desert sun after a summer rainstorm. "I forgive you," she intoned with a regal air befitting a baroness.

Noah had to ask. "Are you really a baroness?"

"Of course. At least I was, in my beloved Hungary. My family owned a vineyard in the Tokaj wine region, where the Great Hungarian Plain meets the Carpathian Mountains. Did you know that those slopes have been cultivated for grapes since medieval times?"

"I had no idea," Noah replied, feeling more and more like a guest at the Mad Hatter's tea party.

She held out her glass for more champagne. When Noah obliged, she took a sip, then continued. "Nine centuries," she reflected, her eyes misting slightly at some unrevealed memory. "For nine hundred years the Levinzski family's wine was world famous. Do you know that Voltaire praised our wine? That Peter the Great cherished it?"

"That's quite impressive. I take it you left when the Communists took over the vineyards."

"Those idiots," she spat out. "They wouldn't know a great wine if it bit off their noses." She tossed her head, finished off her champagne, then held her glass out for more. "I didn't realize California had a decent table wine," she said, eyeing the label. "It's really quite tasty."

"It gets better the more you drink." Noah refilled her glass again, wondering what it would accomplish if the lady got drunk before she told him why she'd followed him from Brand's estate. It was time to stop playing the gentleman.

"Why did you follow me here?"

She sipped on the champagne. "Because I couldn't get in to see you at Malcolm's." He didn't miss her use of the man's first name.

"You know Malcolm Brand?"

She smiled, a slim, secretive smile that brought to mind the Mona Lisa. "Darlink," she replied patiently, "I know everyone."

Somehow, Noah didn't think that statement as far off course as he might have earlier. Her next words chilled his blood.

"Just as I know the reason you've gained admittance to Malcolm's house. And his collection."

Her eyes flashed knowingly, and Noah realized that the baroness, whoever she was, was no joke.

SARA WAS ENGROSSED in the art textbook when she heard footsteps echoing from the hallway. She tensed involuntarily. *Don't be ridiculous,* she told herself. *No one suspects a thing.* She had managed to affect an air of relaxed calm by the time Peter entered the library.

"Sara, what a surprise to find you still up. After all the work you put in today, I thought for sure you'd be asleep."

"It's probably the strange surroundings. I thought I'd read a bit before going to bed."

"Malcolm has an excellent library," Peter agreed. "Did you find something entertaining?"

Sara closed the book, keeping the title out of view as she rose from the chair and returned the text to its shelf.

"Actually, I'm afraid I chose something quite dull."

"That's too bad," he commented easily. "Perhaps I could recommend something. I'm quite familiar with the selections."

Sara stifled a feigned yawn. "Thank you, Peter, but suddenly I'm quite sleepy."

"Then the book served its purpose."

If you only knew, she thought with an inner sense of anticipation. "I suppose it did," she agreed. "Good night, Peter."

She was almost to the door when Peter called to her. "Sara?"

He looked decidedly uncomfortable, and for a moment Sara feared he suspected something. "Yes?"

His hands were shoved deep into the pockets of his gray flannel trousers, and lines of concern creased his forehead. "Do I make you nervous?"

He was very perceptive, Sara realized. She would have to be more careful to hide her feelings when he was around.

"Nervous? Whatever gave you that idea?"

"I don't know," he admitted. "It's just a feeling I've been getting lately whenever we're together. It's as if you're afraid of me."

"Of course I'm not," she hedged.

"Then why do you scurry away like a frightened rabbit whenever I enter a room?"

Sara decided a half-truth was better than an out-and-out lie. "I have a confession to make," she admitted.

"A confession?"

Had his shoulders actually tensed? Sara wondered. What was Peter expecting her to say?

"It's not you I don't trust. It's myself," she admitted softly. She forced herself to meet his questioning gaze straight on. "You're a very attractive man, Peter," she said, "and at this point in my life, I can't allow myself to get involved." That much, at least, was true.

He seemed to relax before her eyes. "I'm very flattered that you'd find me a risk to your heart, Sara. Especially with the availability of young men out there who would jump at the chance to become involved with you."

Sara's answering smile was genuine. "You're certainly not old, Peter. Besides, I'm not really into young men. They all seem so shallow. You, on the other hand, remind me of Cary Grant."

A broad smile of masculine satisfaction split his face, and he preened visibly. "Really?"

Sara's smile turned to a mischievous grin. "Definitely," she assured him. Then, unable to resist the comparison, she tacked on, "It's as if you stepped right out of *To Catch a Thief*."

With that parting remark, she escaped to her bedroom, her heart pounding with excitement. In leaving so abruptly, Sara failed to note the startled expression on Peter's handsome face. His smile had vanished behind a mask of uncertainty.

He went over to the bookcase, easily locating, by its gilt-edged leather binding, the text Sara had returned. His expression grew decidedly thoughtful as he studied the title—*Expressions of Early Christian Art and Architecture*.

Blissfully alone in her room, Sara lay on her back on the bed, staring up at the ceiling. After the past six months of sharing her apartment with Jennifer and Kevin, she'd never again take privacy for granted. She allowed her mind to drift, and in her imagination the crown of Constantine appeared among the white plaster swirls.

It wasn't that she intended to keep it; she wasn't really a thief. Certainly not like Malcolm and Peter. Her mind wandered from its initial path. It was such a shame about Peter. She sincerely liked him. He was handsome and devastatingly suave. But more than that, he was also a very nice person. During the six weeks she had been working at the mansion, he had been friendly and thoughtful; he had even invited her to stay in this luxurious room. She wished he wasn't in cahoots with Malcolm Brand and couldn't help wondering how the two men had ever gotten together in the first place. They were as different as night and day.

Noah Lancaster, however, was a totally different story. Now *there* was a man she could easily envision as a crook. It was a simple matter to imagine him as a pirate, enjoying both his stolen booty and women with the same lusty pleasure.

That vision was oddly disconcerting, and Sara forced her mind back to her own treasure. While she had no idea how she was going to steal the crown away from Malcolm, she knew precisely what she was going to do after she had it in her possession. She would return it to the Turkish government, of course. What on earth would she do with a jeweled, sixteen-hundred-and-fifty-year-old crown?

No, all she really wanted to do was to deprive Malcolm Brand of the treasure he'd been seeking all his adult life. That, plus the fact that he'd be out all the millions he paid to have it lifted from the presidential palace in Ankara, would be sweet revenge for what the man had done to her father.

Of course, the Turkish government would pay a finder's fee—that's the way it always worked in cases of art theft. Sara smiled as she conjectured as to the amount. Certainly several thousand dollars. Maybe they'd go as high as ten. It would be nice to be able to afford a few luxuries. Lord knows, an associate professor's salary was nothing to shout about. Then there was her sister and nephew. Sara couldn't wait until she handed Jennifer her share of the settlement. Oh, yes, she considered, pillowing her head with her arms, it was all going to be so delicious!

Now all she had to do was figure out how to spirit the crown out of Malcolm's secret treasure room. She was an intelligent woman, Sara reminded herself. And she'd always been a big fan of both mysteries and spy thrillers. Surely she could come up with something before the week was out.

As she considered all the aspects of her problem, one unknown variable kept popping up. Noah Lancaster. Who was he, really? Was it merely a coincidence that he had arrived at this time? As the disconcerting image of a swashbuckling pirate returned to mind, Sara didn't think so.

The strident ring of the telephone jarred Sara from her sleep. She groped in the dark for the receiver. "H'lo?"

"Hello. Were you asleep?"

Sara could not mistake the deep voice on the other end of the telephone. Fighting down an unexpected surge of pleasure, she propped herself up on one elbow and peered over at the clock.

"Of course not. I'm always wide awake at three in the morning. I like to remain alert just in case the phone rings."

"I didn't realize it was that late." That was a lie. Noah was just not willing to let the woman know thoughts of her had been keeping him awake.

"I've got a suggestion," Sara said sweetly. "Use your next paycheck from *Art Digest* magazine to buy yourself a watch." She hung up.

Noah grinned as he held the disconnected telephone in his hand. Sara was just one more puzzle in a job that had already taken more twists than Brand's private road. But of the batch, solving the mystery of the lovely blond forger was the most tantalizing. The smile was still on his face when he fell asleep.

Two miles away, Sara tossed and turned, unable to banish Noah Lancaster from her mind. Damn him! She had been sound asleep, immersed in a blissful dream, sipping a piña colada on some scenic tropical beach, surrounded by a trio of attentive, sophisticated blond men who lived only to satisfy her every whim.

Since Noah's call, for some ridiculous reason, she kept picturing the two of them absconding with the crown and sailing off on the high seas. There was definitely nothing sophisticated about the reckless pirate whose dark hair gleamed sable in the sun or whose skin was tanned to the color of teak. They were laughing, giddy with the richness of their plunder. Suddenly, his eyes gleamed with a primitive purpose, and when his lips covered hers, Sara imagined the warmth of desire mingling with the salty tang of the sea.

"Damn him!" She punched her pillow, trying to force it into a shape that would encourage sleep. "Tomorrow morning, I'm going to find out exactly what Noah Lancaster is up to. Then I'm going to figure out what to do with him."

If he *was* here to steal the crown, she could always offer to cut him in, Sara considered. Not that she'd allow him to plan the actual theft; she had first claim. But it would admittedly be a comforting feeling to know that someone as large as Noah Lancaster was on hand in case anything went wrong.

The more Sara thought about that idea, the more she liked it. She was smiling as she fell asleep.

THE RISING SUN burned through the high, wispy clouds, turning them to crimson and gold as Noah drove to the mansion the following morning. Malcolm Brand obviously valued his privacy; his property was situated on the far fringes of the city. As Noah guided the car through the open land, the brown-and-gold terrain gave way to purple-hazed mountains. Paloverde trees dotted the scenery, their silvery green needles glistening in the morning sun.

At the sight of the white van bearing a Mountain Bell insignia, Noah pulled off onto the shoulder of the road and exited the car. The door of the van opened as he approached.

"What do you know about a woman named Sara Madison?" Dan asked in greeting.

"Not as much as I'd like to," Noah replied. "Do you have any coffee? I didn't take time to stop at the coffee shop this morning."

He looked around the inside of the van, seeking a coffee maker. The scene resembled the bridge on the Starship Enterprise; electronic equipment filled the small space.

"Coffee? On a day like this? It's gotta be a hundred and ten in the shade already," his partner complained. He poured a paper cup filled with ice tea from a large Styrofoam cooler.

"Drinking something hot cools you down," Noah said, nevertheless accepting the tea.

"I suppose that's something else you picked up in the Middle East."

Noah took a drink. It wasn't bad. Too sweet for his taste, but beggars couldn't be choosers, his grandfather had always said. "Among others. Why did you ask about Sara Madison?"

"Because I think she's in trouble," Dan reported.

Noah crunched an ice cube, enjoying the cool rush that filled his mouth. Dan was right, he considered. It was as hot as Hades in here. Even with the portable air conditioner.

"I'm not at all surprised," he answered, thinking of the copies filling her studio.

"Then you know she's after the crown?" Dan asked incredulously. "Why didn't you get in touch with me right away?"

Noah choked on a piece of ice. "What the hell are you talking about?" he asked when he could finally talk.

Dan gestured to a large reel-to-reel tape recorder. "I've got it all on tape. Taylor and Brand believe she's planning to steal the crown once it arrives in the house."

Noah muttered a disbelieving oath. "That's ridiculous. She's thick as thieves with those two. In fact, at the moment, she's running a nice little forgery scam."

"You'd have to paint a lot of pictures before you equaled the price of the crown," Dan pointed out correctly.

Noah cursed again, wondering what the fool woman thought she was up to. He took the earphones Mac offered, listening to the conversation that had taken place between Brand and Taylor this morning.

"I'd better get her out of there until I find out what's going on," he muttered, tossing the earphones atop a pile of extra tapes.

Before leaving, he pulled a roll of film from his pocket. He had photographed the baroness last evening, using the minute camera hidden away behind the face of his finely crafted Swiss watch. "Meanwhile, develop this and see if you can get any information on the lady."

"Sure," Dan agreed easily. "What's her name?"

"You're not going to believe this." Despite the lousy way his day was starting out, Noah couldn't help grinning.

"Try me."

"Baroness Gizella Levinzski."

"You gotta be kidding."

"That's what I thought when she showed up at my hotel last night. I figured it was one of your practical jokes."

Dan glanced down at the film in his hand. "What does the lady look like?"

"She's blond, early fifties, good looking, if you like the type," Noah answered.

"What type is that?"

"Rich."

"Very?"

"She could probably buy this entire state with just one of the rocks she was wearing last night."

Dan grinned. "Partner, that's my favorite type. Believe me, if I'd have run into her first, I sure as hell wouldn't have sent her on to you." The smile faded from his face. "What's the story on this baroness?"

"I don't know. She says she only wants *Art Digest* magazine to run an article about her art collection. But apparently there's already one larcenous blond after the crown; I don't like the idea of having to keep an eye on another."

"My heart's bleeding for you," Dan mumbled. "Here I am boiling in this tin can, and you're baby-sitting blondes."

"It's a dirty job," Noah agreed as he left the van.

"Yeah," Dan called out after him. "It's lucky we have you to volunteer."

IT WAS ALL NOAH COULD DO not to cut his morning interview with Malcolm Brand short. He didn't want to waste precious time listening to some egomaniacal racketeer waxing philosophical. He had more important things to do. Like interrogating that lovely forger Brand had working in his studio.

Ten minutes into the interview, Malcolm Brand's secretary announced an overseas phone call, and Noah was given his reprieve.

"I hope you'll excuse me, Mr. Lancaster," Malcolm apologized, reaching for the phone.

"Certainly," Noah agreed immediately. "I want to spend some time photographing the grounds, anyway. Perhaps we can talk again this afternoon."

Malcolm smiled. "Splendid," he agreed.

Less than two minutes later, Noah burst into the studio without knocking.

"I want to talk to you," he said abruptly.

"Good morning to you, too," Sara replied calmly. "By the way, there's something I forgot to ask when you so rudely woke me up this morning."

"That makes two of us with some questions," he countered.

She ignored him for the moment. "Exactly how did you ring my room? There must be thirty phones in this place, counting all the extensions."

"The phones in the guest rooms have private lines," Noah informed her. "I made a note of yours while I was taking a tour of the house yesterday."

She nodded, not particularly surprised. She had called *Art Digest* the moment the editorial offices opened this morning, and although they had confirmed the fact that they did, indeed, have a reporter named Noah Lancaster, Sara still didn't believe his story. In fact, what proof did she really have that this man was the real Noah Lancaster? He could be an impostor, she realized, wishing she'd thought to ask the magazine for a physical description of their reporter.

"You don't miss much," she stated coolly.

"That's right. Including the fact that you're dumb enough to think you can just waltz out of here with Brand's latest acquisition."

His words seemed to knock the air out of her lungs, and Sara struggled to retrieve her composure. "I don't know what you're talking about."

He folded his arms across his wide chest, his stance unmistakably intimidating as he glared down at her. "Next I suppose you're going to try to tell me that a text on early Christian art is light bedtime reading in your circles."

The color fled her face. "How do you know about that?"

Noah shrugged off her question. "It's not how I know about it that should concern you. It's the fact that Brand and Taylor know." He shook his head. "God deliver me from amateurs," he muttered disparagingly.

Angry color returned to flood her cheeks. "At least it's not as bad as being a professional!" she shot back.

He leaned down, his face inches from hers. "You're crazy."

Sarah held her ground. "Am I?" she asked. "Is it common practice for reporters from *Art Digest* to bug the house? Really, Mr. Lancaster, if that *is* your name, which I strongly doubt, you can't believe me to be that naive."

"Anyone who'd try to pull the dumb stunt you have planned is green as grass," he retorted.

A long moment passed as they glared at each other. Noah's scowl could have melted stone; Sara's strong chin jutted out defiantly. Finally, he remembered what he'd come in here for in the first place.

"Look, this isn't the place to discuss it," he said, straightening suddenly. He reached into the pocket of his slacks and extracted a key, which he handed to her.

"What's this?"

"If you can't even recognize a house key, how do you expect to recognize a sixteen-hundred-and-fifty-year-old crown?" he inquired acidly, scribbling an address onto a pad of paper. He tore it off, taking several additional sheets, as well, which he jammed into his jacket pocket.

"You know, you're absolutely irresistible when you turn on the charm," Sara said with saccharine sweetness. "Nice neighborhood," she remarked, reading the piece of paper Noah shoved into her hand. "A bit more class than I'd expect from a thief, but I suppose it lets you work close to home."

She gave him an angelic smile. "Tell me, Mr. Lancaster, do your neighbors lock up the good silver when they invite you to dinner?"

"You're a riot, lady," Noah countered. "Now if you're finished with your comedy routine, how about getting out of here?"

She tilted her chin defiantly, prepared to face him down. "What on earth makes you think I'm stupid enough to go to your apartment without a contingent of armed guards? I don't even trust you."

"Would you rather take your chance with Brand and Taylor now that they know what's going on inside that devious mind of yours?" Noah shot back. "Face it; they know where you live. Until I can figure out how to get you off the hook, you're a helluva lot safer with me than you'd be if either one of those two guys caught up with you."

Noah's gaze was hard and direct. "Don't tell anyone you're leaving; drive straight to that address. When you get there, lock yourself in and don't open the door or answer the telephone until I arrive. Is that clear?"

Sara stared at him. His stony face could have been carved out of the side of Mount Rushmore, but she could have sworn she saw an inkling of honest concern in his eyes. *Ri-*

diculous, she told herself. *That's just wishful thinking.* This man was interested in one thing, and it sure wasn't her. She'd been right about him all along. He was here for the crown. Her crown.

"What? No secret password?" she asked dryly as she turned to leave the room. "How disappointing."

Noah stared after her. He hadn't known what to expect when he confronted Sara, but he sure as hell hadn't expected her to get her back up like this. She was one tough lady. He wondered if she realized exactly how much trouble she could be in.

"Sara?"

It was impossible to believe that such a gentle tone could have come from the same man who'd been barking orders at her only a moment before. Sara stopped and slowly turned around.

"What is it?"

"Be careful." Noah's expression was still grim, but this time she knew she wasn't imagining the worry lacing his brow.

"I will," she agreed softly. Then she left.

Noah's sharp eyes circled the room, studying the paintings Sara had copied. Her level of expertise was that of someone who'd been knocking off forgeries for some time. The little fool. While Sara was definitely no innocent—her work for Brand attested to that—it was a quantum leap from forging paintings to smuggling government treasures. Didn't she realize the danger she was in?

Noah sighed as he closed the studio door, wondering what to do about Brand. The man already suspected Sara of duplicity, Noah knew that suspicion could billow out of control, like wildfire. He hoped that it wasn't already too late.

As he drove across town to the apartment, Noah wondered once again if Sara realized the danger involved in the life she'd chosen. The woman was the most appealing lady in distress he had ever met. But if someone didn't step in and save her from herself, she could also end up the loveliest corpse he'd ever seen.

There were only two problems. The first was that Noah had never thought of himself as a knight in shining armor. The second was that he was here in Phoenix to pull off the heist of a lifetime. And Sara Madison was turning out to be one complication he damn well didn't need

Chapter Four

Sara paced the floor of the apartment as she nervously awaited Noah's arrival. Her mind spun around and around in circles, like a leaf caught in a whirlpool, as she tried to decide what to do. Should she deny any knowledge of the crown? Or did she dare trust Noah Lancaster?

She didn't believe for a moment that he was actually who he said he was. Even though he had managed to cover himself at *Art Digest* magazine, there was every indication that he was nothing more than a particularly skilled thief. And if she was right, if he actually was a thief, then he was no better than Malcolm Brand. Still, Sara couldn't help feeling that under the right circumstances, Noah was a man of his word.

Why had he bothered to warn her about Peter and Malcolm's suspicions? Could he actually care what happened to her? Or was his motive a more selfish one? Perhaps he only wanted to prevent her from interfering with his own plans to steal the crown. He had certainly demonstrated that he didn't believe her capable of pulling off the theft by herself. Not that she hadn't made a stupid mistake.

"Dumb!" she muttered. "I should have taken that book to bed with me and slipped it back onto the shelf this morning. That way Peter never would have suspected anything. Dumb, dumb, dumb!''

She froze at the sudden knock at the door. For the first time since accepting Peter's offer, Sara realized this was no game. Malcolm Brand would not hesitate to rid himself of any obstacle that stood in his way of acquiring the long-sought-after treasure.

Noah's voice revealed impatience. "Sara, open the door."

Relief washed through her like a comforting balm, and she hurried to unlatch the double bolts and heavy chain. "I thought you might be Malcolm," she admitted as Noah entered the apartment.

Noah scrutinized her face, viewing the apprehension in her eyes. "So it's beginning to sink in, is it?"

He certainly didn't miss much, Sara noted as she crossed the room and sat down on the couch. If his interests were of a less larcenous nature, the man would probably make a crackerjack reporter.

She didn't bother to answer what they both knew to be a rhetorical question. "I was just trying to decide whether or not I could trust you," she said softly.

"And?"

She shook her head. "My mind tells me that I'd be a fool to trust you any farther than I could throw you. You're a fraud, a thief and heaven knows what else."

If he took offense at her words, Noah didn't show it. His expression remained unnervingly bland. "Why do I hear a 'but' in that declaration?"

"I've been asking myself that same question."

As she knitted her fingers together in her lap, Noah noted that her knuckles were white with strain. She certainly didn't appear to be the scheming confident woman he'd first taken her for. Those canvases back in her studio came to mind, and Noah reminded himself that appearances were often deceiving. The woman could look like Snow White and that wouldn't change what she had been up to.

He took a chair across from her, leaning forward, his forearms on his thighs. "Okay, let's start with your involvement with Malcolm Brand."

"I'm not involved with him."

"Yet you live in his house. Do you pay rent?"

"I don't *live* there," Sara objected sharply, recognizing Noah's gritty insinuation. "I'm simply staying at the mansion until I finish my work. The situation at my apartment is rather hectic right now, and it was interfering with my painting."

His amber eyes bored into her. "Is that the truth?"

"Of course. And I resent your even asking that question," she answered, with a touch of hauteur.

"You haven't exactly been a paragon of honesty, sweetheart," Noah countered calmly.

Sara flushed at the all-too-accurate accusation. How could she explain that subterfuge and prevarication were alien to her nature after what he'd seen thus far? The answer was that she couldn't. She remained silent.

"Look, you two are peddling forged paintings; you're living upstairs in his house. It was logical to assume that you had something going with the guy, okay?"

"It is not okay. And for your information, Mr. Lancaster—if that *is* your name—you're wrong on all counts. First of all, I am not involved with Malcolm Brand, romantically or any other way. Second, I am not peddling forged paintings."

Sara was ticking her complaints off on her fingertips. "And third, you haven't told the truth once since you showed up at the house yesterday." Her eyes shot angry sparks. "I'd say what we have here is a case of the pot calling the kettle black."

Noah surprised her by smiling. "Are you always this argumentative?"

Sara returned his smile with a falsely sweet one of her own. "I'm usually a model of diplomacy. You obviously bring out the worst in me."

Noah appeared to be giving her answer some thought. He slowly rubbed his chin, and Sara tried not to be affected by a sudden unbidden fantasy of those long fingers caressing her body. That entire idea was ridiculous; she had definitely been working too hard, she assured herself, seeking some answer to these unruly feelings she'd been experiencing toward Noah Lancaster. The man was definitely not her type. He was too strong, too overbearing, too male.

"I wonder why that is," he murmured finally, more to himself than to her.

"Perhaps I don't like people interfering in my business," Sara suggested acidly.

"That's one thing we have in common," Noah replied easily. "Look, honey, you've got a nice little scam going for yourself. Why risk blowing it sky high by getting involved in something you can't possibly pull off?"

Sara didn't like his patronizing tone. "How do you know I'm not capable of getting that crown out of there?"

"Then you're admitting you know about Malcolm's latest acquisition."

"I don't seem to have any choice, since you're obviously after the same thing." She studied him thoughtfully for a moment. "How did you find out about it, anyway? It's never been anything but a rumor."

"Let's just say that I have my own sources and leave it at that." His eyes turned hard. "I'm going to take it, Sara."

She met his challenging gaze with a level one of her own. "Not if I get it first."

Noah muttered a frustrated oath as he rose from the chair to begin pacing the plush carpeting. "Even if your cover wasn't blown with Brand, you'd never be able to pull it off."

"That's your opinion."

Secretly, after examining the detailed security system, Sara had begun to question her ability to steal the crown. But she wasn't about to let Noah in on that little secret.

He dragged his hand through his dark hair. "You're going to get in my way," he complained. "Give it up, Sara. Stick to painting forgeries and let the experts handle the tough stuff."

She was growing extremely weary of his assumption that she was nothing more than a scheming art forger. "I'm not painting forgeries," she repeated firmly.

"Of course you're not. You just get a kick out of copying expensive works of art in your spare time." He shot her a disbelieving look. "You can't possibly expect me to believe that cock-and-bull story about your being an art-history professor."

Now Sara was on her feet, as well, her hands on her hips as she stepped in front of him, halting his forward progress. She had to look a long way up to meet his eyes. "That's precisely what I am."

"So why aren't you in the classroom instead of hanging around Brand's fortress?"

"It's summer vacation, hotshot," Sara retorted. "Classes don't begin until the day after Labor Day."

He looked skeptical, but she thought she viewed a fleeting glimmer of doubt in his eyes. They were lovely eyes, she considered momentarily. A deep, rich golden brown that reminded her of gleaming topaz.

"I suppose you could be telling the truth," he stated finally.

"It's easy enough to check out." She handed him the telephone. "Call the university; they'll confirm the fact that I'm an associate professor in the fine arts department."

He returned the phone to the table. "That's not necessary. Besides, you could have arranged for someone to cover for you. It's not that hard to do, as you undoubtedly discovered when you called *Art Digest* magazine this morning."

Sara stared up at him. Did the man know her every movement? "I suppose you have my studio bugged."

Noah appeared unperturbed by her icy tone. "Of course. But that's not how I know you checked up on me."

"Then how—?"

He smiled. A wide grin that was strangely intimate. Sara found herself warmed by its glow. "Simple. You don't trust me any more than I trust you, lady. If I were keeping score, I'd put that down as one more thing we have in common."

"Along with the crown," she muttered, realizing that of the two of them, Noah was undeniably the expert. She doubted that if the man wanted something badly enough, he'd let anything or anyone stand in his way.

"Along with the crown," he agreed amiably.

A thick silence settled over them as each waited the other out. Sara knew Noah expected her to back down. She also knew she wasn't going to. She had waited years for a chance to avenge the wrong Malcolm Brand had done to her father; she wasn't about to let Noah Lancaster ruin her moment of triumph.

"It seems we're at a stalemate," she said finally.

"It seems so."

"What do you suggest we do?"

"We could always make it a contest," he suggested. "Winner take all."

Sara knew from Noah's self-assured tone that he fully expected to emerge the victor. "I suppose we could do that," she replied unenthusiastically.

Why didn't the man just go find something else to steal? Like the Hope Diamond. Or the British crown jewels. There were plenty of career opportunities out there for a professional thief. Why did he have to insist on her crown?

"You could always go somewhere else," Sara suggested hopefully. "I've heard the Riviera is lovely this time of the year; surely you could find something appealing. And jewels are so much easier to fence than works of art." Sara complimented herself on remembering the proper jargon. Years of reading mysteries hadn't gone unrewarded.

"I could," he agreed. "But to tell you the truth, I've developed a particular fancy for those sparkling jewels in Constantine's crown."

"You're not going to destroy it!"

When she seemed honestly shocked by that idea, Noah grew even more puzzled. She couldn't be planning to sell it intact. The risks were far too great for an amateur; she'd only end up getting herself killed. Now he was going to have to make certain he succeeded in getting the damn crown in order to save this dizzy blonde from herself.

"What were *you* going to do with it?" he asked, dreading her answer.

"Give it back to the Turkish government, of course."

"You're going to risk your dumb neck to steal it simply to turn around and give it back again?"

There he was, casting aspersions on her intelligence again. Sara was growing extremely tired of Noah's high-handed attitude.

"Not exactly."

"Not exactly?" he roared. "What the hell kind of answer is that?"

She shrugged, averting his incredulous expression. "Not that I have to tell you anything, but I plan to collect a finder's fee."

He shook his head. "That still doesn't make any sense. The stones in that crown are worth millions more than any finder's fee you could possibly ever get. In fact, you could earn more than that with one of your forgeries."

He came up behind her, taking hold of her shoulders to turn her around. "What are you really up to, Sara Madison?" he asked softly.

Sara dropped her gaze to the floor, her mind going into overdrive to come up with a logical-sounding explanation. Noah cupped her chin with the fingers of his right hand, compelling her gaze to his. His thumb brushed lightly beneath her lower lip.

"The truth this time, Sara," he demanded softly.

His touch was scattering sparks on her skin, and Sara was stunned by the sensuality she suddenly viewed in the swirling brown depths of his eyes. When those treacherous fingers began to stroke her throat, his thumb rested over her pulse spot, and Sara knew it would be impossible for him to miss the sudden, wild beating of her heart.

A ghost of a smile hovered at the corners of his lips. "Would it kill you to trust me?" he asked in a tone that reminded her of ebony velvet—rough and soft at the same time.

"I could ask you the same question." Though barely a whisper, her voice was easily heard in the suddenly intimate atmosphere pervading the room.

Sara felt suddenly bereft as he released her, returning to sprawl in the chair, his arms folded behind his head, his long legs spread out in front of him. "You could," he agreed amiably, behaving as if that shared golden moment had never occurred. "So, it looks as if we're back to square one."

She was feeling both foolish for nearly succumbing to a seductive moment and angry that the man still believed her to be a woman of scant principles. Sara decided against defending herself any longer. What did she care what this overbearing giant thought of her? She didn't care beans about his approval. Sara sighed inwardly, realizing that prevarication was a dangerous habit. Now she was even starting to lie to herself.

She settled back down on the couch, crossing her legs with a fluid gesture that momentarily captured Noah's attention. Sara experienced a surge of feminine satisfaction as his eyes moved down her calf. So the man was human, after all. Interesting.

"We could work together," she suggested, making an exaggerated project of tugging her skirt over her knees. His eyes remained directed along the length of her long, tanned leg.

"I don't need a partner."

Sara swung her foot idly. "I don't know what you have planned, but surely it would be easier if you had someone on the inside."

At her words, Noah dragged his gaze from her shapely ankle to her face. "You're forgetting that your cover is blown to smithereens as of last night. I have a feeling that you're persona non grata around that household at the moment."

She linked her fingers together around her knees. "Suppose I can fix that?" she suggested with a casualness she was far from feeling.

Sara smiled inwardly as his gaze returned to her legs. "How do you plan to do that?"

"Simple. I'll admit to Peter that I know about the crown and want to be cut in on the deal."

His eyes jerked back to hers. "That's the dumbest idea you've come up with yet!"

"Flattery will get you nowhere." She rose from the couch, moving across the room in long, graceful strides to perch on the arm of his chair. "Just hear me out," she coaxed prettily.

He shook his head. "I've already heard more than I want to. It's too damn dangerous."

"Please listen, Noah." Sara reached out, brushing back a dark wave that had fallen onto his forehead. Her touch was as light as a feather, but when she began to speak again, her voice trembled with unmasked emotion. "I've waited years for this opportunity; I'm not going to let a little danger stand in my way."

"A little danger?" he asked incredulously. "Sweetheart, you are downright certifiable. You're not in the minor leagues any longer; these guys play hardball."

Her fingers trailed down his arm, coaxing acquiescence. "All I need is a coach. Besides, Peter isn't at all like Malcolm. He'd never do anything to hurt me; he likes me."

"In case you've forgotten, he's the one who turned you in this morning," Noah pointed out. His mouth firmed into a grim line. "No way. You're staying out of there if I have to tie you up and sit on you."

Sara expelled an exasperated sigh. Realizing that feminine persuasion definitely had its limits, she rose from the arm of the chair and stood in front of him.

"Noah, I'm going to steal that crown whether you help me or not. You have to believe that."

He dragged his hand through his hair, wondering what he'd done wrong in his life to get mixed up with Sara Mad-

ison. She could test the patience of a saint. And no one had
ever offered up that description of him.

"You're crazy," he said flatly.

"I'm committed," she corrected.

"Now *that's* an idea. You should *be* committed. Into
some nice, quiet sanitarium with rubber rooms."

She was as crazy as a bedbug, Noah told himself. And he
was as loosely wrapped as she was to even be considering her
proposal. Working with Sara would be like playing catch
with a loaded hand grenade. The question was not *if* the
damn thing would go off but *when*.

But if he didn't go along with her featherbrained scheme,
she'd undoubtedly end up at the bottom of one of Arizona's desert lakes. Left to her own devices, this maddeningly
stubborn woman was a homicide just waiting to happen.

"All right," he agreed brusquely. "You've got yourself
a partner. But I call all the plays."

Sara smiled, vowing to be magnanimous in her victory.
Besides, Noah certainly didn't look at all pleased with the
prospect; there was no point in antagonizing him any further.

"Agreed," she replied without hesitation.

He had to know that she was willing to accept his instructions without qualification. But their lives could very
well depend on that.

"And since your only interest is a finder's fee," he continued, "I get sole possession of the crown."

Sara gasped. She had just made another fatal mistake in
judgment. Of course, Noah would have no intention of returning the crown to the proper authorities. What on earth
had she gotten herself into?

Noah's voice broke into Sara's unhappy thoughts. "I'm
waiting for an answer."

"Are you really going to destroy it just for the jewels?" she asked weakly.

"This isn't a negotiable part of the contract, Sara. I promise you'll be well paid. But either you hand the crown over to me without question or find yourself another partner."

Sara knew it was not an idle threat. She'd have to pretend to go along and figure out how to extricate herself from this sticky web she'd managed to get herself entangled in later. She had every intention of returning the crown to its rightful owner. The problem was how to convince Noah to see the light. Sara decided she'd take a page from Scarlett O'Hara's book and think about that little dilemma tomorrow.

"All right," she agreed on a rippling sigh. "You've got yourself a deal."

Noah nodded with overt satisfaction as he extended his hand to her. "Want to shake on it?"

It was more a command than a request, and as Sara obediently accepted his handshake, she understood that she had given him much more than her hand. She had just put her life in the hands of a stranger, a man whose true identity she didn't even know.

"I don't even know what to call you," she complained.

"I've always answered to Noah."

"Is that your real name?" *Please don't lie about this,* her blue eyes begged him.

"My mother gave it to me," he assured her with a smile. "Before I was born. The name's been given to the firstborn son in my family for four generations."

That made her feel a little better. The man had a mother. And a family with traditions. How bad could he be? When Ma Barker came immediately to mind, Sara wished she hadn't asked herself that particular question.

"What about your last name?"

His face shuttered. "You're just going to have to trust me on some things."

"I do," she lied.

His tawny eyes searched her face, seeking answers to questions that for the moment remained unasked. Finally, remembering he was still holding her hand, Noah released her.

"Okay," he said gruffly, "let's get down to work."

AN HOUR AND A HALF LATER, Noah was sitting in the van at the bottom of the hill, waiting for Sara to confront Peter Taylor. He still thought it was a stupid idea, but Sara had been adamant. She had to reestablish her credibility with Malcolm, and she had argued that this was the best way to do it. After all, if Noah was so willing to believe she was capable of larceny, why wouldn't Peter also accept her story?

As she stood outside Peter Taylor's office door, Sara dried her moist palms on her skirt, wondering how an ice-cold hand could perspire. Then she knocked, at first tentatively, then with increased vigor.

"Come in."

He looked up as she entered, his eyes narrowing slightly. "Sara," he greeted her easily, "what can I do for you?"

She stopped in front of the wide mahogany desk, twisting her fingers together behind her back. She didn't want Peter to see how badly her hands were shaking.

"I think we need to talk."

He gestured toward a chair. "I agree. Should I call Malcolm in?"

The suggestion caused her blood to run a little colder, and Sara struggled to maintain her composure. "If you don't mind, Peter, I'd like to talk privately first. Then you can decide whether or not to bring Malcolm into this."

He picked up a pencil, toying with it absently as he appeared to be studying her words. Sara realized she was holding her breath.

"You work for Malcolm," he reminded her. "Any problem should be taken up with him."

Sara took the chair Peter offered, leaning toward him, her body tensed into a straight line. "I don't believe we need bother Malcolm with this. After all, what he doesn't know won't hurt him, now, will it?" She smiled her most beguiling smile.

Eavesdropping on the conversation back at the van, Noah curled his hands into anxious fists as he awaited Peter's answer. He'd blow the entire job if he had to break into Taylor's office, but if the man laid one hand on Sara, that was exactly what he'd do.

Peter's fingers tightened around the ends of the pencil. "You're treading in dangerous waters, Sara," he commented quietly.

She rose, unable to sit still any longer. "I resent the fact that you consider me nothing but a dumb blond airhead."

"Where on earth did you get that idea?" He sounded honestly confused.

Sara shook her head and gave an unfeminine snort. "Really, Peter, if you ever decide to try your hand at writing, I think you'd be a natural for fiction. Especially fairy tales."

"I'm afraid you've lost me," Peter stated patiently. "Why don't you just start at the beginning, Sara, and we'll see if we can untangle your rather muddled thinking."

She crossed her arms over her chest, mentally crossing her fingers, as well. "All right. I know that you lied to me about painting those copies. I also know what you plan to do with them.''

When his fingers tightened even more, Sara wondered if Peter was imagining them around her neck. "I told you, Malcolm is concerned about the possibility of theft. He does a great deal of entertaining and wants to hang your copies in place of the originals whenever the house is filled with strangers.''

Sara fleetingly considered that she might have a career in acting. She couldn't believe how well this was going! She wondered if Noah was proud of her.

"That's a lot of baloney, and you know it,'' she argued, returning her mind to her performance. "You're using my reproductions to smuggle Malcolm's paintings into the galleries.''

"You don't smuggle paintings *into* galleries, Sara, dear,'' Peter pointed out smoothly. "If you're into things like art theft, you smuggle them *out*.''

Sara held her ground. *Are you paying attention?* she mentally asked Noah, knowing he was listening to every word. *Because this'll knock your socks off.*

"Not if you're planning to auction off some of those stolen paintings you've got stashed down in the basement vault.''

A loud crack shattered the expectant silence, and both pairs of eyes moved to the broken yellow ends of the pencil.

"You've got a lively imagination, Sara,'' Peter said quietly. "I'd be careful if I were you. It could end up getting you in trouble.''

Noah half rose from the carton he was sitting on, preparing to run for the car. He'd known all along that Sara's plan was ridiculous. When on earth had he started listening to amateurs? Especially the female kind? It had admittedly come as a surprise that she hadn't actually been painting forgeries. He wondered why she hadn't just told him that she'd been recruited to copy those paintings. He also wondered if she was right about Brand's motive.

"I certainly wouldn't want to get into trouble," Sara assured Peter sincerely. "Actually, to tell you the truth, I want in, Peter."

"You've been working too hard; it's obviously done something to your mind."

Sara shook her head as she began to press her case. "It could work out perfectly. You have the contacts to acquire the paintings as well as connections with potential buyers. And I have the skills to create near-perfect replicas of paintings that are safe to auction."

She grinned, appearing to be thoroughly caught up in the idea. "In fact, I'll bet I could even invent some paintings no one even knew existed just by copying styles. We'll 'discover' paintings." She clapped her hands. "Peter, it could be so exciting."

She sat on the edge of his desk, her eyes liquid blue pools as she sought to convince him. "I'm so bored with teaching dry facts day after day, year after year. I'm sick of living in a tiny garden apartment when I could be living in a penthouse at the top of Camelback Towers. And my six-year-old compact is running on sheer necessity. I want a Porsche, Peter." A dreamy expression resembling a blend of greed and lust came over her face. "No, make that a Ferrari. A fire-engine-red Ferrari. And a Rolls for weekend drives to the mountains."

Noah was disconcerted by exactly how convincing Sara sounded when listing the ways she intended to spend her ill-gotten gains. If he didn't know better, he'd think she'd just stopped acting.

Peter stared at Sara as if seeing her for the first time. "You are indeed a paradox, Sara Madison," he murmured. "When I first met you, I took you for a Girl Scout."

Sara leaned toward him, her voice smoky and seductive. "I'm not a girl, Peter. I'm a woman. With a woman's needs and desires."

Now she was definitely going too far, Noah decided. Why didn't she just rip off her clothes and jump into the sack with the guy while she was at it? Who the hell did she think she was, Mata Hari?

Peter cleared his throat. "I'm beginning to see that." His eyes took a long, leisurely tour of her, from the top of her blond head right down to her toes and back up again. Sara's smile was beatific.

She had to fight to keep from cheering as Peter appeared to be seriously considering the matter. "I assume you'd want to keep this little arrangement between the two of us," he suggested.

"Can you see any reason to split all that lovely money three ways?"

Peter shook his head, giving her a wry grin. "You are one surprise after another, sweetheart."

Sara's eyes lit with a bright gleam. "Do you think you can handle one more?"

His eyes narrowed. "I'm not certain. Why don't you try me?"

She licked her lips, drawing his gaze to her mouth. When assured she had Peter Taylor's full attention, she murmured, "I think we should steal the crown, Peter. And then go away somewhere warm and tropical. Together."

"Dammit!" Noah shouted, causing Dan to jerk his head up from a recent issue of *Playboy* magazine. "She's doing it again. If she gets out of there alive, I've a good mind to turn her over my knee."

"Interesting letter about that in here this month," Dan offered helpfully. "Want to read it?"

"I want her to stop playing games," Noah muttered. "Why the hell doesn't she act like an art-history professor?"

"Exactly how is an art-history professor supposed to act?"

Noah shook his head. "I don't know. Proper. Sensible. This one would drive a man up the wall."

"Sounds as if she's gotten under your skin."

"That's ridiculous. I just don't want her blowing our heist."

"Sounds reasonable enough to me," Dan said agreeably, returning to his magazine.

At the mansion, the silence continued for a very long time while Peter stared at Sara, who was struggling not to flinch under his sharp scrutiny.

"So I was right. You do know about it."

"I do. And I don't understand why you're willing to risk going to prison for Malcolm Brand. He treats you abominably."

"Malcolm and I go back a long way."

Sara sighed as she slid off the desk. "Well, I suppose that's that," she replied briskly. "Thanks for your time, Peter; I'd better go pack."

"Pack?"

She offered a regretful little smile. "There's no longer any reason for me to hang around, is there?"

"You knew all along, didn't you?" he asked with grudging admiration.

"Not in the beginning. I only knew you weren't telling me the truth. Malcolm is having to sell off a batch of stolen paintings to pay for the crown, isn't he? Paintings that are going to be hidden behind my copies."

"You are not only beautiful, Sara, but astute, as well."

"Thank you, kind sir." She dropped into a mock curtsy. *What do you think of that?* she asked Noah silently. *Someone thinks I'm astute.*

"Did you mean it?" Peter asked suddenly.

"Mean what?"

"That you'd go away with me."

Sara considered that she had lied more in the past few weeks than she had in her entire life. Today she seemed to be going for the record.

"Of course," she replied without hesitating a heartbeat's length of time.

"Sara, you've got yourself a deal," Peter said after a long, thoughtful pause.

Her eyes widened. "You're kidding."

Peter Taylor's composure had returned. "Not at all. We're going to take the crown, Sara. Together."

Her head was spinning as she considered how this morning she'd been worrying about how to go about stealing the crown. Suddenly, she had two partners, both of them professionals. How was that for luck?

"I can't wait."

He held out his arms. "Shouldn't we at least seal our partnership with a kiss?"

Sara was saved by the intercom, announcing Malcolm's arrival outside Peter's office. She flashed him a regretful smile. "I'm sorry, Peter. But we'll have lots of time for that once we reach our island." She blew him a kiss, then exited the room, nodding pleasantly to an overtly curious Malcolm Brand as she passed.

Chapter Five

Back at the van, Noah continued to eavesdrop on the conversation between Peter Taylor and Malcolm Brand, relieved when the younger man deftly covered for Sara, exonerating her from having any knowledge of the crown. Despite Sara's success, something bothered him. It had been too easy.

That nagging little doubt continued to tease at Noah's mind as he drove up the winding hillside road to the estate. When he entered the studio, Sara greeted him with a broad smile.

"I told you I could do it! When all this is over, I may move to Hollywood and turn my acting talents to the movie business. What do you think?"

Noah's expression was serious, a direct contrast to her celebratory mood. "I think you'd better give it some more thought before you pack your bags."

"Spoilsport," she complained. "You're just irritated because an *amateur* upstaged you." She grinned impishly.

He repeated the thought that had been running through his mind ever since Sara's admittedly talented performance. "It was too damn easy."

Sara's smile faded. "Boy, are you terrific for a person's ego."

Noah felt a stab of guilt for bursting her bubble. But Sara was too impulsive for her own good. She rushed into things full speed ahead, damn the torpedoes. While he certainly hadn't volunteered for the job, it was going to be his responsibility to keep her pretty neck safe.

She turned away to stare out the French doors. A cactus wren was busily repairing its nest in a tall saguaro, while nearby a jackrabbit browsed on a succulent grouping of wildflowers. Sara envied their uncomplicated existences.

She could feel the heat of Noah's body as he came up behind her; it was as if she were suddenly wrapped in a warm cocoon of pleasure. *This is ridiculous,* she told herself firmly. *You don't even like the man.* Another lie, she admitted. The problem was that she was beginning to like him too much for her own good.

"I'm sorry." His deep voice rumbled in her ear. "You were terrific. Anyone would have believed that you were seriously involved with Taylor."

When she didn't answer, Noah's tone turned decidedly gritty. "Sara? You were acting the entire time, weren't you?"

Sara wondered if Noah could possibly be jealous. Now wouldn't that be something? She turned slowly, looking up into his eyes. They were vacant of expression, reminding her again that this was an individual who lived by a code different from that of other men. Noah lived by his wits. Subterfuge, secrecy and lies were all tools of his trade.

"Would it matter?" she asked softly. *Say yes,* some inner voice inside her cried out.

"You've promised allegiance to two men in as many hours. How do I know you're not planning to double-cross me and take the crown with Taylor?"

Noah's accusation grated on her nerves, and Sara's hand actually itched with the desire to slap his face. That's all he cared about. That damn crown. She was beginning to wish she'd never heard of it.

"You don't," she snapped. "What's that old saying about no honor among thieves?" She flashed him a blatantly false smile. "But that's what makes things so interesting, isn't it?"

Noah had to restrain himself from shaking her until those lovely teeth rattled. "You can't trust Taylor."

Her challenging gaze speared into him. "I can't trust you, either."

"That sure as hell makes us even," he countered roughly, glaring down at her, and Sara returned his gaze with a furious one of her own. Tawny-gold eyes dueled with blue.

"I *knew* this would never work," Noah muttered eventually.

"It would if you stopped minimizing my part every chance you get," Sara shot back. "I should have realized that I was asking for the moon, expecting you to congratulate me."

"I'm sorry," Noah surprised her by saying.

Although he sounded as if he really meant it, Sara studied him suspiciously, waiting for the qualifying statement. She didn't have to wait long.

"It just doesn't make any sense," he explained, shoving his hands into his pockets as he began to pace the floor. "Why should Taylor suddenly decide to double-cross a man he's been thick as thieves with for years?"

"Perhaps he finds me a tempting incentive," Sara suggested.

Noah shook his head. "Come on, Sara. No woman, no matter how appealing she is, could entice a man to switch sides that easily." He was scowling out the French doors. "It has to be something else."

"Thanks a heap," she grumbled. Then his words sank in. "Did you mean that?"

"What?"

"That I'm appealing?"

Noah blinked, appearing surprised by her question. "Of course you are," he replied simply. "But surely you already know that."

If a woman wanted romantic declarations from this man, she'd definitely have to work at it, Sara thought with an inward sigh. While she, personally, wasn't interested, she felt obliged to point out his oversight.

"I suppose I do," she answered truthfully. "But a woman likes to be told from time to time that a man finds her attractive."

Noah appeared to consider her words seriously as his eyes moved over her face, as if memorizing her features for later review. Sara forced herself not to blush as his lingering gaze surveyed her body, moving over her breasts, following the indentation of her waist, continuing over the soft swell of her hips. It was an agonizingly thorough examination, and by the time he'd returned to her eyes, Sara felt as if the man had seen right down to her lacy underwear.

"I'll keep that in mind," he said gruffly. Then he turned toward the door.

"Where are you going?"

He pulled a long, narrow notebook from his jacket pocket. "It's time I began pulling my weight. I'm interviewing Malcolm in five minutes."

"Good idea. I've still got one more painting to do by Friday, anyway."

"I'll see you this evening." He opened the studio door.

Sara reached out a hand as if to stop him. "Wait a minute; what do you mean?"

"I'm staying at the Superstition Resort Hotel downtown. Be there around seven and we'll compare notes over dinner."

"If you're staying in a hotel, whose apartment was that?"

"My partner's. He and I needed a place where we could meet without being seen together. The hotel is too public."

"You have a partner?" Sara asked with a frown. "You never told me anyone else was involved in this."

"You never asked," he reminded her bluntly. "Don't worry; you'll meet Dan when the time is right. I have to go. I'll see you at the hotel at seven. We'll order something from room service."

"That sounds like a cozier partnership than I had in mind," Sara said. "I think I'll pass." She gave him a sweet, entirely false smile. "But thanks for asking."

"It wasn't exactly an invitation."

"Look, Noah, I'll admit I made a mistake with Peter, initially. And I appreciate you warning me as you did. But that still doesn't give you the right to order me around like this. I have no intention of spending the evening alone with you in your hotel room."

"You were alone with me in the apartment this morning," he pointed out with maddening logic.

"That was different. You'd just dropped that little bombshell about Peter and Malcolm; I was frightened out of my wits."

He nodded. "Of course you were. And if you had an ounce of sense, you still would be."

"What makes you think I'm not?" Sara retorted.

His eyes seemed to soften a bit at her admission. "You don't have to be afraid of me, Sara."

"So long as I obey orders, right?" Her tone was laced with sarcasm.

"I don't want to discuss it further," Noah asserted brusquely. When she looked inclined to argue once again, he cut her off. "Look, I have no intention of discussing this in a crowded restaurant where any Tom, Dick or Harry can overhear us. We'll talk about it in my room, at the hotel, at seven o'clock this evening." He crossed his arms over his broad chest, his stance challenging her to object.

Sara never could resist an out-and-out dare. "I have plans for this evening."

"This is more important."

"What if I don't think so?" she challenged, thinking of her promise to have dinner with Jennifer and Kevin.

She could practically see the smoke pouring from his ears. Noah was not used to having anyone question his authority, Sara realized. It was time he learned that he didn't own the world.

Noah exhaled a visible sigh. "Sara, don't be difficult," he coaxed tiredly. "I really don't have time to sit around and cajole an obstinate, hardheaded female."

Her fingers splayed on her hips. "And I have better things to do than to spend an evening with a dictatorial, heartless male."

He arched a brow. "Dictatorial?"

Sara nodded firmly. "You've been issuing orders left and right since I met you.... Obstinate?"

"You haven't *accepted* a single order since *I* met *you*," he countered. He glanced down at his watch. "I've got to go. We'll hash out the details over dinner."

Sara opened her mouth to complain, but Noah continued before she had a chance to object. "Show up anytime you want," he offered magnanimously. Then he winked. "So long as it's around seven."

He was gone before Sara could answer, which was just as well, because she couldn't muster up a single honest argument. It had been the damn wink that had done it, she decided, slapping red paint onto a canvas. He'd appeared almost boyishly charming, a total reversal of his earlier overbearing manner.

The man was impossible to pin down. She had been attempting to categorize Noah from the beginning, but every time she thought she had him figured out, he'd turn around and display a totally different side to this character. The man had more facets than a well-cut diamond. Who was Noah Lancaster? And why was it becoming so important that she know?

Sara couldn't remember a day ever going by so slowly. Finally, at five-thirty, she went upstairs to change. When she came out of her room, she found Peter coming down the hall.

"Sara," he said, taking both her hands in his. "You look absolutely lovely." His eyes held a hungry gleam as they drank in the sight of her. "I hope you went to all that trouble for me."

Sara brushed nervously at a few nonexistent wrinkles on the full skirt of the while eyelet sundress. "Oh, Peter," she stated regretfully, "I'm sorry. I'm having dinner with my sister tonight."

Sara wondered if some divine power was keeping track of the lies she'd been telling lately. Chalk up one more, she acknowledged fatalistically. Actually, she had felt badly about canceling the evening with Jennifer and Kevin, but her sister had brushed it off, telling her that Brian had been wanting to meet Kevin, anyway. In fact, Jennifer had admitted, she had been planning to call Sara and cancel their evening together herself.

"Your family must dress formally for dinner."

Did she detect suspicion in his tone? Sara decided she was overreacting. All this spy-counterspy business would put anyone's nerves on edge.

She ad-libbed yet another falsehood. "It's her birthday. I'm taking her out to the Pointe."

"Oh." He was obviously disappointed. "Perhaps we can have a nightcap when you get home."

She put her hand on his arm. "That would be lovely. But I'm afraid I might be very late."

Peter smiled attractively. "How long can dinner take?"

"Well, not that long," Sara admitted. "But you know how women are when they get together." She gave him a conciliatory smile. "We'll probably girl talk for hours. Jennifer's got a new man in her life, and I'm dying to hear all about him." Finally, she had managed to tell the truth! Sara half expected to hear a flare of trumpets.

"We do need to talk." The smile had turned into a frown.

Sara bobbed her head in agreement. "And we will," she promised. "First thing tomorrow morning. I'll meet you for coffee in the solarium." She reminded herself to ask Noah if he had bugged the plant-filled sun room.

"It's too risky there," he objected. "We'll go riding out on the desert. That way no one will be able to overhear us."

Sara's heart skipped a beat. "It'll be hot."

"Not if we go out about five-thirty," he countered. He bent his head, giving her a firm, hard kiss on the lips.

Sara's eyes opened wide, and when he seemed inclined to pursue the kiss, she placed her hands against his shoulders and pushed.

"You're right about the house being too risky," she said when Peter looked startled by her behavior. "How would we ever explain our relationship to Malcolm?"

"You've got a point," he agreed unhappily. Then his expression brightened. "I suppose I'll just have to wait until tomorrow morning."

"Tomorrow morning," Sara agreed weakly, wondering how she was going to break this latest news to Noah. The man was literally going to hit the roof. As she left the house, Sara tried to remember if her insurance was paid up.

AS SARA ENTERED the Superstition Resort Hotel, she remembered belatedly that she didn't know Noah's room number.

"Excuse me," she said, drawing the attention of a young desk clerk whose sleek brunette locks brought to mind a recent Vassar graduate. "Could you tell me what room Mr. Noah Lancaster is in?"

The dark-haired woman shook her head. "I'm sorry; we're not allowed to give out that information."

Terrific. Sara tried again. "It's all right," she assured the woman. "He's expecting me. I'm—uh—his sister." She had to stifle her inner groan. How many times did this desk clerk hear *that* line? she wondered.

"I can ring his room," the clerk offered without a great deal of enthusiasm.

"Thank you," Sara said with a smile.

The clerk frowned. "I'm sorry; Mr. Lancaster doesn't answer."

He must be in the shower, Sara concluded, since it was now after seven. He wouldn't have made such a big deal about the time if he hadn't been planning to be there himself.

"Thank you, anyway," she said, wondering what she should do next. "I'll simply wait for him in the lounge."

"Why don't you do that," the clerk agreed disinterestedly, turning toward a businessman who'd just arrived at the desk.

Knowing when she was licked, Sara walked away from the counter, considering her options. There was always the chance that Noah hadn't returned to the hotel. If that were the case, she could wait for him in the lobby. But if he had his key with him, he might not stop at the desk. And there were so many entrances to the hotel, he might not see her.

She could wait a few more minutes, then call his room and tell him she was downstairs. Or, she decided, watching another clerk come on duty, she could simply do what the professionals would do. Use subterfuge.

She pulled a pen out of her purse. Digging farther, she found a scrap of paper on which she wrote a few words before folding it in half.

"Excuse me."

"Yes? May I help you?"

As the newest obstacle in her quest to locate Noah turned toward her, Sara wondered fleetingly what modeling school the Superstition was recruiting their employees from. This woman, whose brown-and-gold pin proclaimed her name to be Candi, was even younger and prettier than the first. No wonder Noah chose this hotel, she thought wickedly.

"I'd like to leave a message for one of your guests," Sara explained. "But I'm afraid I've forgotten his room number."

Candi's smile belonged on a toothpaste commercial. "That's all right, ma'am," she assured Sara helpfully. "If you just tell me your party's name, I can look him up on the computer."

Ma'am? Sara doubted that she was more than five years older than the accommodating desk clerk. "Noah Lancaster."

"Lancaster," the young woman murmured thoughtfully, punching in the name on her computer. "Here it is."

"I don't suppose you could give me the number?"

Candi's pink lips firmed, indicating that inside her cotton-candy exterior dwelt a woman who was as immovable as her preppy counterpart. "Oh, no, I'm afraid I couldn't do that! But you can leave your message with me and I'll make certain Mr. Lancaster gets it."

Sara had not a single doubt. She handed over the piece of folded paper. At first, Candi seemed bemused by the bright red gum wrapper, but then she shrugged and walked over and slipped it into his box.

"All taken care of," Candi said with another smile that reminded Sara of a row of perfectly spaced Chiclets.

When she'd seen which slot her message had disappeared into, Sara's stomach had dropped to the floor. She managed a weak smile. "Thank you."

She turned away, leaning against a wall for support. As she closed her eyes, garnering strength, a security guard came up to her.

"Are you all right, ma'am?"

Ma'am? Twice in one day? She opened her eyes, viewing a male version of Candi. Sara was feeling more ancient by the minute.

"I'm fine," she assured the young man, who looked as if he belonged on a surfboard. "I was just trying to remember something."

A flash of white greeted her explanation. "Happens to me all the time. If you just go to where you were when you thought of it last, it'll come right back to you."

"Thank you."

He bobbed his sun-streaked blond head. "Anytime."

As he left, Sara sighed. Then she walked past the bank of elevators to the door marked stairs; *2033*, she groaned inwardly. Wouldn't you know the man would have a room on the twentieth floor? She looked down at her strappy white sandals. Her highest heels. This was turning out to be one hell of a day.

MUCH, MUCH LATER, Sara arrived at Noah's door. Her hair, which had been precariously pinned atop her head in a sophisticated topknot, was tumbling sideways. Her face was flushed, there were spots of dirt on her nose and chin, she'd chewed off all her lipstick, and she had a run from climbing the last six floors in her stocking feet. She had barely tapped on the door when it flew open.

"Where in the hell have you been?" Noah greeted her furiously. As he caught sight of her disheveled condition, his expression instantly changed to one of sympathy and concern. He grabbed her arm, pulling her into the suite. "Good Lord, you've been attacked! I knew this was too dangerous. Was it Brand or Taylor?"

Sara shook her head, dislodging more hairpins. "Neither. It doesn't have anything to do with the crown."

"Are you telling me it was just an everyday mugging? Do you know how worried I've been about you?" he asked as he lead her to the couch.

She sat down, deciding that the strong arm around her shoulder felt rather nice. "Let me get you a cool cloth," Noah suggested, releasing Sara sooner than she would have liked. "Would you like a drink?"

"Ginger ale would be nice," Sara agreed with a valiant attempt at a smile. It must have been a hundred degrees on that staircase. Noah left the room. "Were you really worried?" she called out.

"What do you think?" he asked, returning with a damp washcloth and a glass filled with ice and ginger ale. "I got your note telling me that you ran into a little complication but not giving me any details . . . Here, drink this.''

"Thank you." She took a sip of the effervescent soda. "I can explain."

Noah was too wrapped up in his own agitation to listen. "So I came up to the room to wait for you. At first, when you were late, I was irritated." He began moving the washcloth over her face, and Sara wondered how such large hands could be so gentle. "Twenty minutes later, when you still hadn't shown up, I began to go crazy."

The cool terry cloth moved across her forehead, down the side of her face and along her jaw. Sara decided that the pleasure she was receiving from Noah's tender care was definitely worth whatever blisters she'd gotten.

"Are you sure you're all right?" he inquired solicitously. "Perhaps I should call a doctor."

"I'm fine," she answered happily. The washcloth was now moving down her throat, and she leaned her head against the back of the couch, closing her eyes.

"Are you positive? You don't have to pretend to be brave around me, Sara. You've already proven yourself."

"I have?" She leaned forward a bit, helping as he slipped the white eyelet jacket off before moving the cloth over her heated shoulders.

"In spades," he confirmed in an unusually gruff voice.

"I really am fine. I'll probably have a few blisters tomorrow, but they're certainly not terminal."

The cloth stopped. "Blisters? What kind of mugging gives you blisters?"

Sara's eyes flew open at Noah's harsh tone, her gaze clashing with his suddenly skeptical one. "That's what I was trying to tell you. I wasn't mugged."

His eyes raked over her. "Then why do you look as if you were run over by a Mack truck?" He tossed the cloth uncaringly on the glass-and-chrome coffee table.

Well, it had been nice while it lasted. She sat up, straightening her skirt. "Watch that sweet talk, Noah. A woman might think you're getting serious."

"I *am* serious," he ground out. "What happened to you?"

"Nothing. I always look like this when I hike up twenty flights of stairs."

Noah was staring at her as if she'd just sprouted an extra head. "Why in the blue blazes did you do that? Most people—most sane people—would take an elevator."

She was fed up with Noah continually casting aspersions on her mental capabilities. "Most people don't have claustrophobia," she snapped, jumping to her feet.

He looked at her disbelievingly. "Claustrophobia?"

"That's right. Claustrophobia. An abnormal dread of being in narrow or—"

"I know what it is, Sara," he interjected. "Why didn't you tell me?"

"Because I didn't know you'd have a room on the twentieth floor," she pointed out. "Besides, it's a little difficult to work into casual conversation. 'Hi,'" she mimicked cheerily, "'I'm Sara Madison, and I'm a claustrophobic. How are you?'"

To Sara's surprise, Noah began to laugh and he rose from the couch to draw her into his arms.

"First thing tomorrow I'll change rooms," he promised.

"That would be an enormous help," Sara agreed, trying not to melt as she felt his thighs against hers.

He pushed some damp hair back from her forehead. "Blisters?"

She nodded, unable to drag her eyes from his. "That's what I get for wearing high heels."

"I was wrong." His fingers splayed against the back of her neck as his thumb stroked the delicate skin of her throat.

"Wrong?" she whispered.

"You don't look as if you've been run over by a Mack truck at all."

"I don't?" Sara wondered if the hotel had paramedics on staff. The rapid pounding of her heart couldn't possibly be normal for anyone; she must be having a coronary.

"Not at all," he murmered huskily. "You look absolutely lovely."

As she felt his breath against her lips, Sara gave into instinct, closing her eyes as she lifted her arms around his neck. Her head was spinning, her blood was running warmer in her veins, and her heart was pounding. And pounding. And . . .

As Noah muttered a soft oath, Sara belatedly realized that the hammering was coming from the door. "You'd better see who it is," she suggested, dropping her hands back to her sides.

Noah looked over his shoulder at the door, then down at Sara, then back toward the door. It was one of the few times she had ever seen him vacillate.

"Noah? Darlink, are you in there?"

Noah released her to drag his hand over his face. "I don't believe this."

Sara stared up at him. "Is that who I think it is?"

"Baroness Levinzski," he confirmed with a deep sigh. He began to drag Sara across the floor, then stopped.

"How do *you* know her?"

"I've met her a few times at the local galleries. She's also been to Malcolm's house once or twice."

"You'd better hide in the bedroom."

Sara dug in her heels. "Noah, I refuse to stay here while you romance some phony Hungarian baroness."

"Darlink? Open the door," the baroness instructed brightly. "I have brought champagne and caviar to celebrate our collaboration."

"Collaboration?" Sara hissed. "What in the hell does that mean?"

Noah didn't bother to answer. Instead, he scooped Sara up, carrying her through the bedroom door, where he dumped her unceremoniously on the mattress. "Don't you dare move," he instructed. "I'll explain everything once I get rid of her."

Sara propped herself up on her elbows. "I'm going to love hearing your explanation."

Muttering a virulent string of expletives under his breath, Noah marched from the bedroom. A moment later, her jacket and shoes came sailing into the room. Then he slammed the connecting door.

Sara scowled as she heard Noah greet the baroness. His tone was far warmer, far more welcoming, than the one he had used for her arrival.

Well, his relationship with Gizella Levinzski was certainly not her concern, Sara decided. After all, they were two of a kind. Phonies, right down to the bone. They deserved each other. She allowed herself two minutes of pouting, then went into the adjoining bathroom and retrieved a glass. It wasn't that she was at all interested in the way the baroness was cooing at Noah, Sara assured herself as she heard the champagne cork pop. She was merely safeguarding her interest in the crown. That was the only reason that she was blatantly eavesdropping, her ear pressed to the glass she held against the wall.

Chapter Six

Sara could tell that the baroness was less than pleased with Noah's behavior. They had barely sampled the champagne before he whisked her out the door, promising to get in touch with her tomorrow.

"I'll bet he wouldn't have been in such a hurry if I hadn't been occupying the bedroom," Sara muttered as she returned the glass to the bathroom. She hadn't learned a thing. As Sara exited the bathroom, she found Noah leaning against the bedroom door frame.

"Hear anything interesting?" he asked casually.

Sara didn't bother to deny she'd been eavesdropping. "How could I? You didn't let her stay long enough for the champagne bubbles to go flat."

He grinned. "I was saving it for you."

"Fat chance," Sara returned. "You just wanted to keep me in the dark."

"That's not such a bad idea," he commented slowly, moving toward her. His fingers spanned her waist. "Now, where were we?"

Sara didn't trust his abrupt change in behavior any more than she trusted anything else about Noah. She backed away.

"You were going to explain about your collaboration with the baroness."

His eyes gleamed as he continued to pursue her. "Before that."

And as the back of her knees hit the mattress, Sara realized she had just run out of room. Another step and she would be flat on her back on the bed. "You promised to feed me dinner."

"So I did," he agreed. "Are you as hungry as I am?" He touched her face.

The glint in his leonine eyes did nothing to instill calm, and Sara had the feeling that Noah had her penciled in as an appetizer. The room began to close in on her. Her heart was beating wildly, her head was spinning, and she felt as if she were unraveling from within.

"Don't do that," she whispered tersely.

"You weren't resisting earlier," he pointed out with disconcerting accuracy.

How could the man be so logical about something that defied the very laws of logic? Sara knew that to get involved with Noah would be the very height of folly. He was like the mirages that shimmered so enticingly in the desert heat—all illusion, no substance. Even his name wasn't real. If given the chance, he would steal her heart as easily as he planned to steal the crown. Then, without a backward glance, he'd be gone.

"I wasn't thinking straight earlier," she answered. "Hyperventilating will do that to you."

"Interesting," Noah remarked thoughtfully. "I'll have to remember that." Then he turned away. "I'll order our dinner," he said as he left the room.

Sara stared after Noah, surprised that he had given up so easily. She assured herself that she should be grateful for the reprieve. So why was the feeling oddly disappointed?

"The baroness has excellent taste," Sara commented later as she sipped the champagne. "I hate to think what this stuff costs."

"She can afford it. The lady's art collection makes Brand look like a piker."

"You've seen it?"

Noah spread some caviar on a cracker and offered it to Sara. When she declined, he popped it into his mouth. "She invited me to her house last night for a private showing," he explained when he had finished chewing.

"You certainly don't waste any time. Tell me, does she know you're a thief?"

"I don't believe the matter came up. Would you like some more champagne?"

"I'd like to know what you've got going with the baroness," Sara insisted tersely.

"Jealous?"

Sara felt like hitting Noah over his smug head with the champagne bottle. "Of course not. I just think that you're pushing your luck."

"You think I'm going to abscond with the baroness's paintings, don't you?"

"Yes. And probably everything else in the house you can get your hands on."

His level gaze met hers. "Do you really believe I'm that disreputable?"

Sara felt unreasonably uncomfortable. "I wonder what's keeping dinner?" she said conversationally. "Don't you think you should call down to the kitchen?"

"I asked you a question, Sara." The teasing tone had vanished from his voice.

Sara breathed a silent sigh of relief as the room-service employee knocked on the door. Noah remained silent as the waiter set up the table. He signed the check; then, as they sat down, he returned the conversation to Baroness Levinzski.

"The baroness is eager to get her collection featured in *Art Digest*," he revealed.

"I'm not surprised. She's a terrible snob." Sara turned her attention to her meal. She was suddenly starving.

"Tell me what you know."

"I'm not about to help you rob the baroness blind, Noah. So if that's what you've got in mind, you can just forget it."

"I'm not asking you to break into her house with me, Sara. I simply want you to tell me what you know about the woman." He shrugged. "However, if you insist on being obstinate, I have other sources."

Sara wasn't at all surprised. "She claims to be a member of a royal Hungarian family. But you probably already know that."

"She mentioned it," Noah agreed blandly.

"I'll bet. That's the woman's chief claim to fame." Sara shook her head. "It's amazing how many people are impressed by a title."

"But you're not."

Sara's lips firmed. "Of course not. In fact, while I do sympathize with all those people who have had their countries invaded, the one thing I agree with the Communists about is that royalty should go the way of the dodo bird."

"Has she lived in Phoenix long?"

"Quite a few years; however, she usually only winters here. The rest of the time she jets around the Mediterranean or holds court in her Manhattan penthouse. I'm surprised you haven't run across her before. Her jewels would probably pay your travel expenses well into the next century."

"So I've noticed."

Sara shot him a wry glance. "Somehow that doesn't surprise me in the least."

Noah didn't respond to her unstated accusation. "This is July," he pointed out. "Do you have any idea why she's altered her pattern?"

Sara frowned. "Not at all. Since you and she seem so cozy," she suggested dryly, "why don't you simply ask her?"

"I may just do that," Noah agreed.

"Before or after you rob her?"

"Sarcasm doesn't suit you," Noah responded easily. "Besides, Gizella's motives aren't exactly lily white, Sara. The woman has no qualms about using me to worm her way into the magazine."

"That's still no reason for you to take advantage of her," Sara pointed out.

"What makes you think I'm taking advantage of her?"

"Aren't you?"

He shrugged. "No more than she is me."

"You don't have any principles at all, do you?"

"That's an odd accusation coming from a lady who's told enough lies in one twenty-four-hour period to earn a listing in the *Guiness Book of World Records*."

That hurt. Sara was basically a very forthright individual who detested prevarication and sham. Her parents had brought her up to be an honest, law-abiding citizen. She didn't want to dwell on what they would think of her behavior these past weeks. She reminded herself that in this case the end justified the means.

"I told you that I have my reasons for wanting the crown."

"So do I," Noah pointed out.

Sara squared her shoulders. "Your reasons are based on sheer greed. I'm simply taking care of what the law failed to do."

"It must be nice to see things in such a black-and-white way," Noah replied. "I envy you that ability."

Sara thought she detected a sardonic note in Noah's remarks, but she wasn't permitted time to dwell on it. "Tell me about your father and Malcolm Brand," he requested.

"Why?"

"I'd just like to know what makes a law-abiding art-history professor turn to a life of crime. I'm beginning to believe that under normal conditions you don't even jay-walk."

Sara didn't like his teasing tone. "It's amazing how you can make honesty and integrity sound like character flaws," she muttered, wondering not for the first time what she was doing working with this man.

"You were going to tell me about your father," he coaxed quietly.

Sara sighed as she put down her fork. She had suddenly lost her appetite. "My father was an inventor. He was always puttering away, working on something."

"Was?"

"He died."

"I'm sorry." He sounded as if he really meant it.

"It was a long time ago," Sara said.

"Did Brand have anything to do with his death?"

Sara was distracted by Noah's gentle tone. How could a man who undoubtedly possessed more passports than scruples seem so nice at times, so caring? She reminded herself that in his world charm was a professional necessity.

"Not directly," she answered. "But Dad was never the same after Malcolm stole his patent."

Noah looked at Sara with renewed interest. "You've lost me," he admitted.

"How much do you know about Malcolm Brand?"

"Enough to know that he's dangerous if crossed." His eyes issued her a warning. "You're not keeping anything from me, are you? Some little act of revenge you've forgotten to mention."

"I could ask you the same question," Sara countered. "Are you keeping something from me, Noah?"

A muscle jerked along his jawline. "Let's get back to the patent."

Sara was growing angry. "I don't want to talk about my father with you. In fact, I don't want to talk with you period." She got up from the table.

"Sit down, Sara," Noah demanded. "While you are admittedly beautiful when riled, I'm too tired to fight with you right now."

"I'm disappointed in you, Noah. That cliché is so old, no woman would buy it. I'd advise you not to try it out on the baroness."

"It may be old, and it may be a cliché, but in your case it fits," he argued. "Please sit down. You haven't finished your dinner."

"I'm not hungry."

"Beautiful and stubborn," Noah grumbled. "A lethal combination."

Against her better judgment, Sara took her seat again. "It's not fair that you know everything about me and I know nothing about you," she complained.

Noah seemed to be digesting that. "All right," he agreed finally. "I'll make you a deal. You tell me about your father, and I'll tell you about mine."

"Would you really do that?"

"I will," Noah promised immediately.

"And you won't lie?"

He reached across the table, taking her hand in his. "I promise that I'll never lie to you, Sara. I may not be able to tell you everything, but I'll never lie."

Both his tone and expression were suddenly serious, and Sara wanted more than anything in the world to believe him. His thumb was brushing against the sensitive skin at the inside of her palm, adding to her confusion. How could such a simple touch create such havoc on her senses?

Noah seemed to read her mind. "You know, Sara, appearances can often be misleading. Why don't you try trusting your feelings," he urged with a strange intensity.

Oh, he made it sound so tempting! But Sara knew that if she gave into these sensual feelings, she'd be a goner. "It's not that easy," she protested softly.

He lifted her hand, pressing a light kiss against the inside of her wrist. "I asked you once to trust me," he reminded her. "You agreed, but you didn't mean it." His eyes held hers over their linked fingers. "I'm asking you again, Sara."

"I'll try," she agreed quietly.

Something flickered in the depths of his eyes. "That's a beginning."

A peaceful truce settled over the table as they ate. After they had finished their dinner, Noah placed the table outside the door. When he asked her to join him on the sofa, Sara found the softly issued invitation impossible to resist.

"How could Malcolm Brand steal your father's patent?" Noah asked curiously.

"He's an attorney," Sara divulged, "although he doesn't practice any longer. My father was one of his clients."

"I'm beginning to get the picture. He had your father sign away his rights and applied for the patents in his name. When one of the inventions took off, Brand reaped the benefits."

Sara tried not to become nervous when Noah extended his arm along the back of the couch. "That's only partly right," she corrected.

He looked down at her. "Where was I off?"

"My father never signed away his rights. Those papers were forged."

Noah's brow lifted. "If that were really the case, why didn't your father take the guy to court?"

"He did," Sara revealed with unrestrained bitterness. "My father's attorney was a young man who'd just passed the bar. It was all he could afford. Malcolm Brand, on the other hand, showed up in court with a team of high-priced lawyers. Dad didn't stand a chance."

"What was the invention?"

"It's a valve on the machine that's used to administer anesthesia during operations. I couldn't begin to understand how it works, but somehow it decreases the risk of overanesthetizing patients during lengthy procedures."

Noah considered that for a moment. "How did Brand know it would even work?"

"He was a partner in a firm that leased medical equipment to doctors and hospitals in different states. It was his business to know things like that. In fact, that was one of the reasons my father went to him instead of an attorney specializing in patent law. Dad hoped that Malcolm might see the value in his work and be willing to loan him the money to begin manufacturing the valve."

"Why doesn't Brand realize who you are? Obviously your father's invention gained him a great deal of money."

"That was more than twenty years ago. Do you have any idea how many people Malcolm Brand has stolen from in the interim? He couldn't begin to keep track." Sara tried not to dwell on the comparison that Malcolm Brand and Noah were both thieves. Only their methods differed.

Noah didn't quite buy Sara's explanation, but he decided not to press her. "I take it that was the last thing your father ever invented that could have made money."

"My father died the following year," she said flatly. "He'd always had a heart condition, and the strain of the trial plus the stress put on him by Malcolm's army of attorneys accelerated his illness." Her lips tightened. "It's ironic, in a way."

"What's ironic?"

"Malcolm is suffering from the same heart condition, but he had a triple bypass three years ago that helped him survive." Her voice was tinged with ancient bitterness. "My father's valve allowed the lengthy surgery."

Noah could not remain unaffected by the shadow darkening Sara's blue eyes. "I really am sorry." His fingers curved around her shoulder.

She didn't resist as he fit her into the curve of his arm. "As I said, it was a long time ago. And it's not as if I've been wasting my entire life, hoping for revenge. It was only when Peter offered me the job of painting those copies that I decided fate had stepped in."

"And opportunity dropped right into your lap."

This time her smile was genuine. "Precisely. I didn't know what they were up to, but I knew they weren't telling me the truth about the reason for the copies. After I arrived at the house, I overheard Malcolm and Peter discussing the paintings in the vault. I put two and two together and figured out what they had planned."

"So the original stolen paintings are going to be hidden behind your copies. I suppose the intended buyers have a list of the originals being auctioned."

"They'd have to," Sara agreed, "or they wouldn't know what they were bidding on."

"I can understand why Brand's doing it this way," Noah offered, his fingers absently stroking her arm. "Nobody's going to be suspicious of a gallery auctioning off a few paintings from his collection. But there's got to be a way to keep unsuspecting buyers from ending up with one of the copies."

"Especially since a technical analysis would reveal that it wasn't a genuine painting. Not only would that damage the gallery's reputation, but it would focus attention right back to Malcolm."

Noah fell silent for a moment, considering the matter. Then he snapped his fingers. "The hidden ones will be worth more than what the originals of your copies would earn."

A glimmer of comprehension lit her eyes. "So anyone not knowing about the scheme would drop out of the bidding."

"Exactly." He tapped the tip of her nose playfully. "Not bad, lady. For an amateur."

Sara grinned. "High praise indeed. From the professional," she countered, wishing she hadn't put it quite that way.

The one thing she didn't want to think about was that, despite the way she was drawn to him, Noah was a professional criminal. Eventually, he would be captured and put in prison. As a claustrophobic, Sara could imagine the terror of being locked up behind bars. She hated the idea of that happening to Noah.

"Cold?" he asked, detecting her slight shiver.

She shook her head. "No, I just had a thought."

He eyed her curiously. "It must not have been a very pleasant one."

"Have you ever been in prison?"

He seemed surprised by her direct question. "No, why?"

"I think I'd die if I was ever put in a cell," Sara said with heartfelt anxiety.

Noah's arm tightened around her. "Don't worry," he promised, brushing a light kiss against her furrowed brow. "I'd never let that happen."

Something in his voice encouraged Sara to have faith in his ability to do exactly that. As she searched his face for secrets, Noah drew the shutters over his eyes once again, denying her the opportunity to read his thoughts.

"It's your turn," she reminded him. Sara was determined to know something about this inscrutable man.

During her time alone in the bedroom, Sara had removed the few remaining pins from her hair, brushing it into a sleek curtain that fell straight as rain to her shoulders. Noah's touch was gentle as he tucked the blond hair behind her ear.

"My turn?" he inquired absently, nibbling lightly at her exposed earlobe.

Sara's body tingled with escalating desire, urging her to give in. But those images of prison life were still emblazoned on her mind, and she reminded herself that she was on the verge of making love to a man who could only offer her a future behind bars.

"To tell me about your father." She moved deftly out of his arms.

Noah leaned toward her, one long, dark finger tracing her lips. "I'd rather talk about you." He closed the gap between them.

Feeling incredibly foolish, Sara scooted across the cushions to the other side of the sofa. "We've already talked about me," she declared firmly. "Now it's my turn to learn something about you."

He spanned the distance quickly, placing his hands on the back of the sofa. The gesture effectively fenced her in. "I can think of better ways to get acquainted."

Sara put her hands on his chest. "I don't know what kind of relationship you usually have with your partners, but ours doesn't include bedroom rights."

He grinned unrepentantly. "How about couch rights?"

She pushed against him but found she might as well have tried to move the Rock of Gibraltar. "Not those, either. This is strictly a business arrangement."

"There's always room for negotiation in any business deal," he advised lightly.

"You're incorrigible," she protested, fighting the temptation brimming in his eyes.

"That's what my mother always said," he agreed as he prepared to kiss her.

Sara ducked out from under his arm. "Speaking of parents, I'm waiting to hear about your father."

Noah glanced down at his watch, then rose lazily from the cushions. "Tomorrow," he assured her.

Sara folded her arms over her chest. "What's wrong with now?"

"Because it's late. And we both have to get up early tomorrow morning."

She stared at him. She had completely forgotten Peter's plan to go horseback riding. "We?"

He gave her a knowing grin. "That's right, we. As in you and I, Peter and Malcolm. Oh, and the baroness. We mustn't leave her out."

Sara was too stunned to dwell on the idea of Baroness Levinzski atop a horse. "All of us? Together?"

Noah nodded. "I want all the principal players where I can keep an eye on them." He took her hand in his. "You didn't think I was going to allow you to go off into the desert with Taylor alone, did you?''

"Nothing would have happened," she argued. "I'm perfectly capable of saying no."

Noah picked up her jacket and held it out to her. Sara slipped her arms into the short sleeves. "I'm well aware of your aptitude for avoiding seduction, Sara," he argued good-naturedly. "However, that isn't why I don't trust Taylor alone with you."

As Noah's words sank in, she froze. "You don't really think he'd try to harm me, do you?"

Noah's expression suddenly grew sober. "I still don't buy the way the guy accepted your offer so quickly," he explained irritated by his inability to force that particular piece of the puzzle into place. "But I do know one thing. There's not much a man wouldn't do for several million dollars, Sara. Don't forget that."

I won't, she vowed, reminding herself that in that respect this man was no different from Peter. What would Noah be willing to do to achieve the crown? she wondered. And why did she believe she was any safer alone with him?

"I'll go down in the elevator with you," he offered, his hand cupping her elbow as they left his hotel suite.

"I can't," she protested.

"You can't walk back down twenty flights of stairs," Noah argued with consummate logic. "And I'm sure as hell not going to carry you down."

"I didn't ask you to." She turned toward the stairs.

Noah swore, then grabbed her wrist and pulled her toward him. "Don't be an idiot," he muttered. A moment later, he appeared honestly apologetic. "Look, Sara," he tried patiently, "I promise that it won't be as bad as you think." He pushed the button.

She shook her head. "Noah, I can't do it. Now I'm sorry if you think I'm being childish, but I simply refuse to get in that elevator."

"How long has it been since you've actually been in an elevator?"

"I don't remember."

He gave her an encouraging smile. "Then you don't even know if you're still claustrophobic," he pointed out. "This is as good a time as any to try."

"I don't know," she said uncertainly.

At that moment, the heavy steel doors opened, and before she could protest, Noah pulled her into the elevator and pushed the button designating the lobby.

As the doors closed, Sara's head grew light. The interior of the elevator was decorated in mirror panels, and her reflection resembled that of a frightened ghost.

Noah wrapped her tightly in his arms. "Close your eyes," he instructed.

Sara was all too willing to comply. She squeezed her eyes shut and rested her forehead against his shoulder. "Noah," she begged as the walls closed in, shrouding her in darkness, "please let me out."

"Shh," he murmured into her ear. "All it takes is a little mental imagery.... Try picturing a meadow filled with flowers, green grass blowing in the soft summer breeze."

"Noah..."

"The sun is shining; birds are singing in the trees. The sky is a vast blue bowl overhead," his husky voice continued to drone in her ear. "Can you hear the birds?"

"I don't *want* to hear the damn birds. I just want to get out of this elevator!"

He sighed his surrender. "You can't say I didn't try. We'll just have to resort to different tactics."

Before she could object, he covered her tightly set lips
with his own.

Sara was stunned. At the first touch, her body stiffened,
taken by surprise. A moment later, she found herself thinking that jewel thieves made dynamite kissers. His lips were
neither firm and demanding nor tentative. Instead, they
brushed her own in a manner that was far more tempting
than threatening.

His breath was warm, fluttering against her skin like
angel's wings, and Sara sighed into his mouth. "I still don't
trust you," she whispered.

The tip of his tongue circled her mouth, leaving a ring of
exquisite fire. "I know."

As a liquefying pleasure flowed through Sara, she
wrapped her arms around his neck. "This doesn't change
anything."

"I know." Noah's answer whispered over her lips.

"Good. I just wanted to set the record straight."

Her eyes flew open as he lifted his head, breaking the
heavenly contact. Noah's eyes danced with what appeared
to be both amusement and honest affection.

"You've succeeded," he assured her. "Now will you do
something for me?"

Anything! her impulsive self shouted out. "What?" the
practical side of her nature asked.

He grinned as he traced the delicate lines of her face with
his fingers. "Shut up."

Then her mind went blank. Her lips clung to his, trembling as he kissed her with an intensity that created an ex-
plosion of fireworks behind her closed lids. Her head
whirled with the display of dazzling light and color, and
Sara almost cried out in distress when the mind-blinding kiss
finally ended.

"We're almost at the lobby," Noah pointed out calmly. He had one hand on the button, stopping the elevator in its descent.

"Already?" Sara had entirely forgotten her fear.

His eyes held a warm smile. "Want to take another ride?"

Sara was learning that Noah was at his most dangerous when he put on the charm. "No, thanks," she said firmly. "Once is enough."

Noah cupped her face in his palms. "Now there's where you're wrong, sweetheart."

Sara held her breath as Noah looked inclined to kiss her again. But at that moment the elevator reached the ground floor, and the door opened, revealing a group of conventioneers.

"Going up," Noah commented cheerily as he took Sara's hand and walked out into the lobby.

"I forgot to tell you something," he said as he walked her to the parking garage.

"What?" Sara murmured, her mind still on that devastating kiss.

"We're invited to a party."

"A party?" she echoed absently.

They had reached her car. As Sara unlocked the door and slid into the driver's seat, she wondered what it would be like to make love with a man who kissed with such expertise.

"Brand's throwing a bash Saturday night," Noah revealed. "That's when we'll take the crown."

His words shocked her from her dreamy lassitude. "With the house filled with people? You're crazy!"

He laughed, giving her a quick, hard kiss on the lips. "Trust me." The flare of heat ended far too soon. "Drive carefully." His knuckles brushed her cheek. "And sweet dreams."

She put her hand on his arm. "Noah, you can't just drop a bombshell like that and expect me to get any sleep!"

"It'll be a cinch," he assured her with a rakish grin that reminded her exactly how he earned his living. "By the way, don't get upset if you think you're being followed. It'll only be me."

"I'm already upset," she complained. "And you don't have to follow me back to the house; I'll be fine."

Noah studied Sara for what seemed to be a very long time. Finally, he managed a wry grin. "Sara Madison, you're a great deal more than fine." Then he winked. "Now if you want to get any sleep, I'd suggest you get going."

He closed the car door and disappeared into the vast cavern of the parking garage. Bemused, Sara started the engine and headed up the ramp. A few minutes later, she glanced up into her rearview mirror and saw the glow of headlights behind her. Knowing Noah was back there gave her a strangely comforting feeling.

He turned back shortly before she reached the gates to the mansion, flashing his lights in a private farewell.

"Evening, Ms Madison," the guard greeted her politely. "Mr. Brand instructed me to send you to his office when you returned from dinner with your sister."

"At this hour?" she asked incredulously. Malcolm's heart condition had limited his activities. He was usually in bed by nine o'clock; it was now past eleven.

"He said whenever you got in," the guard stressed.

Sara fought down the spiral of fear that lanced through her. Noah wouldn't have let her return to the house if he believed she was in any danger. Would he?

She forced a smile. "Thank you, John. I'll go right up."

She continued the rest of the way to the house, parking her compact car in the five-car garage. Entering the house, she made her way to Malcolm's private office.

"Sara? Is that you?" he asked as she knocked.

"It's me," she answered, opening the door. "Are you all right? It's very late."

"I wanted to talk to you," he said. "Privately." His smile was not as warm as others she had received since coming to work.

She entered the room on wobbly legs, hoping he couldn't see her knees shaking. "Of course. Is it about the paintings?"

He waved away her concern. "No, you're coming along splendidly. I saw your progress when I came searching for you earlier this evening. Peter told me you'd taken your sister to dinner."

"It's her birthday."

Malcolm appeared distracted. "So Peter said. Did you have a nice celebration?"

It was not in Malcolm Brand's nature to participate in idle, personal chitchat. Sara was growing more apprehensive by the moment.

"Lovely," she said, eager to escape his steady gaze. "Well, if that's all you wanted, Malcolm, I think I'll go upstairs to bed. It's been a long day." She stifled a feigned yawn.

Brand was not about to let her get off that easily. "Sit down, Sara," he instructed firmly. "And tell me everything you know about our Mr. Lancaster."

Sara struggled to maintain her composure as she sank into the nearest chair. Her blood was pounding in her ears, her mouth had gone as dry as the Arizona desert, and she felt as if she might faint.

Chapter Seven

"Mr. Lancaster?" Sara schooled her voice to what she desperately hoped was a casual tone. "I don't know anything about him," she answered, chalking up yet another lie on her mental blackboard. She was becoming as unprincipled as Malcolm. As Noah. Now that was a depressing thought.

Malcolm's steely eyes narrowed. "Come on, Sara. It's your business to know the art world."

"I know all about art history," she agreed. "But I don't have much time for light reading like *Art Digest*. Usually I stick to thick, scholarly tomes." Belatedly remembering the text on Early Christian art, Sara realized she had made a mistake. She rushed ahead to keep Malcolm from dwelling on it. "Of course, I know its reputation, and I think it's marvelous that your collection is going to be featured." She smiled encouragingly. "Just think what it will do for your reputation."

"It won't hurt it," Malcolm responded gruffly. His jaw hardened. "It's about time those blue-blooded snobs realized that they don't have the market cornered."

"They do tend to behave a bit high-handedly."

"Speaking of snobs, why do you think Lancaster's hanging around with Gizella?"

"Gizella? The baroness?" Why did she feel as if she were in the middle of a whodunit, with everyone but her knowing the ending?

"The same—that woman's been nothing but a pain in the you-know-what since she hit town."

"She seems to find Peter attractive," Sara hedged.

"She's been trying to steal him away for the past two years. Not that she has a snowball's chance in hell of succeeding."

"Peter's very loyal," Sara replied, wondering why Malcolm was having this conversation with her. Did he suspect collusion between Peter and her? Or between Noah and her? Sara suddenly wished she had never heard of the lot of them.

"How long has Peter worked for you?"

"Twenty years," Malcolm replied. "And he'll be here another twenty unless I decide he's become useless." He gave her a mirthless smile. "Peter and I understand each other."

"That's helpful, since you work so closely together." When Malcolm didn't answer, Sara realized he was lost in thought. She decided to take this opportunity to beat a hasty retreat. "Malcolm, if you don't mind, I'm exhausted. I'd better get to bed before I fall asleep right here in this chair."

He looked at her as if surprised to find her still sitting there. "Of course," he agreed, waving her away absently. "I have to get up in a few hours, anyway. Lancaster wants to go riding first thing in the morning."

"That sounds like a nice way to begin the day." Personally, Sara couldn't think of anything more unattractive than crawling out of bed at dawn, but Noah seemed to have his reasons for wanting everyone together.

"Why don't you join us?" Malcolm suggested suddenly. "We'll make it a foursome."

"A foursome?"

"You, Lancaster, Gizella and I." He grimaced. "Lancaster invited her along. Said it'd give the article some added punch." His lips were set in a thin line. "It seems that deposed royalty is all the rage these days."

"I suppose Mr. Lancaster know what sells magazines." She hoped her tone was noncommittal.

Malcolm grunted. "I suppose so. I still have half a mind to set the dogs on her. I wonder how she found out he was in town, anyway?"

Sara shook her head. "I couldn't imagine. She does know a lot of people; she probably heard rumors." Sara managed an encouraging smile. "I don't think you have anything to worry about, Malcolm. After all, Mr. Lancaster came to interview you, not the baroness. It's probably exactly as he said. He's just putting her in the article to show that you have colorful, influential friends."

He seemed to accept that. "It does give me a little class at that."

Sara breathed a sigh of relief. "I'm sure it's going to be a wonderful article," she replied enthusiastically.

Malcolm smiled. "I'm going to miss you when you leave, Sara. It's amazing how much a beautiful young woman brightens up the place. These past few weeks I've almost forgotten that I'm a dying old man."

The look he was giving her was definitely not that of an old man, Sara thought. "You're not going to die for years and years, Malcolm," she assured him breezily. "But I'm going to collapse of exhaustion at any moment." She stood up and turned toward the door.

"Good night," she called back over her shoulder.

"Good night, dear. Will you come riding tomorrow morning?"

"I wouldn't miss it for the world," she answered truthfully.

When she entered her bedroom, Sara spent a few moments looking for the listening device she was certain Noah had secreted somewhere in the room. When her search proved fruitless, she undressed, hoping that he hadn't also included a close-circuit camera.

"I don't know if you're listening or not," she said as she climbed into bed. "But if you are, Noah Lancaster, or whatever your name is, I just pulled your fat out of the fire. You can thank me in the morning."

THE SUNRISE RIDE the next morning was for the most part uneventful. While Peter seemed surprised to find the stables occupied when he arrived, he apparently decided not to create a scene in front of his employer. Instead, he smoothed over the initial awkward moments expertly, stating that he'd been too long without exercise and had come down for a ride on a whim. He greeted Sara warmly, but there was nothing in his manner to suggest their secret rendezvous.

The baroness, who had been clinging to Noah's arm, deserted him the moment Peter arrived. Malcolm, apparently taking Sara's words to heart, seemed determined to put on a good front for Noah. There was nothing to suggest that he'd banned Gizella from the estate the previous week.

Noah directed most of his conversation toward Malcolm, paying scant attention to Sara. It should have been a pleasant excursion. The air was fresh and crisp, the scenery without parallel. Majestic cottonwoods, clustered about intermittent water sources, towered into the pristine blue sky, their branches home to birds that filled the air with their cheery morning songs. However, by the end of the ride, the others had paired up, and Sara, left to bring up the rear of the small parade, felt extremely out of sorts. Even the soft cooing of the mourning dove did nothing to lift her mood.

"Excuse me, Ms Madison," Noah said after they had dismounted. "I believe you dropped this." He handed her a pack of cinnamon chewing gum.

She started to speak, but his steady gaze stopped her planned protest. "Why, thank you, Mr. Lancaster. It must have fallen out of my pocket." She slipped the pack of gum into her jeans. "Well, that was lovely, but I think I'd better get to work," she said, wanting to escape the stables before Peter had a chance to speak to her alone.

"Aren't you hungry?" Malcolm inquired. "Mr. Lancaster and the baroness are staying for breakfast. Why don't you join us?"

Sara shook her head. "Sorry, Malcolm, but you know I don't eat breakfast."

"Some coffee?" Peter asked, an unspoken order in his smooth tone.

Sara apologized with a smile. "I *really* do have to get to work. Perhaps I'll see everyone at lunch." With that she took off toward the house on a jog, feeling three pairs of male eyes directed at her back.

Priding herself on escaping without a struggle, Sara showered and washed her hair. When she came out of the bathroom, she stopped short, staring at the man lounging on her bed, his head pillowed by his arms. His chambray shirt fit tightly across his chest, and his long, muscular legs stretched to the end of the king-sized mattress.

"What are you doing here?"

Noah grinned. "Didn't you read my note?"

The short note had been stuck inside the package of gum. "You said you'd see me later," she said firmly, tugging the bath towel more firmly around her body.

The teasing smile reached his eyes, making him look far less formidable than usual. In fact, if she didn't know better, she'd think he was exactly what he was professing to be. A reporter after a story. A reporter with a roving eye, she tacked on, unable to avoid the way he was looking at her scantily clad body.

"That's right. And this is later," he agreed laconically.

Sara didn't like the way he seemed to have taken possession of her bed, as if by some divine right of kings.

"What are you doing here?"

"I came to thank you."

"Thank me? For what?"

"For pulling my fat out of the fire last night." He rose languidly from the bed. "Do you know how tempting you look right now? All flushed and fragrant? You make a man think about risks he shouldn't be taking." He touched her shoulder, and Sara jerked away.

"You're a fine one to talk about dodging risks," she snapped. "If you're not careful, you're going to end up in a prison cell until you're too old to remember what a woman looks like."

Noah heard the tremor in her voice. "Does that prospect bother you?" he asked quietly.

"Of course it bothers me," she answered forcefully. "Do you think I like the thought of you locked up in some dark closed place? Unable to see the sun, feel the breeze in your hair? Do you think I enjoy the prospect of your losing your freedom, of losing—" As an intimate warmth rose in Noah's gaze, Sara realized she had come close to revealing her innermost thoughts. She stopped suddenly, turning away from him.

"Would you please leave? I'd like to get dressed."

Ignoring her gritty tone, Noah reached out to turn her toward him. "Losing what, Sara?" he asked softly. His hands tightened on her bare arms. "What were you going to say?"

Sara shook her head. "Nothing." She wasn't about to admit that she had been going to say that if he was arrested, he'd lose what they had together—a relationship that seemed to be developing despite her best efforts to stop it.

He studied her for a long, thoughtful time. Sara wondered if he could see her heart pounding beneath the royal-blue terry cloth.

"You're doing it again," he murmured as he traced a finger along the top of the towel.

Sara tugged it more tightly around her body. "Doing what?" she challenged in a voice that was far weaker, far more vulnerable sounding than she would have liked.

Noah wished that he could tell Sara something that would ease her fears, anything that might allow her to relax enough to get through the next few days as painlessly as possible. But he knew there was only one thing she wanted to hear from him. She wanted to know that he wasn't really the thief she believed him to be. And that was the one thing he couldn't give her.

"You're lying," he murmured, stroking her fragrant, just-bathed skin. "You do care about me. About us."

Faced with those steady eyes, Sara couldn't deny it. "Oh, Noah," she said with a sigh, "can't we just forget all this?" Her blue eyes pleaded with him. "Why don't we let Malcolm have his stupid crown and leave here before it's too late?"

He framed her distressed face in his hands. "It's already too late, Sara. For both of us."

She couldn't take any more. During that conversation with Malcolm last night, Sara had been overcome with fear for Noah. For his freedom, for his life. She couldn't continue this way; she felt as if she were drowning.

"I've changed my mind." As she pulled away from him, the towel started to slip, and it took all her concentration to hitch it up again. "I want out. In fact, I'm leaving as soon as I can get packed. If you insist on doing this, Noah, you'll do it without me." She grabbed a handful of clothes from the closet, throwing them onto the bed.

"I need your help, Sara," Noah pointed out quietly. "My plan depends on both of us going to that party Saturday night."

"Then come up with another plan," she retorted. "Because as of right now, I'm out."

"What about your father?"

Sara shot him a blistering glare that accused him of unfair tactics. "My father would hate the fact that his eldest daughter had turned into a liar and a thief. It was a stupid idea, anyway."

Noah strode to the window, gazing out over the estate. When he didn't answer, Sara hardened her tone. "Would you please leave?"

He turned around, pinning her with a particularly censorious gaze. "So you're just going to let Brand go on cheating others like he did your father? You're not even going to try to stop him?"

Sara was offended by his moralistic tone. "Stop him? What on earth makes you think I could stop him? I just wanted to cause him some discomfort, some feeling of loss. I never, in my wildest imagination, thought I could stop him."

"We could, you know," Noah said slowly. "You and I could see that he went to jail for a very long time." His expression was deadly serious. "It wouldn't help your father, Sara, but it might help some other child's father. It might help all the other people he will steal from in the future if he isn't stopped."

The idea was too enticing. Oh, the man certainly knew which buttons to push, Sara considered grimly. "Why should you be bothered by the way Malcolm Brand earns his living?" she asked. "What makes you any better?"

Noah sighed, dragging a hand through his dark hair. "Sara, you're going to have to—"

"I know," she interrupted. "Trust you." She heaped an extra helping of scorn on the request she'd heard far too often in the past two days.

"Look," he suggested, "I promise that as soon as we have the crown, I'll tell you everything."

"Everything?" she asked suspiciously.

He nodded. "Everything."

Sara considered that offer, wanting more than anything in the world to believe him. "I need to know one thing first," she demanded.

"Sara," Noah objected, "can't you just take me at face value for a couple more days?"

"Are you married?"

He appeared honestly startled by the question. "Would it matter?"

She held her ground. "It would to me."

Noah's expression softened. "Sara, you're a lovely, spirited woman. I would probably fantasize making love to you even if I did have a wife and a houseful of kids waiting for me at home."

Sara told herself that she'd asked for the truth. So why did she feel so lousy?

Then his tawny eyes moved over her in a way that warmed her as much as if he'd used those strong, wide hands. "The difference is, if I *were* married, I wouldn't have actually tried to make love to you. I'm a one-woman man, Sara Madison. The unlucky lady who gets me is going to be stuck with me. For life."

Stuck. That was a funny way of putting it, Sara mused. Yet, oddly enough, that was precisely how she felt. She didn't want to care for Noah. And she certainly didn't want to spend her life worrying whether or not he was going to return safely to her at the end of the day. But she couldn't turn her back on him. Not right now.

Maybe, she considered hopefully, once she helped Noah take Malcolm's crown, she could convince him to give up his life of crime. She knew nothing about him. Perhaps he stole because of a deprived childhood. If that was the case, there was always the chance that once Noah realized someone actually cared about what happened to him, he would find it sufficient compensation for past hurts.

"I'll stay," she agreed finally, "until after the party."

As Noah pulled her into his arms, Sara tried to evade him, but his fingers tangled in her hair, holding her still as his mouth unerringly found hers. His lips claimed hers with a passionate intensity tempered by a tenderness he had never felt toward any other woman. A soft sound broke from Sara's lips—half sob, half sigh—as she was engulfed by a storm of need unlike anything she had ever known. The world spun dizzily around her, and she had no alternative but to hold tightly to Noah, his kiss, his touch, overwhelming all of her intended objections.

"You're not going to regret this," he promised when they finally came up for air.

Sara sighed, retrieving the towel that had fallen unheeded to the floor. "I already am." Grabbing some clothes from the mattress, she went into the bathroom to change.

When she came out, Noah was gone. Sara didn't know whether to feel relieved or irritated by his disappearance. Unwilling to dwell on the question, she went downstairs to her studio and began putting the finishing touches to a copy of Marc Chagall's *The Large Grey Circus*.

"That's exactly how I feel," she growled. "Like I'm in the middle of a damn three-ring circus."

"Talking to yourself, Sara? I thought that was a sign of old age."

She looked up to see Malcolm standing in the doorway. "It's a sign of frustration," she countered.

As he entered the room, she could see that the morning exercise had taken its toll. He looked far older, far weaker, than usual. Sara found herself almost feeling sorry for him. Then she reminded herself that Malcolm Brand had been given far more years than her father. That thought strengthened her resolve.

Intent on studying the painting, Malcolm missed Sara's hardened expression. "I don't know why you should be frustrated. As usual, you've done a remarkable job. Lancaster's right," he murmured almost to himself. "You could probably become a master forger if your mind possessed a more criminal bent."

His words hit a little too closely to home. "I don't have the nerves for it," Sara answered honestly. "I'd always be waiting for the FBI to show up on my doorstep."

"Some people obviously find such risks exhilarating," he offered.

"Some people like jumping out of planes and racing Indy cars, too. I'm not one of them."

"Play-it-safe Sara," he teased. "Hasn't anyone ever told you the facts of life? It's a cruel world, little lady. You have to be tough to survive."

Sara dabbed orange paint onto the crescent-shaped moon. "I'd rather just muddle along in my own fashion," she replied. "I seem to lack the killer instinct."

"Such naiveté must run in the family."

Sara's hand jerked, sending a slash of orange into the blue background. "What does that mean?"

"Your father didn't have the killer instinct, either," Malcolm said easily, as if they were discussing nothing more controversial than the weather.

Sara stared at him. "You remember my father?"

Malcolm looked amused by her shock. "Of course I do. How could I forget the man whose invention paid for my first van Gogh?"

"And you still wanted me to work for you?"

"Of course."

"Why?"

"Because you're the best copyist I've even seen," he replied simply.

"How do you know I won't steal some of your originals, now that I've seen them, and replace them with my own copies?"

He gave her a grim, mirthless smile. "Because, my dear, as you so succinctly put it, you lack the killer instinct." Malcolm glanced over at the painting in progress. "You've smeared that moon."

Sara nearly shook with restrained fury. "You really are a bastard, aren't you, Malcolm?"

He laughed at her indignation. "Of course I am. But it's made me very, very wealthy, little one. After all, I'm not the one forced to work for the enemy just to gain a few extra dollars to support my poor widowed sister and her fatherless son."

"If you hadn't stolen my father's patent," Sara accused heatedly, "Jennifer would have money of her own, and I wouldn't even be here."

"True," he agreed. "But as you've already discovered, *ifs* don't pay the bills very well." His gray eyes resembled two pieces of flint. "Life is nothing more than a balance sheet, Sara; you have to go for the bottom line. In your father's case, his loss was my gain." He turned to leave. "I'll let you get back to work."

Sara stood frozen to the spot, wondering what to do now. She wanted more than anything else to pack up her things and leave this house forever. But another, more primitive instinct had her hoping that Noah was right—that together they could see that this man received the punishment he deserved.

Malcolm turned in the doorway. "Oh, Sara, you will be staying for the party Saturday night, won't you?"

"I'm surprised you want me to."

He arched a white brow. "Why wouldn't I?" When she didn't answer, he continued. "Besides, I have plans for you, Sara Madison. You're going to prove quite an asset to me."

Her blood was like ice water running through her veins. "What do you mean by that?"

"Mr. Lancaster hit upon an interesting idea. One we need to talk about."

Sara stiffened. "I'm not going to help you sell forgeries," she countered heatedly. "I'll admit I need money. But not badly enough to help you cheat innocent people."

His gray gaze hardened to cold steel. "I think you'll change your mind, Sara."

"Never!"

Instead of answering, Malcolm went over to the desk and picked up the telephone, dialing a two-digit number. "Peter? Please come down to the studio."

Now Sara was growing extremely frightened. Could it be that Peter had told Malcolm about her desire to steal the crown? If so, what would happen to her now?

A heavy silence hovered over the room as they awaited Peter Taylor's arrival. Sara was afraid to utter a word that might get her in deeper than she already was. Malcolm seemed disinclined to continue the conversation. He did, however, look like a poker player who had been dealt a hand of aces.

Peter's expression revealed nothing as he entered the studio. "What can I do for you, Malcolm? Sara?" he asked pleasantly, as if the tense atmosphere did not exist.

"Tell Sara where that painting she completed last month is," Malcolm instructed. "The Manet."

Peter's eyes engaged Sara's with an intensity she found more unnerving than Malcolm's calmly threatening gaze. "It's at the Hudson Gallery in Philadelphia." He smiled at her. "You should be quite proud, Sara. It went for a very good price."

White dots swirled on a background of black velvet, and Sara was afraid she was going to faint. Through the roaring in her ears, she heard Malcolm instruct Peter to help her to a chair and get her a glass of water. She wanted to shake off the hand that gripped her arm but found herself powerless to do so. Instead, she was forced to allow him to lead her to a white wicker chair. She slumped into it, covering her face with her hands.

"Here," Peter instructed, squatting by her side. "Take a drink. You'll feel better."

She shook her head.

He peeled her fingers from over her eyes, folding them around the glass. His gaze seemed almost sympathetic as he lifted it to her mouth. Sara sipped slowly, her dizziness gradually subsiding.

"You can't possibly involve me in anything like this," she protested. "I'll tell the police the truth. That I had nothing to do with it."

Malcolm sighed. "You are making this extremely difficult, Sara. Peter, tell our stubborn young friend who signed the bill of sale."

"Sara Madison," he stated quietly.

The idea that they'd try to frame her made Sara so angry, her head cleared instantly. "That doesn't prove a thing," she argued. "I've never been to Philadelphia."

"Show her the plane tickets," Malcolm instructed gruffly.

Peter reached into an inside pocket of his gray suit jacket, pulling out what was obviously a Xerox of a round-trip plane ticket for Sara Madison from Phoenix Sky Harbor International Airport to Philadelphia. She noted the date. It was the first night she had spent at the mansion.

"That's why you offered to let me stay here, isn't it?" she accused hotly. "Without a witness, I can't prove I was here in Phoenix the entire time."

Malcolm's thin lips curved in a smile. "You were gone overnight," he corrected. "That was just enough time to fly to Philadelphia, sell the forgery and return home again the following afternoon."

It was a very neat frame, Sara considered. But there was something Malcolm didn't know. There was one person who could testify that Sara had been home in the early hours of the morning—Noah. He had called her, waking her from a sound sleep. Her spirits lifted at the idea until she remembered what Noah was. How likely would the authorities be to take the word of a thief? They'd undoubtedly believe she and Noah had been working together.

"You're despicable," Sara charged heatedly, her flashing eyes moving from Malcolm to Peter. "Both of you."

"I told you, Sara," Malcolm stated carelessly, "one must possess the killer instinct to survive." He shot her a cold, triumphant smile. "Unfortunately, I have some business to attend to the next few days that will preclude discussing our future collaboration. The party, the interview with *Art Digest* magazine and something else that doesn't concern you. But you can rest assured, my dear, that we will be getting down to brass tacks very soon."

With that he left, leaving Sara alone with Peter. "How could you do that to me?" She jumped from the chair and turned on him. "I thought you, at least, were my friend."

Peter shook his head regretfully. "You're discovering something very basic about this business, Sara. You don't have friends; you have interests."

"And it was in your interest to help Malcolm weave his nasty little blackmail web?" she inquired acidly.

"Exactly."

"So where does all this leave me?"

A conciliatory shadow darkened his eyes. "Right now, up a creek," he admitted. "But it doesn't have to stay that way."

She eyed him suspiciously. "What does that mean?"

"You already know about the paintings," he said. "The illegally acquired ones he keeps in the basement vault."

Sara nodded.

Peter's eyes blazed with passion. "We're going to take them, too. With those paintings and the crown, we'll have enough money to live the rest of our lives in luxury in Brazil, where neither Malcolm nor the authorities will ever find us."

Sara studied Peter's uncharacteristic expression. "You really hate him, don't you?"

His mouth was set in a grim, taut line. "I have good reason. You're not the only fly he snared in his sticky little trap, Sara. But this time Malcolm Brand is going to learn that even he can be outsmarted."

He bent his head and kissed her heatedly, his lips pressing against hers with an almost-frightening strength. When Sara would have pulled away, Peter wrapped his arms around her, holding her helpless in the wake of his escalating passion.

Chapter Eight

Sara had just decided to kick Peter's shin as hard as she could when she heard a wonderfully familiar voice.

"Excuse me for interrupting, but I was wondering if I might have a word with Ms Madison?" Noah was leaning against the door frame, his expression amazingly bland, considering the circumstances.

Peter released Sara so abruptly that she almost fell back into the chair. "We'll finish this later," he promised under his breath before directing his attention to Noah. "She's all yours," he said agreeably as he left the room.

"He's one cool character," Noah observed as he ambled into the studio.

"You weren't the one he was manhandling," Sara snapped. "Believe me, there was nothing remotely cool about that kiss." She shook her head. "This entire thing is getting out of hand; you won't believe what happened just a few minutes ago."

Noah folded his arms over his chest and looked down at her. "Try me," he invited.

Sara crossed the room, looking out into the hallway. "Not here," she whispered nervously.

"Your room?" Noah suggested.

"No, not in the house. Not on the grounds. It has to be someplace else."

"My hotel?"

She remembered the pointed questions Malcolm had asked about Noah last night. What if he had someone staking out the hotel? "No, not there, either."

"My partner's got someone staying at the apartment right now. How about your place?"

Sara considered that for a moment. "That's good," she agreed. "Kevin should be at the sitter's, and Jennifer will be in class. Let me write the address down for you."

"Don't bother; I know it."

She wasn't really surprised. "All right. I'll meet you there in fifteen minutes."

"Make it a half hour," he countered. "I have a little business to take care of first."

"I hate to ask."

He grinned. "Don't worry that pretty little head. I'm just going to check out the security system in the basement."

"There's only one key," Sara informed him. "Malcolm keeps it locked in a wall safe."

Noah nodded. "Behind the Picasso."

Her lips tightened. "I should have known you'd have already discovered that."

"It's my business."

Sara groaned as she picked up her car keys from a nearby table. "Don't remind me."

Noah watched her as she left the studio, a thoughtful expression on his face.

THE FIRST THING Sara noticed when she entered her apartment was the suitcase standing by the front door. The next thing she saw was her nephew as he walked into the room, a peanut-butter-and-jelly sandwich in his hand.

"Hi, Aunt Sara," he greeted her. "We didn't expect you back this soon. Mom was just getting ready to call you."

"Hi, Kevin," Sara answered absently. "Where is your mother?"

"I'm here," Jennifer said, as she entered the room. She was followed by a tall, good-looking man in his mid-thirties. "Sara, this is Brian Stevenson. Brian, this is my sister Sara."

Brian held out his hand. "Sara, it's good to meet you. Jennifer has told me what a help you've been to her."

"You're her tutor," Sara guessed. "I may have shared some frozen dinners, but Jennifer gives you credit for rescuing her from that clinical psychology course."

"Your sister's an intelligent, capable woman," Brian replied. "She just needed someone to help her see that." Sara couldn't miss the fond gaze he and her sister exchanged.

"Brian's taking us up to his cabin in Strawberry for a few days," Kevin offered. "He's going to teach me how to fish."

Sara directed her words to Brian. "That's very nice of you."

"Not at all," Brian disagreed good-naturedly. "I'm looking forward to having Kevin and Jennifer along. Most of the time I'm stuck with a noisy old owl for company."

"I was just about to call you," Jennifer explained. "I didn't expect you to stop by."

"Something came up."

Jennifer's blue eyes focused on Sara's pale face. "Sara, are you all right?"

She managed a slight smile. "I'm fine."

"Are you sure? I don't have to go away if you'd like me to stay home."

"Mom," Kevin objected, "you promised I could catch our dinner tonight!"

"Don't worry about me," Sara assured her sister. "I'm just a little tired. I've been working too hard. I'll be glad when I can get back to the blissful chaos of the classroom."

Jennifer looked doubtful. "If you're sure," she relented hesitantly.

Brian's arm went around her waist. "Honey, did you ever think that your sister might appreciate a little peace and quiet?"

Sara gave him a grateful smile. "You've hit the nail on the head. That's all I need. You three have a wonderful time. Catch lots of fish," she said to Kevin.

"I will," he promised. "I'll bring one back for you, Aunt Sara."

"That will be lovely. Goodbye, Jen. Brian, it was nice meeting you."

"Terrific meeting you, too, Sara," he said, giving her a warm smile. "I hope we'll be seeing a lot of each other." He picked up the suitcase.

"Oh, you will," Jennifer trilled, waving goodbye to her sister. "We'll be back Sunday evening."

So it was serious, Sara mused. She was glad something was going well for someone these days. She went into the kitchen to make a pot of tea. It wasn't that she really wanted anything to drink, but the ritual of heating the pot and steeping the tea leaves would keep her busy while she waited for Noah. She was on her third cup when he finally arrived.

"You're late," Sara said the moment she had opened the door. "I've been going crazy!"

He gave her a lazy grin as he entered the apartment. "Miss me?"

"You know better than that," she scolded. "I was worried you'd gotten caught sneaking around in the basement."

"I never get caught."

She couldn't keep the distress from her tone. "There's always a first time."

They exchanged a long glance. "Don't worry about me," Noah said finally. "I know what I'm doing."

"Did you get into the vault?"

"Not exactly," he hedged. "But don't worry; I've got everything all worked out. All we need to do is come up with some type of diversion before Saturday." He looked at the cup she was still holding in her hand. "What are you drinking?"

"Tea."

"Sounds great," he said amiably. "Do you have another tea bag?"

"I brewed a pot," she answered, leading the way into the kitchen.

"Will wonders never cease," he teased, sitting down in a chair at the table. "A beautiful, talented woman who's also domestic. Now that's my idea of heaven."

"Don't get your hopes up," Sara advised dryly. "Tea and peanut butter sandwiches are the apex of my culinary skills." She took a cup down from the cupboard, filling it with the robust Irish breakfast tea.

"I like peanut butter sandwiches," Noah divulged agreeably. "Tell me what happened between you and Taylor. Besides that passionate clutch I caught you in."

"He's planning to take the paintings along with the crown," Sara divulged. "He wants us to run away to Brazil."

Noah took a drink of tea. "How's your Portuguese?"

She was irritated by his blatant lack of concern. "Nonexistent. But it's a moot point, since I'm not going."

"I didn't think you were. Is that what had you so upset? Surely you've survived an uninvited pass or two before today."

Sara assured Noah that she was more than capable of surviving any seduction attempts by Peter Taylor. Then she revealed Malcolm's sinister plan to make her continue to paint forgeries he could sell to the booming art market.

"I was wondering when he was going to bring that up to you," he said, sounding not at all surprised.

"Then you knew he'd tricked me?" She couldn't believe how calmly Noah was taking all this.

"Of course I didn't," he assured her. "But the guy would have to be stupid not to realize that you're a very talented woman. You could be quite an asset to the right man."

Sara wondered if Noah had entertained the idea of using her to paint copies for him. She was certain he'd never stoop to anything so vulgar as blackmail. He had probably planned to seduce her into working for him.

"Do you happen to be referring to anyone we know?" she inquired archly.

His grin was unrepentant. "You have to admit, we make a pretty good team, sweetheart."

She stiffened visibly. "This partnership is not going to continue past Saturday night," she warned. "The only reason I'm agreeing to help at all is because you said we could get Malcolm put away where he belongs." There was another reason, but Sara was loath to admit, even to herself, how much she had begun to care for Noah.

"What about the money?" he inquired curiously. "I thought you were all fired up about that ten-thousand-dollar finder's fee."

Sara couldn't help the smile that softened the tense lines on her face. "I wanted that money more for Jennifer than for myself. But I think my sister has found another champion."

"Lucky lady," he murmured.

Sara bobbed her head in agreement. "Brian seems very nice," she said. "I had hoped Jennifer would learn to stand on her own two feet before she got involved with another man. But Brian seems willing to help her learn to do that."

Noah ran his finger around the rim of his empty cup. "What about her sister?"

"Me? What about me?"

"Do you have a man in your life, Sara Madison?" he asked quietly.

The warmth of his gaze was heating her face. "No," she whispered.

He caught her chin in his fingers, holding her still as he kissed her lightly. "You're lying again, lovely Sara," he argued lightheartedly, his breath fanning her lips. "We both know that you do have a man in your life."

She fought against the way he could make her melt with a single touch, a mere look, the softest of kisses. Right now she felt like butter that had been left in the hot desert sun. "I suppose you're talking about yourself."

He traced the outline of her lips with his thumb. "Of course."

"It's not that easy, Noah."

His touch was creating havoc on her skin. "Of course it is," he corrected gently. "Or it would be if you'd stop fighting me at every turn."

"I'm not going to get involved with a thief, Noah. I couldn't live that way."

He refused to let the matter drop. "What if I *weren't* a thief?"

Sara felt herself weakening more with every passing second. "That's an impossible question to answer," she argued. "If you weren't a thief, you wouldn't be who you were, so how do I know how I'd feel about you?"

"How *do* you feel about me?" he asked, sounding honestly curious. His firm lips were just inches from her own, and Sara found herself longing to feel them against hers. She tried to muster up one more lie.

Noah perceived her intention. "The truth," he instructed softly.

She sighed, breaking the contact as she rose from the table. "I've never met anyone like you. Your life is so different from mine—I've always preferred the safe and narrow path, while you seem addicted to dangerous pursuits.... Of course I'm attracted to you," she admitted. "But I don't enter into casual affairs, Noah. And that's all it could ever be between us."

Noah rose, as well, leaning back against the kitchen counter, crossing his legs at the ankles. "Let me see if I get this straight," he said slowly. "You're attracted to me because I'm a thief. But you're not going to do anything about that attraction. Because I'm a thief."

"I know it sounds ridiculous," she protested weakly. "But you asked for the truth, Noah. And that's the way I feel."

He surprised her by smiling. "Far be it from me to argue with such convoluted thinking," he said agreeably.

Sara was stunned by his easy acceptance. "That's it?"

"That's it," he confirmed. "Unless you change your mind. I'm always willing to renegotiate the terms of this partnership."

"Speaking of partnerships, how do I get out of this mess with Malcolm?" she asked, redirecting her attention to her very real problem.

"The first thing to do is to stop that gallery from selling your forgery." At her glare, he held his hands up in mock surrender. "Excuse me. I meant to say your *copy*."

Sara nodded her approval. "That's better. It's certainly no crime to copy a painting."

"Of course it's not," he concurred. "However, if the copyist signed the original painter's name to the copy, then peddled it to a gallery in Philadelphia, the authorities might feel she'd perpetrated a fraud."

"Since you called me the night I was supposedly in Philadelphia, you know very well I couldn't have possibly sold that painting."

"Want me to go to the FBI with you?" he asked helpfully.

"Not on your life!"

Noah looked affronted. "I was simply trying to help."

"You're the damn expert," she snapped. "So come up with something else."

"We could steal the painting back from the Hudson Gallery."

Sara threw up her hands in disbelief. "Don't you *dare* even suggest such a thing!"

He gave her a devilish grin. "Spoilsport."

Sara took a bottle of aspirin from the cupboard, pouring two white tablets into her palm. As an afterthought, she added a third before filling a glass with bottled water from the refrigerator.

"Headache?" Noah asked solicitously.

"A dilly. It's been one hell of a day."

"You need to lie down."

Noah rose, looping his arm around her shoulders as he directed her from the kitchen. The first door he opened revealed a baseball mitt and bat on the floor.

"Whoops." He moved a few feet down the hall. "This is more like it," he noted, taking in the wallpaper sprigged with yellow flowers. "Get into bed and I'll bring you the phone."

"The phone?"

"You're going to call Brand and tell him that you've thought it over and you'll paint his forgeries."

"I will not!"

"For a share of the profits," he continued, as if not hearing her heated protest. "Then you will tell him that you've moved back home."

"What if he objects?"

"He won't. He's getting exactly what he wants, Sara. There isn't any need to have you staying at the house any longer." His expression firmed. "When does your sister get home?"

"She's away until Sunday," Sara admitted without thinking as she crawled under the comforter.

"That's even better. I'll stay here until the job's over."

"You're not staying here!"

"Of course I am," he corrected easily. "Unfortunately, I have some more work to do at Brand's mansion this afternoon. But I'll arrange to have a friend stay with you until I get back."

"I don't need a baby-sitter."

Noah muttered a low oath. He sat down on the edge of the bed, holding her face firmly between his hands. "In case it hasn't dawned on you yet, lady, you're running with a pretty rough crowd these days. All it would take is for Brand or Taylor to get the idea that you're not playing straight with them and you could be in a lot of trouble. I'm not taking that chance."

His low tone managed to frighten her more than any shout could have. "You're serious, aren't you?" she whispered, feeling as if an icy hand had suddenly gripped her heart.

"Deadly."

Sara shivered under the warmth of the flowered comforter. "I wish you hadn't put it that way," she objected.

"Don't worry; I won't let anything happen to you."

Noah looked inclined to kiss her again, and Sara found herself wanting him to. Instead, he reached out and picked up the telephone from her bedside table. "Call Brand," he instructed gruffly. "Then I'll call Dan."

It went exactly as Noah had predicted. Malcolm did not appear at all disturbed by Sara's moving out. Nor had he expressed surprise that she had agreed to his proposal. As to her receiving a percentage of the profits, he stated that the details could be worked out later. After Noah had made his call, he closed the draperies, telling Sara to get some sleep. A while later, she was dimly aware of voices in the living room. One she recognized as Noah's; the other belonged to a stranger. She tried to listen, but the stress of the past few hours caught up with her, and she drifted off to sleep.

As NOAH SAT in Malcolm Brand's private office, he forced himself to remember that nothing would be served if he allowed the fury surging through his veins to get the best of him. What the man had done to Sara was unconscionable, but from what Noah had learned about Brand, he was not particularly surprised. What did surprise him, however, was the overwhelming urge he had to break every bone in that aged body.

Midway through the bogus interview, Brand excused himself and disappeared into an adjoining room for a moment. When he returned, he was carrying a cage of white mice.

"You're just in time to watch Carmen eat her dinner," he said with an expectant smile. Reaching into the cage, he pulled out one of the squirming rodents, holding it up by its tail.

As Noah watched, Malcolm moved aside a decorative screen, revealing a large glass vivarium, home to a brown-and-gray-marked snake. As he dropped the unfortunate mouse into the vivarium, the pit viper immediately came to life, uncoiling her three-foot length.

"Carmen is a fer-de-lance," Malcolm advised. "She's extremely deadly. Do you know that they have fully formed fangs at birth? Natural-born killers," he murmured as the frightened mouse raced to one corner, trying vainly to scramble up the slick glass sides. A wave of repulsion washed over Noah as he observed Malcolm Brand's fascination with the scene. The man was smiling, his eyes bright and alert.

Noah flipped his notebook shut and rose from his chair. "I think I've got all I need for today."

The older man did not take his eyes from the cage. "Sit down, Mr. Lancaster," he instructed with a wave of his hand. "I assure you, Carmen can be very entertaining."

"I'm sure she can, but I really should get back to my hotel room and transcribe these notes."

"A snake's teeth are too sharp for chewing," Malcolm continued, as if he had not heard Noah's objection. "So they must swallow their prey whole. Fascinating, isn't it?"

"Fascinating," Noah echoed. "I'm sorry, Mr. Brand. I must go. I'm expecting a call from my office."

While the older man's eyes remained riveted on the drama taking place behind the glass walls of the vivarium, Noah left the office, wiping the sweat from his brow with his handkerchief.

It was not so much the snake's behavior that had disgusted him. He'd observed far larger snakes than Carmen devouring their prey in the wilds. It was Malcolm's obviously sadistic pleasure that had Noah wishing he had never gotten involved in this job in the first place. But then he remembered that if he hadn't shown up at the house to steal the crown, Sara would still be under the man's roof. She would have about as much chance of surviving in Brand's snake pit as that unfortunate mouse had had with Carmen.

He drove straight to her apartment, suddenly needing to see her. To make certain she was safe.

Chapter Nine

It was dark in the room when Sara awoke. Her headache was still with her, throbbing away with a vengeance, but at least she felt more rested. More relaxed. The apartment was silent, a vast change from the past six months.

"It's as quiet as a tomb," she murmured, wishing immediately that some other comparison had come to mind. Rising from the bed, she moved cautiously into the living room.

A man was sitting in her wing chair, reading the evening newspaper. His back was to her, but from his iron-gray crew cut, Sara guessed him to be somewhat older than Noah.

"You're awake," he said, suddenly turning toward her with an expectant smile.

Sara looked down at her bare feet. "You must have amazing hearing."

"Occupational hazard," he answered easily. "You get a certain radar about people coming up behind you."

"I can imagine," she replied. "Could I get you something? I was just on my way to the kitchen." It crossed her mind that if anyone had told her six weeks ago that she'd be entertaining jewel thieves in her apartment, she would have told them they were crazy.

He declined her offer. "No, thanks, I'm fine." Steady gray eyes observed her. "You look as if you still have that headache."

Sara was surprised by the sympathy she noted in his gaze. "I do," she admitted. "It's been a rather weird day."

"So Noah told me."

He put down the newspaper and rose from the chair. Sara observed that he was amazingly fit for a man of his age. His body was firm, his shoulders nearly as wide as Noah's. But he stood several inches shorter. And while his smile was warm, it didn't affect her the way Noah's could.

"I'm Dan Garrett."

"Hello, Mr. Garrett." Sara took the hand he offered. "I guess Noah's already told you who I am."

"Sure has," he agreed cheerfully. "Oh, and call me Dan. Mr. Garrett was my old man's name."

"Dan it is," Sara agreed weakly, wondering if all jewel thieves were so gregarious. This one reminded her of her insurance man.

"Let me get you something for that head," he offered solicitously. "I used to get migraines myself. Then I learned biofeedback from a swami while working in India and haven't had one since."

"Did you know Noah in India?" Sara questioned, taking the opportunity to delve a little into Noah's past.

The friendly eyes immediately grew blank. "Noah and I go back a long way," he replied noncommittally. "I'll check out your medicine cabinet for some aspirin." He left the room before she could question him further.

Sara was just debating whether to follow Dan and try again when she heard the key twist in the lock.

"If we ever have kids," Noah said by way of greeting, "remind me never to name any of them Carmen."

She shouldn't feel so happy to see him, but she was. Enough so that she wasn't going to argue that she and Noah would certainly never have children.

"Congratulations," she said instead. "Malcolm doesn't show Carmen off to just anyone." She wrinkled her nose. "It *is* gross, isn't it?"

"It's not so much Carmen as the way Brand gets such a big kick out of it. I think he must have been one of these little kids who pulled wings off flies." Noah shook his head. "However, on a brighter note, I have solved our problem concerning the distraction we need during the party."

A shiver of excitement raced up her spine. "Really? Tell me."

"There's something I have to do first." In one swift move, he pulled her against him, kissing her soundly. When his lips released hers, he smiled down into her face, his tawny eyes dancing devilishly. "I needed that."

Sara ran her finger up his chest. "Me, too," she admitted a little breathlessly.

Noah's eyes darkened as he debated his chances of carrying Sara into that frilly yellow bedroom and making love to her right now. A sound from the bathroom reminded him that they weren't alone, and he let out a frustrated sigh.

"You don't know how lucky you are that Dan is here," he said, his voice husky with pent-up passion.

As she looked up at him, Sara felt herself drowning in the warm, inviting pools of his eyes and wasn't all that certain she wanted to be saved. Would an affair with Noah be so wrong? she asked herself honestly. She was an intelligent, modern woman, not some wide-eyed romantic. People jumped into bed all the time these days without exchanging vows of undying love. Why shouldn't she?

"Lucky," she repeated unenthusiastically.

His eyes didn't leave hers as he traced the shape of her face with his fingertip. His expression was suddenly serious, no trace of his earlier teasing remaining. "Sara—"

"Here you go, lady!" Dan appeared, carrying a glass of water and the aspirin bottle. "Oh-oh," he interjected, his sharp eyes surveying the scene. "Sorry, guys; my timing's lousy."

Sara felt as if she'd just been snapped from the yawning jaws of a hungry lion. What on earth had she been thinking of? Noah hadn't even wanted to get involved with her in the first place. They were only together now because she'd refused to agree to give up her treasure without a fight. Well, in another two days Noah would have the crown and be gone. Out of her life. She'd be crazy to give him reason to remember her as the naive art-history professor in Phoenix who'd mistaken a one-night stand for anything substantial.

"No, Dan," she corrected with false brightness. "Your timing is absolutely perfect."

As she went to take the glass Dan offered, Sara refused to acknowledge Noah's frustrated look.

Dan appeared oblivious to the tension swirling about them. He sat down and fixed Noah with an expectant gaze. "Well, what's the scoop on the alarm system?"

"There's only one control switch," Noah said. "It's at the top of the stairs."

"Can we cut the power?"

Noah shook his head. "He's got that covered; the backup generator switches on automatically."

Dan rubbed his chin. "Is the floor weight sensitive, or is he using photoelectric beams?"

"Both."

Sara didn't know why Noah seemed so pleased with himself. Not that she was any expert, of course, but she had read enough spy stories to know that Malcolm had thought of everything.

"I see why you decided to take the crown during the party," Dan said.

Noah nodded. "It's the best way."

Dan rose from his chair. "Well, since you've gotten everything under control, I'll get going. See you Saturday night." He turned to Sara with a warm smile. "Goodbye, Sara. It was nice meeting you. I can't remember ever having such an attractive member on our team."

"It was nice meeting you, too," she responded, surprised to find that she meant it. He might be only another thief, but Dan actually seemed quite nice. Sara wondered what was happening to her sense of ethics.

As Noah walked with Dan to the door, Sara strained to hear what they were saying, but they were speaking too low for her to discern the words.

"So," Noah asked as he rejoined her, "how's the head?"

"Better," Sara answered absently. "If I'm a member of the team, how come I'm the only one who doesn't know what's going on?"

He looked at her as if he didn't know what she was talking about. "You know everything you need to know."

Sara stiffened. "I'm getting damned sick and tired of everyone believing they can use me for their own nefarious purposes," she complained.

"Do you have anything in the kitchen that'll make a decent dinner?" he asked suddenly.

"I don't know. Damn it, Noah, I want you to be straight with me."

"I'll tell you all I can, Sara. After dinner."

It wasn't much. But it was something, she decided. "All right," she agreed with a sigh. "Let's check out what Jennifer has in the refrigerator. But I'm warning you; don't hold your breath.''

They found the makings for hamburgers, and Sara began shaping the patties. "You know," she reminded him, "you still owe me a story about your family."

"So I do," Noah agreed easily, his head inside the refrigerator. "Hey, I just found some potatoes; we can have French fries."

"If you want to go to that much trouble, be my guest. The potato peeler's in the top drawer."

"This'll be great," he responded happily as he began to cover the bottom of the sink with curling pieces of potato skin.

"I'll give you this much," Sara allowed. "You're handy to have around a kitchen."

He winked. "You'll find I'm handy to have around the rest of the house, too."

Sara couldn't miss the seductive gleam in his eyes as she handed him a cutting board. "I believe you were going to tell me about your father."

He began slicing the potato into long, thin slices. "You're not going to let me off the hook, are you?"

"No way." She put the hamburger patties on a plate and searched around in a bottom cupboard for her deep fryer. "You owe me one, Noah."

He sighed heavily. "My family is not exactly my favorite topic of conversation, Sara."

Pots and pans came tumbling out onto the floor when Sara tried to extricate the fryer from the far reaches of the cupboard. Noah put down the potato and squatted down beside her to help.

"Nice filing system you have here."

"You're the one who invited yourself to dinner. If you don't like it, you can always go eat at the hotel."

He rocked forward on the balls of his feet, pressing a quick kiss against her firmly set lips. "Don't get on your high horse. I was only making an observation." Noah watched as she began throwing pans back onto the shelves. "They'll stack better if you put the little ones inside the big ones," he suggested helpfully.

Sara glared up at him. "Why don't you keep your observations to yourself? Besides, you were about to tell me about your family. What's the matter, are they professional crooks, too?"

He laughed at that. "Let me put it this way," he suggested, handing her a lid that had skidded over into a corner of the small kitchen. "My parents refer to me as their prodigal son."

"I can certainly understand that." She tossed the lid onto the pyramid of cooking utensils, then quickly slammed the door shut. Sara and Noah both eyed the cupboard expectantly.

"I think we've got it," Noah said.

"Of course," Sara agreed airily. "It's my own system. It never fails." She plugged in the fryer, filling it with cooking oil. "If your father's not a crook, what does he do?"

"He's a banker." The stainless-steel knife blade flashed as Noah sliced the potatoes with quick, deft strokes. "All the men in my family have been bankers. My grandfather, my great-grandfather—the line goes as far back as anyone can remember.

"Except my Uncle David," he added as an afterthought. "Anyway, Dad's always been annoyed that I didn't go into the family business."

Sara watched, fascinated by Noah's skill. She wondered if he had ever used such a weapon on anything other than a potato—like a person. Deciding she didn't want to know, she turned her mind back to the subject at hand.

"Your father is lucky you didn't. I can't imagine you resisting all that money."

He appeared honestly offended. "Can you really see me as a bank robber? You've hurt me, Sara. Deeply."

Actually, Sara found that as difficult as thinking of Noah as a jewel thief. But that's precisely what he was, and no amount of wishful thinking on her part was going to change that.

She shrugged. "Excuse me. I didn't realize that thieves had their own particular pecking order. I take it stealing jewels is a more prestigious occupation than robbing banks?"

"You are one funny lady," he muttered, dumping the raw potatoes into the stainless-steel basket. The oil sizzled as he lowered the basket into the pan.

"What does your uncle do?" Sara asked as she put the hamburger patties under the broiler.

"He's into art," Noah responded noncommittally. He took a jar of salad dressing, a bottle of catsup and a jar of sweet-pickle relish from the refrigerator. "You're going to love this; it's my own recipe for secret sauce."

Sara wasn't about to let him evade the question that easily. "Does he paint, sell or collect?"

Noah shrugged as he began beating the ingredients together into a small bowl. "A little bit of each."

"Would I know him?" Sara pressed.

"I doubt it; he's only a Sunday painter."

"So how does he earn his living?"

"He doesn't have to. He's rich."

"Oh." She allowed that thought to settle in for a moment. "Are you rich, Noah?"

"Would it make a difference?"

Sara considered the question. "Well, if you were stealing because you needed the money, that would be one thing."

She held up her hand, anticipating his next words. "Although I still wouldn't approve of what you do, at least I might be able to understand it."

"And if I were independently wealthy?" he asked casually.

"Then you'd just be doing this for kicks." She shook her head as she began shredding the lettuce.

"And you would approve of that even less," he guessed.

"Do you want onions on your hamburger?" Sara asked, changing the subject.

"Are you going to have them?"

"Of course. It's not a real hamburger without onions."

"A woman after my own heart," Noah said with a grin. "Make it two."

Sara began slicing the thick bermuda onion. "You still haven't answered my question."

His expression turned intensely serious. "Sara, why don't you stop looking for obstacles?"

Her fingers began to tremble. "I don't know what you're talking about," she protested.

"Of course you do. You're trying to find out something about me that explains this attraction we have for each other. You've always been an upright, law-abiding citizen, and it's too abhorrent for you to admit you want to make love to a common criminal. So you're seeking some excuse that will allow you to give into your feelings."

His amber eyes turned dark as they swept over her face. "I'll bet that overactive imagination even came up with some scenes right out of Dickens. You tried painting me as a modern-day Oliver Twist, deprived as a child, forced to steal in order to survive."

That was hitting a bit too close to home for comfort. Sara sliced viciously at the onion, cutting the tip of her finger in the process.

"Damn! Now look what you've made me do!"

Noah grabbed her hand, sticking it under cold running water. "Hold it there," he instructed. "I've got to save our dinner."

Sara fought back her tears as she watched him turn the hamburgers and dump a pile of golden French fries on a paper towel.

"Now let's see what we need to do with you," he said, returning to her. He lifted her finger from the water. "It's not very deep. But you should have a bandage on it."

"They're in the cupboard next to the glasses."

He located them immediately, drying her hand with a spare paper towel before wrapping the adhesive strip around the cut. Then he lifted her finger to his lips.

"Is that better?" he asked softly, eyeing her affectionately over their linked hands.

Sara nodded.

"I'm sorry I upset you."

"It wasn't what you said," she lied.

Noah gave her a little half smile. "Of course it was," he corrected easily. "For the record, Sara, I'm not stealing the crown because I was deprived as a child. Or because I'm rebelling against my upper-middle-class New England background. Or even for kicks. I'm long past the age of silly fraternity pranks."

"Then why are you doing it?" she asked quietly.

He pressed his finger against her lips. "You ask too many questions."

Sara jerked away from him, marching over to yank open the refrigerator door. "There's cola, milk, white wine or beer. Take your pick."

"Beer'll be great," he agreed without enthusiasm.

"Fine," Sara spat out, slamming the bottle onto the table.

The easy mood had evaporated, and neither seemed inclined toward conversation as they ate their dinner in silence. Sara knew that his French fries were cooked to perfection—crisp and golden on the outside, tender inside. Even so, they were forming into a hard ball in the pit of her stomach, along with the rest of her dinner. After two glasses of wine, she felt no more relaxed.

"Are you going to sulk all night?" Noah asked finally as they cleared the table.

Sara put the rinsed plates into the dishwasher. "I don't sulk."

Locating the detergent, Noah filled the dispenser cups. "You're giving a damned good imitation."

She turned to him, her wet hands dampening her white jeans. "I've had a bad day, Noah. Correction—I've had an absolutely lousy week. I've been threatened, blackmailed and spied upon. I'm expecting the FBI to show up at any moment and cart me off to jail for selling a forged Manet to some gallery in Philadelphia that I've never even heard of. And when they do arrive, it's going to be damn difficult to prove my innocence when I'm in the company of a man who's probably wanted by every law enforcement agency from the FBI to Interpol to the KGB."

Sara didn't like the guilty expression that flitted across Noah's face. "Oh, God, Noah, not the KGB?"

He gave her a lopsided grin. "Sara, I think this is one of those things you don't really want to know."

She sank down into a chair, covering her face with her hands. "You're right," she groaned. "I don't. I don't want to know what you stole from the Russians." She lifted her head. "They wouldn't happen to know where you are, would they?"

He shook his head. "Last I heard, they were celebrating my demise in the mountains of Afghanistan."

Her eyes widened. "Afghanistan?"

Noah shrugged. "It's a little difficult to explain,"

"Don't bother," Sara replied with a deep sigh. "I've never held up very well under torture, Noah. I'd probably tell them anything they wanted to know." Her blue eyes were laced with very real distress. "And on top of everything else, in two days I'm going to risk my neck to steal something that rightfully belongs to the Turkish government! Can you imagine what life must be like in a Turkish prison?"

"Room service probably leaves a lot to be desired," he agreed.

Sara threw her hands up in the air. "This is all a nightmare," she affirmed impatiently. "If I just stay calm, I'll wake up in the morning and not remember any of this. Jennifer will be burning the toast, and Kevin will be relating the latest adventures of Conan the Barbarian in agonizing detail over his cornflakes."

"Would you like some coffee?"

"I'd like you to go away. Back to Afghanistan or wherever it is you came from." She blinked, as if hoping the action would cause him to dematerialize. She wasn't that lucky.

"I will," he promised. "As soon as I get the crown."

"That damn crown again," Sara said heatedly. "A month ago I'd never even heard of it. Now it's turned my entire life upside down."

Noah stroked her hair with a wide, ineffectual hand. "It'll all be over in two days," he promised soothingly.

"We could both be dead in two days."

He perched his hip on the edge of the table, cupping his fingers around her chin as he lifted her distressed gaze to his solemn one. "I promised I'd never let anything happen to you, Sara."

"Unless it was a choice between me and your precious crown," she argued.

His fingers tightened. "That's a rotten accusation. You're a helluva lot more important to me than any damn crown!"

Sara wanted to believe him. "You sound as if you actually mean that," she said softly.

"Lady, the day I get my priorities that mixed up is the day I retire and take up fly-fishing."

She couldn't allow the opportunity to pass. "You could do that, anyway, you know," she said hopefully. "Right now. Tonight."

"You can't fly-fish at night, Sara," Noah said patiently. "Besides, to tell you the truth, I hate fishing. It's boring; there's not enough challenge."

And Noah was a man who lived on challenge, Sara thought sadly. He was never going to change. "You're not going to give it up, are you?"

His eyes gave her an apology. "I can't, Sara. Not even for you."

Well, that was that. The legs of her chair scraped against the floor as she stood up. "I think I'll go to bed," she announced stiffly.

"I take it that's a negative on the coffee."

It took all Sara's vast store of willpower to meet Noah's strangely disappointed gaze. "That's a negative on everything."

His lips tightened, but Noah merely nodded in response, saying nothing as she left the room. Once she was gone, he slammed his fist into his palm. Not one thing about this heist had gone as planned, and it appeared that the situation could only get worse.

In order to succeed, he needed Sara's help. There was no other way; he'd gone over it a thousand times in his mind. And while she had already agreed in theory, Noah knew he would have one hell of a fight on his hands when she discovered what she was going to have to do.

"I'll just take a little tactful persuasion," he told himself. "She'll come around. In time."

Noah continued to assure himself of Sara's eventual capitulation long into the night. But as hard as he tried, he never could quite get himself to believe his own encouraging words.

Sara was still awake when Noah entered her bedroom several hours later. She'd found sleep impossible, for her mind continued to mull over and over the events of the past few days.

"What do you want?" she asked, propping herself up on her elbows to look at him.

A shaft of moonlight streamed through the slit in the draperies, illuminating Noah's face. He looked tired, Sara thought. Drawn. And decidedly tense.

"Some sleep," he answered as he began to unbutton his shirt.

"Well, you're certainly not sleeping in here. Use Kevin's room."

"I tried that. I'd have to be a contortionist to fit on that roll-away bed you've got the kid sleeping on."

He pulled off the shirt, tossing it uncaringly onto the nearest chair. When his fingers went to his waistband, Sara experienced a disturbing jolt of need. She turned away.

"I haven't changed my mind." Sara wasn't certain whom she was reminding of that fact—Noah or herself.

"Don't worry," he assured her, his tone thick with sarcasm. "I'm much too tired to do anything even if I wanted to. Besides, considering your prickly attitude, I'd just as soon make love to a porcupine."

"You are so complimentary," she muttered into her pillow.

She heard a clunk as his belt buckle hit the floor. "Just calling them as I see them," Noah stated blandly. The cool breeze from the air conditioner feathered across her back as he pulled the sheet back. "Scoot over; you're hogging the whole bed."

As Sara felt his long legs brush against hers, she needed no further encouragement. She inched her way to the very edge of the mattress, holding on with her fingertips. She held her breath, waiting for Noah to touch her. But moments later she heard the steady sound of breathing and realized he had fallen asleep. Sara didn't know whether to feel relieved or insulted.

THE HARSH DEMAND of the phone shattered the predawn darkness. Sara groped for the receiver. "Hello?"

"Ms Madison?"

"Yes. Who is this?"

"I'm sorry to wake you, Ms Madison, but it's important that I speak with Noah."

Noah was awake, sitting up beside her, watching her with expressionless eyes.

"It's for you," Sara said, handing him the receiver. She turned on the bedside lamp.

As he listened, his eyes beamed with satisfaction. "Good work, Joe. I appreciate your taking care of it so quickly. I know Ms Madison will be relieved." He gave her an encouraging smile. "Yeah, I will," he agreed, returning his attention to the caller. "Give Ellen my love."

Noah handed the receiver back to Sara. "Sorry about the phone call waking you up." He turned off the lamp, then stretched out on his side, his back to her.

"Hey, just a minute," Sara complained as she hung up the disconnected telephone. "What am I going to be relieved about?"

"I'll tell you in the morning," Noah mumbled, pulling the sheet up to his chin. "Let's get back to sleep."

Glaring down at his chestnut head, she yanked the sheet off him impatiently, discovering too late that he was stark naked.

Noah observed her patiently over his shoulder. "Change your mind?" he asked agreeably.

Sara kept her eyes steadfastly on his face. "I want to know what I'll be relieved about."

Noah sighed as he sat up, his back against the headboard. "Your Manet is no longer at the Hudson Gallery."

Relief mixed with dread flowed through her. "Noah, you didn't have anyone steal it, did you?"

His gaze was fond as he reached out and tousled the disarray of blond hair. "Not exactly." His wide palm was moving down her throat, and she knew he could feel her swallow under his touch.

"What does that mean?"

His voice was dark, warm and all too enticing. "Sara," he whispered as his fingers toyed with the strap of her nightgown, "why don't you try trusting me? Just this one time."

His clever hands smoothed over her shoulders, encouraging her acquiescence. A warmth infused her blood, moving through her veins like heated honey.

"You're a thief," she complained softly, closing her eyes to the tender torment of his increasingly intimate caresses. When his hand slid between the silk of her nightgown and the satin of her skin to cup her breast, Sara trembled.

"I'm a man," he corrected huskily, pressing his body down on hers to allow her to feel the strength of his need. "Why can't that be enough for you, Sara?"

As she opened her mouth to try to explain, Noah covered her lips with his. It was a deep, drugging kiss, and when he finally lifted his head, all Sara could manage was a long, shuddering breath.

Noah's eyes were brilliant gold flames as they burned down into her softly glazed blue ones. "Tell me I'm not imagining things," he demanded. His voice was rough and unusually gravelly. "Tell me that you want me as much as I want you."

Sara was teetering on the brink of insanity, struggling to overcome the primitive responses created by the feel of his warm, hard body pressing her deeper and deeper into the mattress.

Noah could feel Sara's body trembling against his; he could feel the wild beating of her heart and saw the raw, answering desire in her wide, frightened eyes. Even as he pressed his advantage, he sought to reassure her.

"Don't be afraid of me, love," he crooned into her ear while his fingers glided along the soft skin of her inner thigh. "I'd never do anything to hurt you."

His slow hands were so deft, so practiced, as they roamed her body under the blue silk nightgown. Sara luxuriated in his touch, no longer caring whether her behavior was unwise or imprudent. She only knew that she had never experienced such golden pleasure.

When his lips pressed against her skin, Sara cried out at the fire his open mouth created. Her body tensed.

"Shh." His stroking hands soothed the tension from her body, and Sara relaxed, languidly accepting his fluid caresses, wherever they chose to roam.

She was floating on a calm, tropical sea of pleasure. Her limbs were heavy, suffused with a soothing warmth, while her mind drifted on tides of lazy passion.

Noah took his time, allowing Sara to grow accustomed to his touch, his taste, giving her time to relinquish her emotional objections to their lovemaking. As he stripped the nightgown from her body with one hand, the other never ceased its gentle caresses, moving from her shoulders to her knees with an expertise that owed far more to feelings than experience.

Her body flowed like liquid silk under his touch, her creamy flesh glistening in the silver moonlight. Her eyes were closed, her lashes resting on her cheeks, and were it not for the way her body had begun to move, Noah would have thought Sara had fallen asleep.

In the beginning, Sara had been content to lie still, allowing Noah's seductive hands to explore her body at their leisure. But an alien sensation began to hum through her, dark and insistent, creating a need just this side of pain. She arched her back, reaching for his touch, her hair splayed on the pillow as she tossed her head back and forth.

Sara heard the soft moans and realized they were coming from her own lips. The pressure within her was building to explosive heights, and she reached for him blindly, pleading wordlessly for fulfillment.

"Not yet," he commanded, his breath filling her mouth as his thumbnail scraped against one taut, tingling nipple. "You're not ready yet."

He seemed intent on possessing her, his hands and lips continually seeking out flash points of pleasure Sara had never known existed. She writhed on the bed, her body vibrating with need, her skin hot and moist. Pinpoints of a strawberry flush darkened her chest, creating a vibrant contrast to her creamy complexion as it spread between her breasts, down her rib cage and across her abdomen. As Noah followed the heated path with his tongue, a mindless excitement took hold of her, searing away the last remaining vestiges of reason.

Noah thought he'd explode as he tasted the passion emanating from Sara's every pore. He could not remember wanting a woman more. He could not recall a time when it was more important to bring a woman pleasure.

The power shifted so abruptly that Noah was given no time to understand how he had lost control. Suddenly, Sara's slender hands were moving over him, her avid mouth teasing, tasting and tormenting him until she had coaxed a ragged groan from the depths of his chest. When he would have pulled her onto him, Sara eluded him, intent on learning Noah's secrets as he had learned hers.

Time ceased to exist as Sara sought to display feelings she could not put in words. But she was telling Noah, with her heated caresses, with the kisses she rained over his body, that whoever he was, whatever he did, she trusted him. With her life.

Unable to take any more, Noah utilized his superior strength, turning Sara onto her back as he hovered over her expectant body. As their eyes held, Sara's pupils widened, appearing like gleaming obsidian moving over sparkling sapphire.

"Yes," she murmured, wrapping herself about him. "Yes, yes, yes."

Chapter Ten

Sara awoke to the sound of birds twittering outside her window. As she opened her eyes, she found Noah propped up on one elbow, looking down at her, a self-satisfied smile on his face.

"If I could paint," he said. "I'd want to capture you just like this."

Although Sara knew she should feel uncomfortable by the presence of a naked thief in her bed, the lingering memories of last night's lovemaking caused her to smile.

"No woman in her right mind would let any man paint her first thing in the morning," she complained with a smile. She lifted her fingers to brush a cloud of blond hair from her eyes.

Noah caught her hand, pressing a kiss against her palm. With his other hand he tucked her hair behind her ears. "On the contrary," he argued, "that's when a woman is the most beautiful. She hasn't had time to don her proper, civilized mask, so her eyes are filled with passion, and her lips are warm and enticing." He ran his finger down her face. "Especially if she's been well loved the night before."

"You sound like quite an expert on women the morning after," she argued, attempting to sound cool and detached. Instead, her voice held a soft question.

"I'm an expert on you," he corrected. "You work over-time to create the image of a strong, independent female, Sara Madison. But deep down you're a warm, passionate woman. You need a man who can match that passion."

"And you think you're that man."

His lips brushed hers in a tantalizing caress. "I know I am. We're two of a kind, sweetheart. I've never met a woman I wanted more than you. Needed more than I do you. You're mine now, Sara."

Sara was startled by the depth of feeling in his voice. "Noah, what we shared last night was wonderful; I've never experienced anything like it," she admitted. "But we shouldn't misinterpret what it was."

He arched a brow. "And what, exactly, was it?"

Sara moved out of his arms, feeling unreasonably vul-nerable as his eyes turned hard. He gave her a mocking look as she reached down, pulling the tangled sheet up around her.

"Sex," she answered softly.

His expression turned gentle as his finger traced her skin above the yellow flowers. "You know better than that."

She shook her head. "Noah, there can't be anything else between us."

"Why not?"

"Because it's too soon." When he looked inclined to ar-gue, Sara took a deep breath. "And because I don't want there to be anything else," she confessed.

Noah frowned. "You trusted me last night, Sara. You can't deny that."

She couldn't. But that didn't mean she approved of him.

"Two days," he reminded her. "Two more days and all this will be over and we can concentrate on us."

"There can't be any us," she persisted. "After the party, you'll have the crown. That's what you've always wanted."

"That was before I met you. Before we made love."

His warm gaze threatened to be her undoing. "Don't do this, Noah. You're being unfair."

He sighed. "You win," he relented, throwing back the sheet as he gave up the pleasure of lying beside her. "We'll take it one day at a time."

Sara didn't quite trust his easy acquiescence. "Promise?"

His answering smile didn't quite reach his eyes. "I promise. But I'm not going to give up without a fight, lady."

He was towering over her, and Sara tried not to be affected by his uncompromising strength, his seductive stance. He was an intimidating man under the best of circumstances. Nude, he radiated a masculine power that reminded her of a Greek statue. *Two days,* Sara reminded herself. Surely she could keep from falling under his spell again for that short period of time.

"I didn't expect you would," she said quietly.

Noah had no intention of letting Sara get away. He was leaving Saturday after they had taken the crown. And she was coming with him. He'd let her believe what she wanted to for now; this job depended on their ability to work together. But the game would be over after Brand's party, and he was playing to win.

"I'd better get dressed," he announced abruptly. "I've got some things to take care of before the party." He scooped up his clothes from the floor, leaving the room. Moments later, Sara heard the sound of the shower in the adjoining bathroom.

She rose, her body unusually stiff as she slipped into a white eyelet robe. She had the coffee made by the time he entered the kitchen.

"That smells great," he greeted her warmly, as if the tense scene in the bedroom had never occurred. He was buttoning his shirt, and she had to jerk her eyes from the beads of moisture nestled in the crisp dark hair covering his chest.

"Help yourself," Sara offered. "I want to brush my teeth and take a shower."

"Go ahead; I'll make breakfast," he offered.

"I don't eat breakfast."

"Really? I thought that was just something you told Brand so you wouldn't have to hang around after the ride."

"I never eat a thing before noon."

"We'll have to work on changing that," he offered amiably. "Didn't your mother ever tell you that breakfast is the most important meal of the day?"

Sara held up her hand. "Noah, I'll make a pact with you. I won't try to change you if you'll agree to let me muddle through life in my own way."

He shrugged. "Whatever you say."

She eyed him suspiciously, but his answering smile was absolutely guileless. Still feeling it was too easy, she left the room, wondering what surprise Noah was going to pull from his little bag of tricks next.

When she returned to the kitchen, Noah was seated at the table, eating an enormous stack of hotcakes as he studied a set of blueprints. He smiled a greeting.

"I like that dress; you look like a breath of spring."

Sara returned his smile, pleased by his response. She had admittedly chosen the flowered sundress with him in mind.

"Thank you, although we're well past spring. It's supposed to get up to a hundred and twelve today."

"Maybe we should fill the bathtub with ice cubes and stay in the apartment all weekend," he suggested with a friendly leer.

Sara poured herself a cup of coffee and refilled Noah's empty cup. "Good try, but I thought you had work to do today."

He ran his hand up the back of her leg. "I do. But I can always make time for a little R and R."

His touch was enticing, and it was all Sara could do not to drop the coffeepot. "Are those plans of Malcolm's house?" she asked, refusing to submit to the ache of pleasure that his touch had created.

Noah sighed, returning his attention to the blueprints. "Yep. Here's your studio, here's Brand's office, and here's the vault where he stashed the crown."

"He has it already?"

Noah nodded. "It arrived last night."

Sara stared at him. "How do you know that?"

"It's my business to know," he answered cryptically. "Now, the way I see it, the only sure way into that room is through the air-conditioning ducts." His finger traced the path. "There's an access in the ceiling of Brand's office. That particular duct runs across the length of the house, right down into the gallery."

Sara sat down beside him and studied the blueprints thoughtfully. She lifted her gaze to Noah's broad shoulders. "I'm no expert, but those ducts can't be that large. How can you possibly fit in them?"

His answering silence was ominous. The sky outside the kitchen window was a clear, endless blue, but Sara felt as if a thundercloud had suddenly moved across the sun.

"I'm not going to do it," she announced firmly, pushing her chair away from the table.

He caught her hands, refusing to let her get away. "Sara, it's the only way."

She shook her head, her hair swirling between them. "Noah, you can't possibly ask me to do such a thing. I can't even get into an elevator. I'd never be able to crawl through that maze of ductwork." Her blue eyes pleaded with him.

His fingers tightened around her ice-cold ones. "I'm counting on you."

Sara stared at him, frightened by the intensity of his expression. Her eyes widened as all the pieces of the puzzle suddenly seemed to fall into place.

"That's what last night was all about, wasn't it?" She tugged furiously in an attempt to free her hands. "You thought you could seduce me into going along with your wild schemes?"

His jaw hardened. "That's a ridiculous accusation."

"Is it?" she blazed. "You're good, Noah. I'll give you that. But I still won't do it."

He couldn't believe she could actually misconstrue what they had shared last night. His fingers tightened even more, but at Sara's sudden gasp of pain, Noah loosened his hold on her, allowing her to yank her hands free and stand up from the table.

"What happened last night had nothing to do with this," he insisted.

"Didn't it?" She rubbed her fingers as she gave him a cynical smile.

Noah dragged his hand through his hair. "Of course it didn't." He wore a look of frustration. "Sit down, Sara. Let's discuss this rationally."

She held her ground. "I'm not getting near you. You've already nearly broken my fingers. How do I know you won't beat me?"

"I'm almost tempted to do exactly that," he admitted, his voice hinting at his barely restrained impatience.

Sara couldn't resist goading him. "I'm not surprised. After all, a man who earns his living the way you do is undoubtedly not above hitting a woman."

She realized she had gone too far when flames burst to life in the amber depths of his eyes. He was out of the chair before she knew what was happening. A moment later, she was in his arms, held tightly against him.

"Take that back," he commanded gruffly.

Sara thought she saw a shadow of pain behind the remoteness of his eyes, but her acute sense of betrayal refused to allow her to acknowledge it.

"No."

He pressed his body into hers. His chest flattened her breasts; his buckle dug into the soft swell of her stomach; his thighs were hard and implacable. She staggered, and they both fell back against the wall. The strength of his body was both intimidating and sexual.

"Then tell me that you honestly believe last night was nothing but a lie."

There was nowhere to go, no way to escape the increasingly sexual demand that was invoking an unwanted response from her rebellious body. Sara tried to think of a blistering response, struggling to remind herself that this was a man without scruples, a man used to taking whatever he wanted from life. As he had taken her last night. But a thick fog was settling over her brain, and all she could think about was the warmth of his body pressing against her, fitting itself so perfectly against her responsive female softness.

"Let me go," she insisted softly.

"I will," he agreed, his breathing strained as he fought to remember that force never solved anything. "As soon as you prove to me you don't want me."

He ducked his head, his intent clear. Instead of turning away, Sara closed her eyes as their mouths met blindly, insistently, passion scorching away reason, need dissolving antagonism. Her body arched against his; her cries were swallowed by his mouth; her shaking legs turned to rubber. Were it not for Noah's strong body holding her against the wall, Sara knew she'd fall to the floor.

Just when she thought she'd explode, Noah broke the kiss. His expression was less harsh than it had been earlier, but his eyes still held a blazing intensity. His mouth was inches from hers, his even breath wafting against her lips.

"Tell me you don't feel it," he dared in that rough, gravelly voice that pulled at something deep within her. "Tell me that I'm the only one going crazy."

She had told too many lies. She could barely live with herself now. And as she gazed into Noah's eyes, Sara knew she could never lie to him. Not after last night.

"You're not," she whispered. "God help me, Noah, I don't want to feel this way about you. But I do."

His mouth lightly brushed hers. "That's all I ask."

Sara felt bereft when he suddenly released her. "Noah?"

His gaze was warm, a smile of contentment softening his expression. "I'll be back," he promised. "I have a lot of work to do if we're going to change the plan at this late date." He turned and headed toward the kitchen door.

Sara's heart swelled as she realized that Noah wasn't going to ask her to do the impossible. He was willing to risk his precious crown to save her the discomfort he knew she'd suffer if forced to crawl along the narrow black tunnels of the air-conditioning ducts. Then another thought occurred to her. He could also be risking his life, his freedom. While she still had every intention of persuading Noah to return the crown to the proper authorities, she knew that she could not stop him from carrying out the theft itself. The challenge had become paramount, surpassing even the riches represented by Malcolm's plundered booty.

She rubbed absently at her wrists, knowing that her skin would bear bruises from his strong fingers. But that thought did not bother her; Noah had branded her his own in a far more elemental manner last night.

"Is it really impossible to do it any other way?" she asked softly.

Noah stopped in his tracks, turning slowly to look at her. He experienced a stab of guilt at the sight of her pallid complexion.

"It's not going to be easy." Then he winked, encouraging her to smile. "But don't worry that pretty little head. I'm renowned for doing the impossible."

Sara took a deep breath. "I'll do it."

It was at that moment Noah understood the feelings he had been experiencing for Sara Madison. He loved her, he realized with a sense of surprise and wonder. Even as that idea surfaced with the crystal clarity of a mountain stream, Noah knew that Sara was not ready for any emotional proclamations. She had good reason to hate what he appeared to be; she would not admit her own feelings easily. But although she might not realize it, by agreeing to enter those ducts, she had proclaimed her own love as loudly as if she had shouted it from the rooftops.

He crossed the space between them in two long strides, holding her by the shoulders as he looked down into her pale, uplifted face.

"You're one helluva woman, Sara Madison," he proclaimed huskily. He have her a swift, hard kiss. Then, before he could change his mind and take her back to bed, Noah turned to leave.

"Lock the door behind me," he instructed firmly. "And don't open it for anyone."

Sara nodded. "Good luck."

His eyes sparkled, and he shook his head, as if bemused by his good fortune. "With you in my corner, I don't need luck."

Sara was still smiling long after he'd gone.

Despite Noah's warning, as the day dragged on, Sara found herself thinking of tomorrow night. While she knew she should be concentrating on the theft, her mind kept wandering to Noah and how his eyes had lit up when he'd viewed her wearing the feminine sundress.

A perusal of her closet revealed what Sara already knew. She owned two items of formal evening wear—a floor-length sea-green crepe for summer and a black wool for winter functions at the university. She'd had both for years, and the kindest thing she could say about them was that they were made of serviceable material and wore well. They were certainly not the type of attire worn by the fashionable women who moved in Noah's world of precious jewels and fine art.

Deciding she had better let Noah know where she was going, Sara placed a call to the mansion, pretending to be a secretary from *Art Digest* magazine. Surprised when the phone was answered in an unmistakable foreign accent, Sara forgot her plan to disguise her voice.

"Baroness?"

"Yes," the woman replied, her voice unnaturally high. "Who is this?"

"Sara Madison. Is everything all right?"

"It's absolute chaos," the older woman related. "Those horrible mice of Malcolm's have gotten loose, and they're running all over the house."

As Sara heard a muffled shriek, she realized one of the rodents had obviously made an appearance.

"Sara, I can't talk right now," the baroness said. "I'll tell Malcolm you called."

"Don't do that," Sara said quickly. "Tell me, is Mr. Lancaster at the house?"

"Noah? No, he left some time ago. Why?"

Sara's mind went into overdrive to come up with an acceptable excuse. "I was just wondering if the mice were going to make it into the article."

"Unfortunately not," Gizella stated dryly. "It would give me great pleasure to see *the* Malcolm Brand embarrassed in a national publication."

"Baroness," Sara asked suddenly as inspiration struck. "Where do you get your clothes?"

"My clothes?"

"I need an evening dress for tomorrow night." Although Gizella could be a royal pain, Sara had to admit the woman had exquisite taste in clothing.

"I go to Paris twice a year," Gizella revealed.

That was farther than Sara had in mind. "Oh," she replied, her disappointment evident.

The baroness appeared to take pity on her. "However, there is one boutique downtown that is suitable in a pinch. Although I really don't think you could afford it, dear," she tacked on solicitously.

Sara was in the mood to throw caution to the winds. "The name, baroness?"

"Gallant's." A sudden squeal threatened to shatter Sara's eardrum. "Really, Sara, I have to go." The phone went dead.

Imagining the sight of the baroness dodging the small white mice, Sara grinned as she hung up the phone. She next tried Noah at the hotel, but there was no answer. Deciding that she could conclude her shopping before Noah returned, she retrieved her purse from the bedroom and left the apartment.

Gallant's was located downtown, near the convention center. The obvious intent was to lure wealthy tourists who had both excess time and money to spend. The small boutique was filled with one-of-a-kind designer originals, none bearing anything so plebeian as a price tag. As Sara's gaze returned again and again to one particular evening gown, she worked up her nerve to ask the saleswoman the price.

Sara stifled a groan at the woman's answer. She'd have to work at the university for three months to pay for the exquisitely designed dress. But then, recalling the way Noah's eyes could light up with such seductive warmth, she decided to try it on.

"It's you," the saleswoman gushed as Sara exited the dressing room.

Sara twirled in front of the three-way mirror, holding out the skirt of the unabashedly romantic gown. Fashioned in the style of a Mexican wedding dress, it was crafted from the sheerest ivory gauze. Worn off the shoulder, it fell to the floor in tiers, each tier edged with delicate, hand-sewn lace.

"I'll take it," she decided, handing the woman her charge card before she could change her mind. A few minutes later, she left the shop a poorer but decidedly happier woman.

As she was getting into her car, Sara caught a glimpse of a familiar face entering the Federal Building across the street. She tossed the dress box onto the back seat, locked the door and raced across the street, mindless of the heated protests from drivers as she crossed against the light.

Fortunately, Daniel Garrett was visiting an office on the first floor, saving Sara from having to take one of those dreaded elevators. However, as she viewed the bold black lettering on the door, her heart froze. What on earth could Noah's partner be doing at the FBI?

There was only one possible answer, and it wasn't at all palatable. Dan was obviously working with the authorities to trap Noah. She ran from the building, hastily scooping up the dress box from the car seat.

"I'm sorry," the saleswoman announced firmly. "But I can't allow you to return the dress for cash." She pointed toward a sign that stated in gilt calligraphy, "No refunds. Store credit only issued on returns."

"But I haven't even worn it," Sara objected.

"I'm sorry, dear. But that's our policy. You're welcome to exchange it for any equivalent dress in the store."

"But I need the credit applied to my charge card," Sara explained. "An emergency has come up, and I need the money I can draw from my credit line."

The woman's green eyes displayed sympathy, but she remained firm. "If it were up to me, I'd take the dress back in a minute. But I'm only the manager."

Realizing she was only wasting time, Sara put the box under her arm and left the store. Five minutes later, she was at the bank, closing out both her checking and her savings account, grateful that the disinterested teller offered no objections. Not that she was depriving the bank of that much working capital, she concluded as she drove across town. She had one more step to make.

When Sara finally returned to the apartment, she found Noah waiting, his face ashen, his eyes wild.

"Where the hell have you been?" he demanded the moment she entered the room. His fingers dug into her shoulders.

"I went out to buy a dress," she began to explain.

Noah cut her off before she could continue. "A dress? You risked your neck over a damned dress?" His expression was incredulous.

"For the party," she answered, as if that explained everything.

He released her, dragging unsteady fingers through his already tousled dark hair. "Do you realize I've been going crazy? Do you have any idea what was going through my mind? Couldn't you have at least left me a note?"

"I wasn't expecting to be gone that long," she explained. "But something happened, Noah."

He crossed his arms, glaring down at her. "This had better be good," he warned.

Sara dug into her purse, pulling out an envelope, which she extended toward him. She couldn't remember ever seeing Noah so angry. Not even this morning. There was not a glimmer of warmth in his hard eyes.

"For me?" he asked brusquely.

She nodded, words failing her.

Noah opened the envelope, staring at the slender stack of bills and the packet of airline tickets. "To Brazil?" he asked, frowning.

"It's all I have in the entire world," she explained. "But it'll have to do. You have to leave here, Noah. Right now. Tonight!"

"Why?"

"Because the FBI knows everything. If you try to steal the crown tomorrow night, you'll be arrested."

His expression remained inscrutable as he flipped through the airline packet. "There are two tickets here."

She was on her way into the bedroom. "I'm going with you." A moment later, she was yanking clothes from the closet. Noah sat on the edge of the bed, silently watching her frantic actions.

"Noah, you have to go back to the hotel and pack right away," she protested. "Our plane leaves in two hours. We fly to Los Angeles, then from L.A. to Miami. By tomorrow morning we'll be in Rio."

She dumped the contents of her lingerie drawer on the mattress and had dropped to her knees to drag her suitcase from under the bed when his silent shaking caught her attention.

"Noah? Are you all right?"

Sara knelt on the carpet, her hands pressed against his thighs. She'd known that he would be disappointed, but she had certainly never expected him to cry over losing the crown. Sara stared, stunned by the huge tears rolling down his cheeks.

"Oh, Sara—" he gasped as he pulled her into his arms "—you are the most marvelous woman I've ever met." His body shook against hers.

Sara tilted her head back. "Noah," she asked hesitantly, "are you laughing?"

He couldn't help himself. His relief that she was safe had overwhelmed him, and gales of laughter racked his body.

"I'm sorry," he said, wiping at his free-falling tears with the back of his hand. "But I was worried out of my mind about you, and all the while you're cashing in all your chips just to rescue me."

Sara stood up, her expression solemn. "It's not funny, Noah. Dan turned you in. I saw him. He double-crossed you!"

Noah took a deep breath, forcing air into his lungs. "And that's why you're willing to leave your work, your family, your students at the university, to run away to Brazil?"

She nodded.

"You don't even speak Portuguese," he pointed out.

"So I'll learn," she assured him blithely. "I'll learn to speak the language, and I'll get a job teaching art, and you'll never have to steal again. You'll see, Noah; we can make it work."

All signs of laughter vanished from his face. "You'd do that? For me?"

She placed her hand against his face. "We're a team, Noah. Remember?"

He turned his head, pressing his lips into her palm. "I don't think I'll ever be able to forget," he answered.

Noah couldn't remember ever being so moved. She had been willing to sacrifice everything for him without a backward glance. Sara Madison, a woman who, under normal conditions, wouldn't even jaywalk, was willing to live the shadowy existence of a fugitive in order to protect an internationally sought after jewel thief. He couldn't believe his luck.

"You have to get going," she insisted weakly, melting as his lips scorched the tender skin of her palm. "They won't be expecting you to make a move until tomorrow night. It should be safe to return to the hotel to pack."

He ran his hand up her arm. "I'd rather stay here. I can think of far more interesting ways to spend my evening than packing."

She shook her head emphatically. "We don't have time. There's only one flight out tonight, Noah. I was lucky to get us on it."

He pulled her onto his lap, his lips nuzzling the nape of her neck. "Is there a flight out tomorrow night?"

Sara sighed as his teeth tugged on her earlobe. "Yes, but—" As his words sank in, she pushed firmly against his chest. "You can't possibly be thinking of staying until tomorrow night!"

He kissed the curve of her jaw. "At the moment, I'm not thinking past the next few minutes."

She jerked her head back, her eyes brimming with distress. "It's not fair to tempt me," she complained. "I'm trying to save you, Noah."

He traced her trembling lips with his finger. "Why don't you concentrate on loving me instead," he suggested.

"But what about Dan?" she asked, weakening as his hand moved down her throat.

"I'll take care of Dan," he promised. As his lips brushed against the pulse spot at the base of her throat, Noah felt Sara's blood quicken in response.

She could not surrender that easily. "But the FBI," she argued. "What about them?"

"I'll take care of them, too," he promised. "Tomorrow night." His deft fingers began to manipulate the tiny pearl buttons on the front of her sundress. "Right now I'd rather concentrate on taking care of you."

Sara shuddered as he pushed the material aside. "Damn you, Noah," she fumed. "You're going to make me crazy."

He pushed her back against the mattress. "I'm going to try," he promised.

As she linked her arms around his neck, Sara surrendered, unable to think of a single remaining argument.

Chapter Eleven

When Sara awoke the next morning, she found herself alone in bed. Pulling on her robe, she went in search of Noah. When she found him in the living room, perusing her bookcase, she breathed a soft sigh of relief.

"You're still here."

"Of course," he said simply.

Sara jammed her hands into the pockets of the white robe. "I was afraid you'd gone."

Noah's answering expression was half affectionate, half censorious. "Did you really think I'd leave without saying goodbye? Besides, I came here to do a job, remember?"

How could she forget? In twelve short hours, her life would be unalterably changed. She'd be a thief. What had ever made her believe she could agree to such a thing, then continue on as if nothing had happened?

As a shadow moved across her face, Noah experienced a sharp stab of guilt. It was certainly not the first he'd suffered since bringing Sara into the scheme. Last night he had almost told her everything. But he couldn't take the risk. He tried assuring himself that it was for her own good, but that didn't ease the nagging feelings. He wondered what she'd do when she found out the truth. Sara Madison might be able to love a thief. But how would she feel about a liar?

"Sara," he said softly, "it's going to be all right."

She sank into an easy chair. "I wish I could believe that."

"Let me get you some coffee," he offered.

Sara only nodded in response. Coffee was not what she needed. What she wanted to hear was that Noah, when faced with the enormity of their situation, would give up this ridiculous plan before it was too late.

He returned to the room, handing her a cup. Sara smiled her thanks, unwilling to trust her voice. Where would he be tomorrow morning? she wondered. Where would they both be? In prison? In Brazil? And most importantly, would they be together?

"You've got quite an eclectic taste in books," Noah remarked conversationally as he studied the bookshelves, which were filled with everything from textbooks on art history to paperback copies of classic literature to modern fiction.

She owned only a few romances; her overwhelming favorites were adventure novels and spy stories. Noah wondered if they were left over from some previous occupant of the apartment. He didn't like the idea of some other man living with Sara, sharing her life and her bed.

"I like to read," she answered absently, sipping her coffee.

"I can see that."

He arched a dark brow as his gaze settled on one particular novel. He pulled it from the shelf, eyeing the cover art designed to appeal to masculine fantasies. The hero, Jake Hawke, clutching a machine gun, was clad in camouflage attire, his harsh, blackened face set in a grim, forbidding scowl. The flames and smoldering buildings behind him hinted at the mayhem that had filled over two hundred pages of text.

"Isn't Jake Hawke a little earthy for an art-history professor?" Noah smiled. "Do your esteemed colleagues at the university know about this side of your nature?"

"I love that book," Sara declared, irritated that Noah seemed to be teasing her. "Jake Hawke is exciting, and I enjoy a little danger in my life." A small frown furrowed her brow.

"What you mean is that you enjoy living vicariously," he guessed correctly.

Sara put her cup down onto the coffee table. "I used to. Then I think I went a little crazy when I decided to turn the tables on Malcolm Brand." She shrugged. "It was probably the result of an overdose of all those adventure novels."

"And now?" he probed gently. "How do you feel now?"

Sara shook her head. "I just wish it was all over so I could go back to my safe, boring little life."

"Do you honestly believe that's possible?"

"Probably not," she agreed with a sigh. She fixed Noah with a level gaze. "There's still time to call this off. You can still get away, Noah."

He sat down on the couch across from her, stretching out his legs. He stared down at the paperback novel in his hands and began flipping idly through the pages.

"Now we're back to me. I thought last night this was a joint effort."

Sara wished she hadn't brought the subject up in the first place. There was one key ingredient she'd forgotten yesterday in her panic. Noah had never stated that he viewed their partnership as a lifelong endeavor.

"I don't know what I was thinking. After all, you certainly didn't invite me to go to Brazil with you."

"And if I had?"

"Last night I would have gone."

He closed the book. "How about this morning?"

"I don't know," she admitted. "I don't know how I feel about anything right now. I think I'm numb." She managed a lopsided smile. "Do you think that's what's meant by scared stiff?"

"Perhaps." He began leafing through the paperback novel again. "This looks well read," he said, more to himself than to her.

"I read it three times," Sara revealed.

Noah lifted his head. "Three times?" he asked disbelievingly. "Why?"

Sara shrugged. "I don't know. I guess I find Jake an intriguing character. Each time I read it, I get a little more insight into his personality."

"So, do you have him figured out yet?"

"Not really. He's a very complex man." She studied Noah thoughtfully. "Actually, now that you bring it up, he reminds me a great deal of you."

Noah looked down at the grim, unyielding man on the cover. "I'm not certain how to take that."

"I meant it in the very best way, Noah," Sara assured him.

He looked unconvinced. "If I remember correctly, Jake Hawke is a loner. He doesn't trust anyone or anything. That sounds like a hell of a way to go through life."

"He has to be that way," Sara argued. "He has to survive in a world of international intrigue, where life is cheap and loyalty is something that's awarded to the highest bidder."

Noah had to smile at Sara's earnest expression. "Sounds like a man in need of a good woman."

Sara shook her head. "What woman could possibly stand being married to someone like Jake? I mean, I know he's officially army intelligence, but let's face it, Noah, the man definitely doesn't go by the book. His methods are a far cry from standard operating procedure. Sometimes he's as ruthless as the bad guys. Even more so.''

"Unusual circumstances often call for unusual tactics," he pointed out.

Sara realized that they were no longer talking about the fictional Jake Hawke. It was Noah they were discussing now. A man whose methods were every bit as unorthodox as the novel's roguish army intelligence officer. The difference, she considered sadly, was that while Jake had at least had the excuse of serving his country, Noah's goals were entirely self-serving.

"And unusual men," she admitted. She leaned forward, her expression intense. "Noah, isn't there anything I can do to get you to change your mind?"

"Only about your participation. If you don't think you can go through with it, Sara, tell me now. Too much is riding on you."

"I can't bear the idea of prison," she confessed in a soft, unsteady voice.

"Neither can I," Noah agreed amiably.

"But with the FBI just waiting for you to make your move, I don't see how you can escape."

"Trust me."

Sara was on her feet, pacing the floor. "Damn it, Noah, if I didn't trust you, I wouldn't have agreed to go this far." Her eyes softened momentarily as they settled on his inscrutable face. "After all, you did get me off the hook with Hudson Gallery, although I shudder to think of what you had your friend Joe do."

Her expression firmed. "I know it sounds horribly selfish, but I can't help thinking what it would do to Jennifer and to Kevin if they came back to find me arrested by the FBI." Her voice rose several notes higher, her distress obvious. Sara was beginning to have doubts about the wisdom of her plan. Why should the FBI believe that she had every intention of seeing that the crown was returned to Turkey?

Noah was on his feet, as well, his hands around the top of her arms, halting her agitated movement. "Look, Sara, we're not going to get caught. But I promise, if we do, I'll tell them that I forced you to go along with it. I'll tell them all about the forged Manet and admit to selling it myself to blackmail you into cooperating." His mouth firmed. "Hell, I'll even tell them I threatened to harm your nephew."

"They'd never believe that," she protested quietly.

"Why not?"

Her open gaze told Noah more than words ever could. "Because you would never hurt anyone," she whispered.

Noah flinched inwardly. He could only hope Sara was as forgiving as she seemed, for in a few hours she was going to have one hell of a lot dumped on her.

"Then you're still in?" he asked, almost wishing she would change her mind.

He'd been crazy to mix her up in all this in the first place. But then, remembering her own resolve to take the crown, Noah reminded himself that she had given him no choice.

"I'm in," she agreed, sighing. "Now don't you think it's time you told me exactly what I'm going to be doing?"

This was sheer lunacy, Noah decided, not for the first time. "I suppose you're right," he agreed unenthusiastically. "I'll go get the blueprints."

He released her and walked to the kitchen. Sara picked up the paperback novel, intending to put it back on the shelf. She studied the cover, mentally comparing the rugged hero to Noah. Jake Hawke was not as tall as Noah, and his shock of hair was black instead of Noah's gleaming chestnut. The eyes, glowering out of the blackened face, were dark brown, in contrast to Noah's tawny amber.

But Sara would recognize that steely gaze anywhere. She'd certainly seen it directed her way enough times in the past few days. The artist had captured a feeling of power—a smoldering sense of danger—that Noah definitely shared with Jake Hawke. In spades.

As Noah returned to the room, blueprints in hands, his determination wavered once again when he viewed her slumped shoulders. *Unusual circumstances,* he reminded himself. It was certainly not the first time he had used someone to accomplish his goal. But it was the first time he had ever felt so damned lousy about it.

He sat down on the couch and spread the plans out on the coffee table. "I hope you don't have a thing about mice. Some women do; I probably should have asked you that yesterday."

"Mice?" she echoed.

"Mice. You know, those little white furry things running loose all over the mansion."

Sara stared at him. "You let them out, didn't you?"

He grinned. "Guilty."

"But why?"

"They're going to be our diversion," he explained. "In fact, one of those little guys is going to trip the alarm for us."

"You *want* the alarm to go off?" Sara knew that Noah enjoyed living dangerously, but this was ridiculous.

"The room is too well secured for us to be able to get in and out without either triggering the floor sensors or the photoelectric beams."

"I know you're the expert on all this," Sara offered tentatively, "but since you know where the key is, why can't we just turn the alarm off?"

"Because the key isn't in the safe any longer," he informed her. "It was already gone when I checked it out."

"I knew you were going to break into that safe," she grumbled. "Tell me, did you happen to find any jewels stashed there?"

His eyes were unreadable. "I only found a bunch of papers," Noah informed her grittily. "There were some corporation balance sheets and the old guy's will. And before you get all high and mighty, lady, remember that I only broke into that damn safe because I was trying to save you from having to crawl through those ducts."

Sara managed a slight apologetic smile. "I appreciate that, but if the key isn't in the safe, where is it?"

Noah shrugged. "Brand's unusually jumpy these days. With good reason. My guess is that he probably has it on him."

"I don't suppose your checkered career happened to have included pickpocketing," Sara suggested hopefully.

"Now that really hurts," he grumbled.

"It was just a thought," she apologized. "So, since we can't get the key, what's the plan?"

He looked at her thoughtfully before answering. "There's still time for you to change your mind."

"If I do, will you try to steal it alone?"

"Yes."

That single word sealed her fate. "I'm not changing my mind," Sara affirmed. She was moderately surprised when Noah seemed less than thrilled with her declaration. *He probably thinks I'll blow it,* she decided.

"You're going to make your way down to the basement. There's a vent in a wall near the ceiling that blows the cold air into the vault. You'll have to loosen the grille in order to lower the mouse onto the floor."

"And he'll trip the alarm?"

"If he's not heavy enough to set off the floor sensors, he's bound to get caught in one of the photobeams."

"And then?"

Noah didn't answer right away. "Let me ask you a question," he said instead. "What's the first thing Brand will do when the alarm goes off?"

"Go check to see who has broken into the gallery," she answered instantly.

"Before he does that."

Sara thought for a moment. "He'll have to turn off the alarm."

"Exactly. He'll want things quiet enough that he can hear someone moving around down there."

"But all he'll find is our mouse."

"One of several little escapees who have been making their way into every nook and cranny of that mansion," Noah confirmed. "He'll see the crown, decide it was a false alarm and go back upstairs."

"And turn the alarm back on," she pointed out.

"That's why you have approximately sixty seconds to get into the room, snatch the crown and get back up into that duct."

Sara was doubtful. "Noah, that's cutting it very tight."

"You can do it."

Sara certainly hoped so. "And where are you during all this?"

"I'm providing your cover. The mood around that place is definitely getting more tense by the day. I think Taylor suspects something, and while Brand is eager to get coverage in *Art Digest*, if I'm not standing beside him when the alarm goes off, he could figure out the entire interview was a hoax. Let's face it, Sara; he didn't amass that fortune by being stupid."

"No," she agreed. "Malcolm is a lot of things, but he definitely isn't stupid." Then something occurred to her. "But if I'm not around, won't he suspect me?"

"Brand won't; he doesn't think you have the killer instinct, remember?"

"All too well," Sara replied grimly as she recalled that distasteful conversation. "But what about Peter?"

"You have a point there," Noah admitted. "But don't worry; the baroness will be keeping Taylor's mind on other things."

"Are you telling me that the baroness is involved in all this?"

"Only that she's been after Taylor for both personal and professional reasons for some time. If I know the baroness, she'll be hanging on to the guy the entire evening."

An uncomfortable suspicion assailed Sara. "You'll use anyone, won't you?"

Noah's expression hardened at the accusation in her tone. "I don't like what you're thinking, Sara."

"That makes two of us," she agreed in a deceptively calm tone of voice.

Noah's mouth tightened almost imperceptibly, but by now Sara was familiar with his every expression. This one was definitely not one of his more encouraging ones. Jake Hawke immediately came to mind.

"I haven't used you, Sara."

"Of course you have, Noah," she replied tranquilly.

"All right," he admitted. "I have. But it's still not what you're thinking."

"Are you a mind reader as well as a thief?" Her smile was cool and remote. "I didn't realize you possessed so many talents."

Damn her! How could she be so soft and approachable one minute and as hard as nails the next? Part of him wanted to shake her, while another part of him admired her stubborn strength.

"And I didn't realize you were an idiot."

Doubts flittered through her mind, tantalizing thoughts that encouraged her to forget the times Noah had appeared genuinely interested in her welfare—those instances of intimacy that had nothing to do with his admittedly wonderful lovemaking.

As their eyes held, Sara realized that she was not nearly so angry that Noah was using her as a willing accomplice as she was worried that he might not love her as she loved him. The realization of that love had not struck instantly; it had crept up on her gradually, growing stronger whenever she reaffirmed her commitment to his cause or allowed herself to be drawn further into this crazy scheme.

"Damn you," she muttered. "If I had any sense at all, I'd kick you out of this apartment, double bolt the door after you and forget I'd ever met such an insufferable man!"

"That's precisely what you'd do," Noah agreed, "if you had any sense."

"I could always turn you over to the authorities and collect the reward," she threatened, knowing she would never do it. "Then I wouldn't even have to share the money with you and Dan."

Noah shrugged. "That's another alternative," he said pleasantly. "Although for some reason your obsession with money seems to have lessened lately. The woman I met a few days ago wouldn't have handed over all her worldly goods to help a man she hardly knew. A common thief."

He leaned back against the couch, fixing her with a steady gaze. "So, what's it going to be, Sara? Do I leave now or wait for you to call the cops?"

Sara closed her eyes as she drew in a deep, steadying breath. "Where is this damn mouse I'm going to be working with?" she asked finally.

Chapter Twelve

Later that evening, Sara was dressed for the party, waiting for Noah to return from whatever secretive mission he'd gone on this time. It still annoyed her that he wasn't telling her everything, but she had given up pressuring him on the subject. When he walked in the door, attired in evening clothes, Sara decided the wait had been worth it.

"You look every bit as sophisticated as Peter," she said, staring at him.

Noah grimaced. "I hate these things," he muttered. "And I sure as hell don't like the idea of Taylor as a role model."

Sara laughed. "Well, like it or not, you look terrific. The baroness won't be able to keep her hands off you."

"Then you'll just have to protect me," he said with a grin. "You, by the way, look even better than terrific. Is that the dress you bought yesterday?"

Sara twirled, displaying her outrageously expensive purchase like a young girl showing off a new party dress. "This is it," she confirmed. "Like it?"

He tossed the packages he was carrying onto a table and drew her into his arms. "I love it," he said against her lips. "But I like the lady inside all that lace even better."

She rested her head against his shoulder. "You continually infuriate me, Noah," she declared truthfully. "But just when I decide I don't want to have anything else to do with you, you say exactly the right thing."

He pressed a kiss atop her head. "I try."

"What's in the packages?" she asked absently, wishing they could just forget the party and spend the evening alone.

"Something for you." As he inhaled the sweet scent of her perfume, Noah wished that he could say the hell with the heist and spend the evening making love to the luscious woman in his arms.

Duty before pleasure, he reminded himself grimly. He'd lived by that code long enough that it had become second nature. But never had he been so tempted to disregard it for more personal pursuits.

Sara lifted her head, her smile beatific. "For me? You bought me a present?"

The obvious pleasure gracing her beaming face made him feel like a first-rate jerk. "Not really a present," he confessed regretfully. He released her to retrieve the packages. "More like equipment."

"Oh." Sara's smile wobbled a bit as she realized Noah was still far more wrapped up in this theft than he was in her. "Well, let me see what you've got," she replied with forced enthusiasm.

Noah held up a black nylon jump suit. "This should fit," he said, his eyes skimming over her body.

Sara glanced at the tag as she took the jump suit from his hands. It was her size, she agreed mentally, not wanting to know how Noah had become so adept at guessing women's sizes.

"I hadn't realized your tastes ran to things like this," she teased, pulling at the stretchy material.

Noah laughed. "It's not what you think. As delightful as that little frock is that you have on, I can't picture you crawling through all that ductwork in it."

Sara glanced down at her full floor-length skirt. "I never thought of that." She studied the thin nylon. "You're right, of course. But can't I just wear a pair of jeans and a T-shirt?"

"This will be better," he assured her. "There's nothing to catch on the hardware. I wouldn't want you to get stuck in there."

Sara shivered visibly at the thought. "Neither would I," she agreed fervently.

"It's got a hood to keep your hair from getting dirty," he offered helpfully.

Sara managed a weak smile. "It seems you've thought of everything."

"That's my job."

She wished Noah wouldn't keep reminding her of that unpleasant fact. "Won't I look a little conspicuous wearing this to the party?"

"You're not wearing it to the party. You can change in Brand's office right before you go into the ducts. After you get out, we'll stash the crown, you'll change back into your dress, and no one will be the wiser."

"Then we walk right out the front door with the crown."

He nodded. "That's the idea."

Sara took a deep breath. "Well, I suppose it's time to get this show on the road." Her tone was unenthusiastic.

"We'd better not show up together. You go on ahead, and I'll follow in about fifteen minutes. Give me your evening bag," he instructed.

Sara handed over the white beaded purse, watching as Noah rolled the jump suit into a tight ball. That it could fit into such a small space didn't make her feel any better about wearing it. Then he looked down at her feet.

"Shoes," he grumbled thoughtfully. "I don't suppose you could get away with wearing running shoes under that dress, could you?"

Sara shook her head. "I'm willing to do a lot for you, Noah, but that's out." She lifted her skirts, revealing a delicate pair of high-heeled sandals. "These are what I'm wearing."

He studied the full, tiered skirt. "How about stashing a pair of practical shoes under that skirt? It should be full enough to hide them."

"Don't even suggest that! Why don't you stash them under your jacket?" she suggested sweetly.

"Because they'd ruin the line."

"Better your line than mine," she retorted.

Noah didn't like not having complete control of things, Sara realized, certainly not for the first time. Viewing the aggravation washing over his face, she took pity on him.

"Don't worry," she said, patting his arm reassuringly. "I never retrieved all my things from Malcolm's house. I've got a pair of running shoes up in my room."

"You could have told me that right off the bat, Sara." His irritation was all too evident.

She went up on her toes, pressing a kiss against his firmly set lips. "I could have," she agreed, "but then I would have missed the fun of seeing you at a loss for once."

His answer could only be described as a growl.

"I'll see you in a few minutes," Sara said, heading toward the front door of the apartment.

"I'll walk you to your car," Noah offered, putting his arm around her waist.

As she slid into the driver's seat, Noah tucked the volu-minous folds of the skirt inside the car. "Sara—" he said hesitantly as she put the keys into the ignition.

She looked up at him. "Yes, Noah?"

"I really appreciate this."

She nodded. "I know you do."

"When it's all over, we need to talk."

"We will."

Sara was curious at the despair visible on Noah's fea-tures and hoped that he wasn't going to give her a long-drawn-out farewell speech. If he was going to disappear from her life, she'd rather have it done quickly.

"Will you promise me that no matter what happens, you'll hear me out?" His voice was tinged with a hint of desperation that didn't make her feel any more secure.

"I promise," she agreed.

His eyes held a lingering shadow of doubt. "That's all I can ask," he mumbled. He bent his head, kissing her with a burst of passion that sent her head spinning. "I'll see you soon," he promised when the kiss finally ended.

"Soon," Sara echoed softly.

Noah closed the door and stood on the curb, his hands jammed into his pockets as he watched her drive away. Then he muttered a short, harsh oath.

SARA HAD BEEN HOLDING the glass of champagne for the past half hour. She didn't want to drink anything before the theft; it was going to be frightening enough crawling through those narrow black ducts. She certainly didn't need alcohol to intensify those feelings. She continued to cast surreptitious glances toward the doorway, watching for Noah.

"My dear," the baroness was saying, "I see you took my advice, after all. That's a precious little frock. So virginal."

Sara smiled as she took in the baroness's skin-tight gold
lamé gown. It crossed her mind that perhaps Gizella should
be the one to retrieve the crown. There certainly wasn't any
loose material in that dress to catch on a bolt. But then
again, Sara considered, she doubted that the woman would
be able to sit down, let alone crawl on her hands and knees.
It was amazing that she could even breathe.

"Thank you," Sara replied absently. Where was Noah,
anyway? "You were right about Gallant's."

"It's not exactly Paris, but one can find a decent dress
there if one is desperate enough," Gizella agreed.

"So," Sara asked conversationally, "do you go to Europe often?"

"At least twice a year," the baroness confirmed. "While
I love America, my roots are still in the old country."

"I've heard you can trace your family back several generations. I envy you that. Most Americans can't."

"Oh, my dear," Gizella said, "my family's roots were
always very important to us." As a waiter passed by, she
plucked another glass of champagne from the silver tray,
replacing it with her empty one. "We were part of the Ma-
gyars, the very first Hungarians who invaded in the ninth
century after migrating from the Urals."

"The ninth century," Sara remarked, her attention still
glued to the door. "Imagine that."

"We added the Venetian branch to the family when Zara
rebelled against the Venetian Republic and put itself under
the protection of my ancestor, King Bella the Third," she
continued.

"If I remember my history correctly, that was a long time
ago. Before the Venetian Crusades."

"The twelfth century," the baroness confirmed. "Oh,
yes, the Levinzskis go back a very long way. Did I ever tell
you that Peter the Great adored my family's wines?"

"I believe I've heard that story," Sara replied. "Excuse me," she said as she saw Noah finally enter the room.

Knowing that the baroness was watching them, Sara greeted him politely, as if they were nothing more than business acquaintances.

"Mr. Lancaster, how nice you could make it this evening."

"I wouldn't miss it for the world" was Noah's response. "Where's Brand?" he asked Sara under his breath.

Sara pretended to sip her now-warm glass of champagne. "I have no idea. I've been here a half hour, and he still hasn't shown up."

Noah frowned. "That's interesting."

"I thought so. Do you think he suspects something?"

"I don't know. Where's Taylor?"

"He was here a little while ago, but I haven't seen him lately. I got stuck listening to the baroness's illustrious family tree. Speaking of which..." Sara's voice trailed off as she viewed the woman crossing the room toward them.

"Noah, darlink," Gizella enthused, "now the party can begin." She placed both her hands on his face, giving him a kiss.

Sara wasn't about to stay and watch this woman climb all over Noah. She had an overwhelming urge to pull the baroness's hair out by her dyed roots. Wouldn't that create a diversion? she considered with an inward smile.

"If you'll both excuse me, I believe I'll freshen my drink," she said.

"Of course, dear," the baroness returned uncaringly. "Have a good time. I'll keep our guests entertained." She linked her arm through Noah's.

"I've no doubt," Sara mumbled. Deciding this was as good a time to retrieve her shoes as any, she left the room and headed down the hallway toward the stairs. As Peter came out of Malcolm's office, Sara had no place to hide.

He seemed surprised to see her. "Sara, what are you doing here?"

"I left my favorite lipstick upstairs. I was just going up to get it."

He appeared to accept that. "Did I tell you how lovely you look tonight?"

"You did," she agreed, forcing a smile. She looked past him. "Is Malcolm in there?"

"He's in his room," Peter explained. "He's not feeling very well this evening, I'm afraid. He asked me to bring him some papers."

"He's well enough to work but not well enough to join the party?"

Peter's smile was condescending. "You know what a workaholic the man is, Sara, dear. He'll probably be drafting memos from his deathbed."

"What about the party?" Sara asked, her mind spinning as she wondered how this would affect Noah's plan.

"I'll just take these papers up to him; then I'll extend his apologies to our guests. With all that free liquor and food, no one will even miss him."

"Probably not."

Peter took her hand, his thumb rubbing sensuous little circles against her palm. "You haven't been around the past two days."

Sara bit down the revulsion his touch created. "I explained that to Malcolm. I may have agreed to work with the two of you, but that doesn't mean I have to like it."

He clucked his tongue. "Are you still angry at me? I thought we'd come to an understanding about that?"

Sara forced herself to meet his censorious eyes with a level gaze of her own. "I don't really trust you, Peter. You've worked with Malcolm for years, but you're willing to double-cross him. Why should I receive any better treatment?"

He ran his finger down the side of her face. "Because, my love, you are far more enticing than Malcolm Brand."

"What about the baroness?"

His eyes narrowed. "What about her?"

Sara shrugged. "You certainly seemed to find her intriguing enough while we were all out riding the other morning."

He surprised her by laughing. "So that's why I've been receiving the cold shoulder. You're jealous!"

Sara opened her mouth to insist that she certainly wasn't any such thing. Then she realized that it would be a tactical error to clarify her feelings.

"Can you blame me?" she asked, forcing a pretty pout. "After all, the baroness has a title, money, and I hear her art collection rivals Malcolm's. How can I possibly compete with all that?"

He shaped her bare shoulder with his hand, and Sara tried not cringe as his fingers trailed down her arm. "I'm surprised you even have to ask," he said huskily.

As he looked inclined to draw her into his arms, Sara backed away. "Peter, someone could come by," she protested.

He studied her thoughtfully. "I haven't decided if you're the world's greatest tease or if you're actually afraid of me."

"It's not you," she stammered, trying to come up with an excuse for continually putting him off. Something the baroness had mentioned when commenting on her dress popped into her mind, and Sara jumped at it. "It's just that I'm not as experienced as you seem to think, Peter. I need a little time."

She could practically see the wheels turning in his head as he tried to decipher her words. "Are you telling me that you're a virgin?" he asked incredulously.

Sara kept her eyes directed on the marble floor as she nodded.

"At your age?" he probed. "Why?"

She lifted her head. "Perhaps I was waiting for the right man."

The message swirled between them, and Sara held her breath as Peter seemed to be digesting it. Finally, his eyes lit with a gleam that appeared both sensual and triumphant, all at the same time.

He took her hand, linking their fingers together as he lifted it to his lips. "Stay after the party."

"I don't know," she demurred.

His fingers tightened. "It will be good, Sara. I promise."

She knew Noah would kill her for asking the next question, but she had to know. "And the crown, Peter. What about it?"

He gave her a mirthless smile. "You're definitely a self-serving little lady, aren't you, Sara Madison?"

She smiled sweetly. "So are you, Peter. That's why we're probably a match made in heaven."

"Or hell," he muttered brusquely. "I'll make you a deal, my greedy little tease. Stay with me tonight and we'll take the crown in the morning, before Malcolm wakes up."

Sara pretended ignorance. "It's here? Already?"

"It's in the vault.... I want you Sara."

She glanced down at the papers in his hand. "Don't you think you ought to take those papers up to Malcolm before he comes looking for you?"

"I'd better," he agreed reluctantly. "I'll meet you in the pool house after everyone has left."

Sara nodded. "I'll be there."

As he left her, his heels clicking on the marble floors, Sara exhaled a deep breath. Then she continued down the hallway, taking the stairs to the second floor as fast as she could.

NOAH HOPED he was answering the baroness at the right intervals. She was babbling away about her family, and the art she had escaped with when fleeing Hungary after the Soviets crushed the uprising in 1956. Her hands fluttered against his chest, and her fingers played with his hair, her seduction attempts grating on his nerves more with each passing minute. Where the hell was Sara, anyway? She'd been gone far too long.

For a while he had been afraid Taylor had caught up with her, but the man entered the room and explained that their host was feeling too tired to come downstairs. After a polite murmur of regret from the guests, the party had continued.

"Darlink, it's getting so warm in here." The baroness pouted prettily. "Why don't you come out for a walk on the grounds with me?"

"Perhaps you just need a cool drink," Noah suggested.

He was never as relieved to see anyone as he was Peter Taylor, who joined them at precisely that moment. "I would be honored if the baroness would take a stroll with me," he suggested smoothly. "Have I shown you Malcolm's newest acquisition?"

Noah found himself holding his breath. He couldn't possibly be going to reveal the information about the crown?

"And what is that, Peter, dear?" Gizella asked absently, her gaze flitting back and forth between the two men as if she were attempting to make up her mind which gentleman promised a more fulfilling evening.

"There's a new Arabian stallion in the stables. He only arrived today."

The baroness made up her mind. "I adore Arabians," she said, clapping her hands. She turned to Noah. "You won't miss me, darlink?"

"Of course I'll miss you," Noah responded smoothly. "But I'll struggle to survive."

She laughed—a light rippling sound. "You are such a magnificent liar, Noah." Her eyes surveyed the room. "Why don't you go visit with Miss Madison? She looks a little lost."

Noah glanced over at Sara, who was standing by herself by the buffet table. "Perhaps I will."

"Tell her you like her dress," the baroness instructed. "On her miserable wages, the poor little thing probably won't be able to afford to eat for a month. It will make the expense worthwhile if a handsome man compliments her."

"I'll try to fit it into the conversation," Noah agreed.

The baroness patted his cheek. "Have fun, darlink. But not too much. I don't think our Sara is capable of handling a man like you."

Sara proved otherwise the moment Noah approached her at the table. "I thought Peter was suppose to be keeping the baroness occupied," she snapped as she crunched on a bread stick.

"He saved me just in the nick of time," Noah related with a wry grin. "I was just about to dunk my head in the punch bowl and drown myself if I had to spend another second listening to all that feminine drivel."

"I could see how horribly you were suffering." Sara popped an olive into her mouth.

"I was. Actually, I was worried about you."

"Really? Funny, it didn't look like it." She bit into a stuffed mushroom.

"Do you always eat when you're angry?"

Sara swallowed. "Always. I figure it's better than throwing things."

"Probably so. But if you keep it up, you won't be able to fit into those ducts."

"I'll fit," she muttered, piling a thick slice of ham and two pieces of Swiss cheese onto an onion roll. "So when are we going to do it?"

Noah took the sandwich from her hands and put it on the table. "Now," he informed her calmly.

Chapter Thirteen

As Sara accompanied Noah down the hallway toward Malcolm's office, her legs felt as if they had turned to wood, her feet to stone.

"Nervous?" he asked, aware of her slight shiver.

"Nervous doesn't begin to describe it."

He stopped, his hands cupping her shoulders as he looked down into her pale face. "You know I wouldn't let you do anything dangerous."

How she would love to believe that. But despite her wish that circumstances were different, she couldn't shake the feeling that Noah's first love was the crown.

"Wouldn't you?"

His fingers lightly massaged her bare skin. "You still can't trust me, can you?"

"I want to," she answered truthfully.

"Just another hour," he promised. "Then we'll have that long-overdue talk."

Sara sighed. "I still can't believe I'm doing this."

"No one's forcing you," he pointed out.

Some little part of her wished that he would. It would make everything so much easier. "Let's just get it over with."

He glanced down at her feet. "Where are your shoes?"

Sara managed a weak smile. "I'm getting pretty good at this spy stuff. I hid them in an urn outside Malcolm's office."

His smiling eyes rewarded her. "Just like Mata Hari."

Sara cringed as she started walking again. "You would have to bring her up. Wasn't she executed for collaborating with the Germans?"

"Don't worry about it," he assured her blithely. "According to the international rules of war, in order to be condemned as a spy, you have to be captured within enemy lines in disguise or while representing to be other than what you are." He smiled. "I'd say you're safe enough."

"I'm not even going to ask how you know that," she muttered.

They'd reached the door of the office. As Noah turned the knob, a frown darkened his brow. "It's locked."

"That's not so surprising. Malcolm often locks his office when he's not working."

"Makes sense." Noah pulled a piece of wire from his breast pocket. Two seconds later, the door opened. "Piece of cake," he murmured with self-satisfaction.

Sara shook her head. He was too handy with that lock pick for comfort. But what had she expected? Those were obviously tools of his trade. She plucked her running shoes from the urn and entered ahead of him.

Her shoes dropped unheeded to the floor, and she opened her mouth to scream at the scene that greeted her. Noah's wide hand clamped over her mouth.

"Don't make a sound," he warned, his breath rasping in her ear. "Not one peep. Understand?"

Sara's eyes were wide with horror as she stared at Malcolm Brand seated in his leather chair, his glazed eyes seeming to stare right through her.

"If I take my hand away, will you promise not to scream?"

She nodded dutifully.

He released her mouth, catching her as she sagged. "Take a deep breath," he instructed on a harsh whisper.

Sara tried to do as directed, breathing in a ragged gasp of air.

"Again."

This time she was more successful, and the oxygen cleared away the black fog clouding her brain. "Is he—" She couldn't make herself say the word.

Noah's mouth was a grim slash. "I'm afraid so."

Sara couldn't stop looking at Malcolm's face. His eyes appeared almost colorless, his face was ashen and his mouth slack.

"I've never seen a dead person before."

"Believe me, Sara," Noah grated, "it doesn't get a helluva lot easier no matter how many you've seen." He looked down at her. "If I let go of you, will you be all right?"

As she shifted her gaze from the body to Noah's eyes, Sara was strengthened by the concern she viewed there. "I think so."

He moved to close the door behind them, locking it with a swift twist of the wrist. "The first thing to do is check the safe for the key."

Sara wondered how he could be so businesslike when confronted by such a sight. Surely jewel thieves didn't run across that many dead people in their line of work. She watched as his fingers deftly twisted the combination lock.

"It's empty."

Her heart fell.

"We'll have to check his pockets," Noah announced.

Sara caught his arm as he headed toward Malcolm's body. "You can't!"

Noah covered her icy hand with his. "If he has it on him, we can simply turn off the alarm ourselves and take the crown right now."

"You can't still be thinking about stealing the crown," she protested. "Noah, we have to get out of here. Malcolm's dead. Someone might think we did it."

Noah pried her fingers loose, going over to squat down beside the body. "He's been dead for some time," he said, his fingers on the man's limp wrist. "I'd guess at least two hours."

"Was he murdered?" Her voice was a thin thread of sound.

Noah shook his head. "I don't think so. There aren't any signs of foul play. You did say he had a heart condition; it was probably natural causes."

Sara turned away, looking out the window into the well of darkness, unable to watch as Noah began going through the dead man's pockets. "It's not here, either," he muttered. "We'll have to go back to the original plan."

She spun back around to stare at him. "You can't be serious."

His level gaze held hers. "Of course I am. It's too bad the bastard's gone; I would have loved to have seen him spend the rest of his life in prison. But we came to do a job, Sara. This doesn't change a thing."

She shook her head, backing away from him. "I really can't believe you can be so unfeeling.... Noah, a man is dead. I don't care how bad he was, the fact remains that he can't possibly ever hurt anyone again. Why can't we be satisfied with that?"

Noah's eyes were unreadable. "Because by tomorrow morning, this place will be swarming with people—cops, lawyers, press. They're bound to find the vault. And the crown. I can't allow that to happen. If I have to try those ducts myself."

She took in the wide shoulders that stretched the seams of his custom-tailored tuxedo. "You'd never make it."

His expression could have been carved in stone. "I have to try. There's too much riding on this."

Sara's expression was challenging. "A few jewels? You'd risk your freedom, your life, for a few damned stones?"

"It's more than that," he countered brusquely. "You have to understand, Sara, I'm not working solo on this one. There are individuals who have a good reason for wanting that crown. They hired me because I'm the best, the only one who can get it." His jaw firmed. "I have a responsibility to do exactly that, with or without your help."

"And what about your responsibility to me?" she asked quietly. "To us? I thought I meant something to you, Noah." Sara knew she was pleading, but she couldn't stop herself.

Noah wished he could just take Sara away from here now. Back to his mountains. Back to where the sky overhead was a remarkable cobalt blue, where the eagles soared with an amazing grace and the air was crisp and clean. Where life was pure and simple. But he couldn't do it. Not yet.

And after tonight he doubted that he would ever be able to convince her to come of her own free will. He wondered how she would accept being kidnapped. Something flickered in the depths of his eyes, but it was gone too quickly for Sara to decipher its meaning.

"This has nothing to do with us," he assured her quietly.

"You're wrong," she corrected on a soft but firm tone. "This has everything to do with us, Noah."

"I gave my word."

"Dammit, now you sound exactly like that stupid Jake Hawke!"

"I thought you liked the guy."

"I do. In fiction," she qualified. "Real life isn't something out of a spy novel."

He exhaled a weary breath. Then he bent down, picking up her shoes. "Go home, Sara Madison. You're right. This is not any place for you. It never was." There was no censure in his voice, only a deep regret.

Sara took the shoes he was holding out. *Don't do this,* she begged silently. *Come with me. Now, before it's too late.*

"Goodbye, Noah," she said softly.

He pressed his hand against her cheek. "Goodbye, Sara. Have a good life." As his eyes softened, she expected a kiss, but instead Noah dropped his hand and turned away. His hands were deep in his pockets, his wide shoulders slumped as he stared out the window.

Sara reached out her hand, debating going to him. Then, changing her mind, she unlocked the door and left the room. She had gone no more than three feet when she knew she couldn't do it. She couldn't walk away from Noah. Not like this. She had no idea what he was involved in—his admission about working for others had come as a surprise— but whatever it was, she had to do whatever she could to keep him safe.

"Let's go," Sara announced abruptly as she reentered the office.

Noah was standing on a chair, removing the grille from the air-conditioning vent. As he took in Sara's unexpected appearance, every muscle in his body tensed.

"When all this is over," he said slowly, "remind me to tell you how much I love you."

Sara nodded. "I have every intention of doing exactly that." Her own voice was low but strong and certain.

He climbed down from the chair. "You'll have to change."

Sara pulled the jump suit out of her purse. "Turn your back."

Noah couldn't resist smiling despite the gravity of the situation. "Isn't this a little late to be developing a sense of modesty?"

"I'm only offering to steal your precious crown for you, Noah," Sara answered firmly. "A floor show doesn't come with the admission." She stole a quick glance at Malcolm's lifeless body. "And turn that chair around," she instructed. "It was bad enough when he was alive. I won't have those pale eyes leering at me after he's gone."

Noah immediately obliged. It took his entire store of self-restraint not to cheat and watch Sara undress, but she had already taken more than a woman should have to accept from any man.

"I'm ready," she announced shortly.

Noah slowly turned, his eyes widening as he viewed Sara in the skintight jump suit. The black nylon jersey caressed her curves like a second skin; he couldn't remember ever seeing anything so seductive. He had to fight his body's automatic response.

"You sure don't look like any jewel thief I've ever known," he said in a rough, gravelly tone.

Sara blushed. "You've got some weird taste in women's apparel; I feel as if I should be on a runway with a band playing some pounding bump-and-grind music."

He shook his head. "You look sexy as hell, but I think it's the comparison of that suit on such a classy lady."

She couldn't resist a smile. "Always ready with the perfect line, aren't you, Noah?"

"Only for the perfect lady."

They exchanged a long glance, then Sara drew in a deep breath. "Well, let's get this show on the road," she announced abruptly, "before I come to my senses."

"Here's a map of the ductwork so you won't get lost," he said, handing her a piece of paper.

"Don't even mention that!"

"Don't worry, it's all right turns." He reached into his pocket. "And a penlight so you won't be crawling along in total darkness."

She shivered as she considered that scenario. "Noah," she said suddenly, "there won't be any spiders in there, will there? I can handle mice, but spiders are another story."

"Too hot," Noah assured her as he tied a length of rope around her waist. "You'll need this to get back up into the duct. All you have to do is attach this suction cup onto the top of the duct, tie the rope through the eyebolt, and you'll be all set."

"What makes you think I can climb a rope?" she asked curiously as he strapped a pair of pads, much like those worn by athletes, around her knees.

He seemed surprised by the question. "It's only an eight-foot ceiling, Sara, and I've tied knots in it for you to hold on to." Then his brow furrowed. "Perhaps we could make some kind of ladder."

"I can do it," she admitted. "When I was little, Dad built me a rope swing. I climbed it all the time, although in those days I never considered it career training."

"You never know what'll come in handy," he agreed amiably. "Here's a walkie-talkie. I'll talk you through the ducts until you get to the vault."

"Thank you; I appreciate that."

His expression was grave. "You know that if there was any other way—"

Sara pressed her fingers against his lips. "I know," she replied softly.

They exchanged a long glance that expressed more than mere words ever could. Finally, Noah shook his head, as if clearing his thoughts.

"We don't want to forget your little friend." He reached into a cupboard, pulling out a small cardboard box with holes in the lid.

"You stashed him in there when you let the others out, didn't you?"

"I wanted to make certain we'd be able to find one when we needed him."

"It looks as though you've thought of everything," she replied. Then her gaze slid to Malcolm's body. "Noah, who's going to turn off the alarm?"

"I'm counting on Taylor to have the missing key. Didn't you say you saw him earlier, coming out of this office?"

Sara nodded.

"Malcolm had to have been already dead. Taylor probably saw his opportunity to get the key and took it."

"That makes sense," Sara agreed thoughtfully. "He promised that if I spent the night with him, he'd have the crown in the morning."

Noah's eyes narrowed. "You didn't tell me that."

Sara shrugged. "I didn't think it was necessary."

His jaw could have been carved from granite. "I'm going to break that guy's face when all this is over," he announced.

She couldn't help laughing. "I love it! Here we are, in a room with a dead body, about to pull off an international jewel heist, and you're worrying about my honor."

"Someone has to," he grumbled. "You didn't agree, did you?"

She patted his cheek. "Don't worry, Noah, I can only handle one thief in my life at a time." Her eyes softened.

"Do you happen to remember how you cured me of my claustrophobia in the elevator?"

A smile tugged at his lips as he remembered Sara's unrestrained passion at that kiss. "How could I ever forget?"

Her palms framed his face. "I think I need a booster," she said softly.

Noah pulled her into his arms. The kiss that began as a gentle, reassuring gesture quickly turned urgent and possessive. Her senses whirled at the onslaught of his mouth, and her lips parted, her tongue meeting his, desperately, passionately, heatedly. This was what she needed, something that would continue to grip her senses during the time in the ducts and focus her mind on where she was and what she was doing, all in the name of love.

"Sara." Her name was husky on his lips as his hands moved down her back, raking her skin through the thin jersey.

The tip of her tongue traced his lips. "I do love you," she whispered.

Unexpectedly, his hands moved to her shoulders as he gently moved her away from him. "I hope you always will."

Sara stared up at him, trying to read the secrets shielded behind his expressionless gaze. The silence lingered between them for a long, immeasurable time.

"We'd better get this over with," he urged finally.

Sara swallowed, nodding bravely. "Wish me luck."

As he lifted her up to the open vent, Noah's fingers tightened on her waist. "Always."

IT SEEMED as if she'd been crawling through the darkened tunnel forever. It was as hot as Hades, and her hair was plastered to her forehead, but her skin was ice cold from fear. Every so often, at Noah's instruction, she would stop and take a few deep, calming breaths. It was at those times she fantasized about his kiss, and for some reason she could not fully comprehend, that memory gave her the strength to carry on. He had kept his word, continuing to reassure her as she made her way through the maze of ductwork.

"We should be coming up to it soon," she whispered to the mouse she was carrying. "It can't be that much longer."

The muffled squeaks from the cardboard box assured her that the tiny mouse was no more pleased than she by these circumstances.

"Look at it this way," she continued to whisper, finding comfort in having some company in the darkened ducts. "It's got to be better than ending up as Carmen's dinner."

She stopped again momentarily, checking her map. If Noah was right, one last turn, then a few more feet and she should be there. Drawing in a deep breath, she continued.

"Eureka," she said with a ragged sigh.

"Sara?" Noah's voice was remarkably calm considering the circumstances.

"I've reached the vault," she answered. "Now all I have to do is attach the suction cup and remove the grille."

"I hate to leave you—" his tone was thick with regret "—but I'd better get back to the others."

Sara opened her mouth to speak, but no sound escaped. She swallowed and tried again. "That's all right," she managed finally. "Doug and I will do fine."

"Doug?"

"My accomplice," she explained, feeling rather foolish. "I named him after Douglas Fairbanks, Jr. It seemed to fit."

His deep chuckle was warmly reassuring. "You are one of a kind, lady. Now remember, you've only got sixty seconds. Don't get carried away drinking in the sight of Brand's hot masterpieces."

"Don't worry about me," she retorted. "You just take care of Peter."

"I'm on my way. And Sara—" His voice deepened.

"Yes, Noah?" Sara whispered.

"I don't know how I'm ever going to make this up to you," he admitted gruffly.

"Don't worry," she assured him with far more aplomb than she was feeling at the moment. "I have a myriad of suggestions in mind that we'll discuss later tonight."

Noah chuckled appreciatively. Then, as the small hand-held receiver went dead, Sara realized she was on her own.

"Okay, Doug," she whispered. "Now it's all up to you."

It took some doing, but she managed to dislodge the grille. Noah had explained that the slip knot around the mouse would pull free easily once she'd lowered him to the ground. She certainly hoped Noah was right. She didn't think that Peter would accept the idea of a mouse running around the vault wearing a leash.

Her heart raced as she went to work, attaching the suction cup to the smooth surface of the duct before looping the rope through the eye hook. She tugged experimentally and it held.

Next Sara lifted the lid on the cardboard box and took out the mouse, stroking his furry white back comfortingly as he tried to wriggle free.

"I know," she said softly. "This has been rough on all of us. But it all will be over soon. Then you can join your friends."

Slowly, inch by inch, she lowered the mouse to the floor, holding her breath as she tugged on the cord. The knot loosened just as Noah had promised it would, allowing her to pull the cord into the duct. She had just managed to replace the grille when a loud siren sounded. Sara held her gloved hands over her ears and peered through the grating of the vent. The noise was deafening; she could only hope that Noah was right about Peter's having a key.

The sound stopped as abruptly as it had begun. The door opened at the top of the stairs, and Sara heard the excited murmur of voices. Obviously some of the guests, alerted by the siren, had accompanied Peter to the door. Sara prayed that Noah was with him. A moment later, the light came on in the vault.

Sara momentarily forgot her mission as she stared down into the vast room that served as Malcolm's private gallery. She recognized several paintings that had disappeared from the world's most prestigious museums. There was a sixteenth-century Safavid, considered one of the finest examples of Islamic art in the world, hanging next to a portrait of Paul Revere that had been painted by the great American artist John Singleton Copley. Her studied gaze took in the striking realism of a Fairfield Porter farmhouse, jarringly placed next to the classical, idealized poses of William Bouguereau's pillowy nymphs.

Shelves lined the walls, and Sara could see a pottery watchdog from the Han period and a Ming water basin that shared space with sixteenth-century Indian miniatures from the court of Akbar. At first, she was puzzled that there seemed to be no order evident in Brand's collection. Then she realized that his tastes had not encompassed any particular time or school. The only thing that the paintings and the figurines in the vault had in common was that they were among the rarest of their kind in the world. Even in Brand's collecting, money appeared to have been the bottom line.

Then her eyes focused on a glass box in the center of the room. There it was, in all its gilt and jeweled glory—Constantine's fabled crown.

Although she knew she couldn't be seen, Sara could not help but pull back farther into the duct as she heard the harsh sounds of footfalls on the stone steps. She held her breath until she thought she would burst. Peter came into view, his face set in a puzzled frown as his eyes swept the large room. When his gaze seemed to linger on the wall where her vent was located, Sara held her hand over her mouth to keep from giving herself away. Her pulse quickened as he began to walk slowly toward her.

She could have literally kissed Noah's mouse when it suddenly scampered across Peter's feet, squealing its fear in a loud, high-pitched voice. As she watched, breathless, Peter's face relaxed.

"It's just one of Malcolm's blasted mice," he called up to the people waiting at the top of the stairs. "Nothing but a false alarm." He scooped the mouse up, holding it gingerly by the tail. Then, with one last look around the vault, he turned and headed back up the steps.

Sara was out of the duct in a flash. She slid down the rope, her feet hitting the floor with only the slightest sound. She froze momentarily, afraid that Peter might have heard her, but there was no sound from the staircase. She crossed the room and lifted the lid on the glass case, not allowing herself to dwell on the beauty of the crown as she hurriedly carried it back to the vent.

She was momentarily bemused as she considered how she was supposed to carry the crown while climbing the rope, but a glance down at her watch warned her that she only had twenty seconds left. A flash of inspiration hit, and she stuck the crown atop her head. Then, hand over hand, she climbed the rope, pulling it back into the duct just as the sweep hand reached sixty seconds.

Sara leaned back against the side of the metal duct, her lungs drawing in huge crofts of air. She'd made it. She, Sara Madison, a respectable art-history professor who had always lived a staid, peaceful existence, had just snatched one of the greatest art treasures the world had ever known. A small smile teased at the corners of her mouth as she flipped the lever on the large suction cup, freeing it from the smooth metal.

As she made her way back through the maze of ductwork, her smile began to grow wider and wider until it split her face. The adrenaline was still surging through her veins; she'd never felt more alive in her life.

Noah was waiting for her when she returned to Malcolm's office. "You're right," she exclaimed as he lifted her from the vent. "It's the most exciting thing I've ever done! I can't believe we did it; I can't believe *I* did it. I can see why you can't give it up, Noah! It's wonderful!"

Noah couldn't help grinning in response as he looked down into her smudged face. Her eyes were as bright as newly mined sapphires, her face was alive with the bloom of late-summer roses, and she was quivering with excitement, like a thoroughbred waiting at the gate. The priceless crown of Constantine was perched atop her head, tilted at a precarious angle.

She was the most beautiful sight he'd ever seen, and even as Noah thanked his lucky stars that she was back, safe and sound, he wondered what kind of Pandora's box he had opened tonight.

He plucked the crown from her head. "We'd better get this out of here."

Sara nodded enthusiastically as she retrieved her dress from the desk and stuck it under her arm. "Let's go."

Noah chuckled, pulling his handkerchief from his pocket to wipe at a smudge on her cheek. "Don't you think you ought to change back into your dress? It would be a bit difficult to explain if we were caught with you still wearing your Mata Hari outfit."

Sara's nose wrinkled in a totally out-of-character gesture but one that Noah found charming all the same. "You're right. I should have thought of it." She began peeling off the jump suit.

Noah decided Sara must have set a record as moments later she was changed, frowning into the mirror of her compact as she combed her straight blond hair into a semblance of order.

"Well," she said, putting the comb into her purse, "this is about as good as it's going to get." Her expelled sigh ruffled her bangs.

"You look terrific," he assured her, putting his arm around her waist. Then he frowned. "Let's just hope no one sees us leaving with the crown."

"I've got a solution for that." Sara lifted her full skirt invitingly. It had two deep pockets, either of which would conceal the crown.

"What about ruining the line of your dress?"

She grinned. "It beats wearing the crown on my head."

They made it out of the mansion without any unforseen problems, and soon Noah was at the wheel of Sara's car, headed back to her apartment. He would send someone for the rental car in the morning. Sara was still flying higher than a kite, and he didn't think it wise to let her drive.

Noah smiled to himself as he remembered how excited he had been on his first assignment. Scared but excited. In the end, burnout had exstinguished those exhilarating feelings. Tonight, however, he found Sara's enthusiasm contagious.

"It's the most beautiful thing I've ever seen," Sara breathed reverently, running her fingers over the stones sparkling in the reflected glow of the streetlights. "I'm going to hate giving it up."

"Speaking of that..." Noah began, deciding the time had definitely come to tell Sara the truth. In fact, he admitted, it was long overdue.

Sara cut him off as they pulled up in front of her apartment. "Noah, I just saw a man standing in front of my window. Someone's broken in!"

He exhaled a tired sigh. He hadn't expected them to show up this soon. Dan had promised to allow him time with Sara. Time to work his way through the tangled web of prevarication he'd spun about them. Obviously something had happened to change the schedule.

"Come with me, Sara," Noah instructed flatly as he opened the car door. "It's time for you to meet the rest of the team."

Chapter Fourteen

Noah's fingers cupped tightly around Sara's elbow as they walked up the sidewalk to her apartment. His mouth was a taut, grim slash, his amber eyes unreadable. Sara felt her excitement sifting away like grains of sand through her fingers.

The door opened as they approached. "You've got it," Dan stated on a pleased note. Sara didn't object as he took the crown from her hands.

"I told you we would," Noah said. "Just like you told me you'd give me some time."

Dan looked honestly apologetic. "Sorry, pal, but the wheels of democracy have to keep on turning whatever the price to our personal lives."

Sara looked up at Noah. "What does that mean?"

"It means Dan isn't exactly what we led you to believe he was," Noah explained slowly.

The pieces of the puzzle began to fit into place. "You're FBI, aren't you?" she exclaimed. Her startled gaze moved to Noah as she attempted to figure out his role in all this.

"Not exactly," Dan said. He reached into his pocket and pulled out his identification, which he handed to Sara.

"Central Intelligence Agency," she read aloud. She lifted her head to stare at him. "CIA? You're with the CIA?"

Dan nodded, looking decidedly uncomfortable by the obvious censure in Sara's tone.

Her eyes were chips of blue ice as they turned to Noah. "Are you a CIA agent, too, Noah?"

"Noah's army intelligence," said a man Sara had not realized was in the apartment until he entered the living room from the kitchen. "Fred Carlisle, State Department," he introduced himself. "We want to thank you, Ms Madison. You've done your country a great favor."

Her hardened gaze could have cut diamonds as her eyes turned on Noah. "Army intelligence?" she asked coldly.

"Retired," he corrected, as if that might soften the glare she was directing his way.

"Retired," she echoed, slowly shaking her head. A sound resembling a gunshot rang out as her palm connected with his cheek. Then she marched into the bedroom, slamming the door behind her.

The three men remained silent for a moment. "Looks as if you have some explaining to do," Dan pointed out finally.

Noah rubbed his reddening cheek. "Now I know how Daniel felt when he was tossed into the lions' den."

"You knew she wasn't going to take it well," Dan reminded his friend.

Noah sighed. "I did. But I also thought I'd have some time to break it to her in my own way." His gaze hardened as it swept over the two men.

"Sorry about that," Carlisle apologized. "But the word's leaked out. Ankara is buzzing with rumors that are getting worse by the hour. There's even one going around that a Greek Cypriot managed to get into the palace and assassinate the president. Democracy is a delicate thing in that part of the world, as you well know. The government can't allow the appearance of a tear in the delicate fabric of their coalition government.''

"So," he continued, "they had no choice but to schedule a press conference for tomorrow to assure the world that everything is fine. It's imperative that the crown be there.''

"Well, since you now have the damn thing, I know you both will excuse me while I try to salvage the flimsy fabric of my own life," Noah muttered, leaving the room.

"Sara?" He tapped on her closed door. "Sara, let me in. I can explain.''

"Go away.''

Noah twisted the knob. "Give me five minutes. That's all I ask.''

When there was no answer from behind the door, Noah took the pick from his pocket. The lock proved no obstacle, and he entered the darkened room. Sara was lying facedown on the bed.

"Go away," she muttered into her pillow.

"I will," he promised, "as soon as you hear me out.''

"There's nothing you can say that will make me feel any less a fool. So just get out of my apartment. And while you're at it, whatever your name is, get out of my life.''

The mattress sagged as he sat down beside her. "Sara—'' He reached out, touching her shoulder.

She shook off his hand. "I'm warning you, if you and your cohorts aren't out of here in two minutes, I'm calling the police.''

"Then you *will* give me two minutes?"

Damn him, Sara thought; he always took things exactly the way he wanted to hear them. She turned her head to glare at him.

"That's not what I meant. I've already given you far more than you deserve.''

"I know that," he admitted. "And don't think I haven't felt like hell about it."

Sara hated the way his raspy voice still had an effect on her after all he had done. "You lied to me, Noah. You promised that was one thing you'd never do."

"I didn't lie, Sara. Granted, I didn't tell you the entire truth. But I never lied."

"You let me think you were a jewel thief!"

"That was your own idea."

"You certainly didn't bother to correct me."

"Sara, try to understand. The entire mission was on a need-to-know security basis."

"And I didn't need to know."

He nodded. "That's right. I wanted to tell you—ask Dan. But I couldn't."

"Why shouldn't Dan confirm your story?" she spat out. "He's as big a liar as you are. You both make me sick."

"I was also thinking of you. It could have been dangerous for you to know too much."

"Dangerous?" She sat up against the headboard, pushing her hair over her shoulder with hands that shook with anger. "You didn't think it was dangerous for me to be crawling through that ductwork? You didn't think it was dangerous for me to be playing games with Peter Taylor? Give me a break, Noah. I may have had miserable judgment where you're concerned, but I'm not stupid!"

The corners of his mouth tightened. "I never thought you were."

Sara dragged her eyes from his. "You made love to me," she protested. "Do you know how that makes me feel?"

"I can guess."

"Used," she said bitterly.

His fingers cupped her chin, lifting her unwilling gaze to his. "I made love to you, Sara," he agreed gently. "That's precisely what it was. If you don't believe anything else, you have to believe that."

Stinging tears of anger and frustration burned her eyes. "I don't have to believe anything," she corrected heatedly. "Your two minutes are up; please leave."

Ignoring her command, Noah drew her into his arms. "I can't do that, sweetheart."

Sara stiffened, fighting against the seductive feel of his wide hands moving up and down her back. "Yes, you can," she insisted. "It's easy, Noah. Just stand up and walk through that door. And take your friends with you."

He brushed his knuckles along her cheekbone. "I think I lost the ability to walk away from you the moment we met, Sara Madison."

Before Sara could come up with a scathing response to Noah's huskily issued statement, his lips covered hers. They plucked teasingly, seductively, as his hands sought to soothe away her anger with a gentle touch.

"This isn't what I want," she protested weakly as he lowered her to the mattress.

Noah lifted his head. "The truth, Sara," he insisted. "At least give me that."

"Why should I?" she retorted. "You never cared enough to tell *me* the truth."

As his palm scraped against her breast, her body responded instantly, a taut bud pressing against the thin gauze fabric.

"How can you honestly believe any of this was a lie?" he asked gruffly.

As his hand moved down her midriff, Sara had to stifle her cry of longing. "It was only sex," she breathed painfully.

He shook his head in mute frustration as he released Sara to lie beside her. "We're both experienced enough to recognize the difference, Sara. We were making love."

"You hurt me, Noah," she said shakily.

He brushed away a glistening tear that was sliding down her pale cheek. "I know. And believe me, I never wanted that to happen."

She did believe him, Sara realized. "But you'd do it all over again, wouldn't you?"

"The truth?" he asked solemnly.

Sara nodded.

Noah sat up abruptly, dragging his long fingers through his chestnut hair. "I probably would," he admitted flatly.

Sara was beginning to understand this man. She wasn't certain she liked what she was seeing, but his admission had triggered some vague feeling of respect. Ever since she'd met him, she had felt uneasy by his seeming lack of ethics. That part of his behavior hadn't seemed consistent with what she had instinctively felt was a strongly moral man. Now she realized that Noah's sense of morality would not allow him to put his own needs, or those of a single individual, before what he considered the greater needs of the majority.

She sat up, tucking her skirt around her bent knees. They remained silent, lost in their own thoughts.

"You're just lucky that I'm a Jake Hawke fan," Sara said finally. "I'm still hurt by what you did, Noah. But I think I can understand your motives."

Noah fought to keep from revealing the blazing hope that her words instilled in him. "Does that mean you believe me?"

Sara nodded. "I believe you. Although I still think I should knock your block off for letting me believe that I was falling in love with a thief. My God, do you realize I broke the law for you tonight?"

He took her hand in his. "You've no idea how good that made me feel. And how rotten."

She sighed. "Well, at least my life hasn't been boring lately." A nagging question had persisted since they'd first met, and Sara decided that now was definitely the time to settle it. "Am I going to have to learn to call you by a different name?" That wasn't going to be at all easy.

He smiled. "The Noah stays. My last name is Winfield."

Sara nodded. "I don't believe I could think of you as anyone other than Noah," she admitted. "Winfield. Where have I heard that before?" She wrinkled her brow as she concentrated on placing the name.

When she did, she stared up at him. "Noah, your Uncle David—the one who's involved with the arts—is he David J. Winfield?"

"Publisher of *Art Digest* magazine," Noah concurred.

"No wonder they covered for you when I called."

"My family doesn't like what I do, or did. But they can be counted on to come through in a pinch."

"Are you really retired?"

"For the past two years," he assured her.

"Then why are you here now?"

"It's a little tricky to explain," he said slowly. "You see, the Turkish government unearthed the crown during a recent subway excavation. Amazed that it actually existed, they decided to make an official announcement on the third anniversary of the end of martial law. There were going to be a lot of state ceremonies, and it seemed like a good time. But then the crown disappeared from the presidential palace."

"I still don't see how that would concern you."

"Our government's ties with Turkey go back a long way," he explained. "They're one of our NATO allies."

"I know that," Sara answered impatiently. "It still doesn't explain your participation. If you're really retired," she tacked on accusingly.

Noah decided not to rise to her sarcastic tone. He took a deep breath, trying again. "When it was learned that the theft was orchestrated by an American collector, that little fact proved embarrassing to Washington."

"Why wasn't it on the news?"

"The Turkish democracy is fragile, at best," he explained. "Many of the people view the country's current economic problems as a direct result of the new regime. They're suggesting that they might have been better off under military rule. Plus, there are always fears of terrorism in that part of the world. It would have been inviting trouble to let it be known that palace security was lax."

"I can see that." It all made sense, but he still hadn't answered the most important question. "But what does all that have to do with you?"

"They needed someone with a working knowledge of art," Noah explained, "and the computer kicked out my name. There wasn't time to train anyone else, and my background was perfect. Not only is my uncle the publisher of the country's most prestigious art magazine, but I grew up surrounded by the stuff. Some of it was bound to rub off."

His gaze was fond. "Of course I'm not as knowledgeable as a certain lovely art-history professor, but I could carry off the charade well enough to convince Brand of my credentials."

Sara leaned back against the headboard. "I still don't understand how you got into the spy business in the first place. It had to be more than the fact that you don't like banking."

Noah frowned. As Sara watched, his fingers curved unconsciously into a tight fist. "After I graduated from college, I was eligible for the draft. My father wasn't about to have his only son shipped off to Vietnam, so he began to pull all kinds of strings to keep me out."

"But you didn't want him to," she guessed.

He sighed. "It didn't seem fair that I should be protected by an accident of birth." His lips firmed, and Sara had the feeling Noah was remembering the arguments he must have had with his father. "Thousands of young men were being sent to Vietnam because their families didn't have the money or political power to keep them out of a war we had no business being in in the first place. I wasn't about to let some poor kid from Omaha or Seattle go in my place while I stayed home and shuffled bank notes."

She wouldn't have expected Noah to do any less. "So you enlisted."

Noah nodded. "My father hit the roof. It was two weeks before he cooled down, but when he did, he began maneuvering to keep me stateside. That's when I requested army intelligence."

"You did it to spite your family?"

"Originally," he admitted with a grim smile. "Then a funny thing happened. After a time, I began to believe that in my own small way I might be making a contribution toward keeping this fragile old earth a decent place in which to live."

Sara was undeniably moved by the emotion in his deep voice. "I do love you, Noah Winfield," she said, brushing a kiss against his lips. "And I'm very, very glad you're not a thief."

"Me, too," he agreed, taking her into his arms. His eyes smiled down at her. "I *was* a little worried that I was going to have to spend the next few years rehabilitating you. You seemed to enjoy our little escapade this evening."

Sara tilted her head back to look up at him. "I loved it. But to tell you the truth, I'm not sure my nerves could take it as a way of life."

Noah looked inclined to kiss her, and Sara parted her lips expectantly. The polite knock on the door captured their unwilling attention.

"Noah?" Dan called softly.

"You've got rotten timing, Dan," Noah returned. "Go away."

"I'd love to leave you two alone to work things out, but we need to see you. Right away."

Noah sighed, relinquishing his hold on Sara. "They probably want to give us a medal," he joked.

As they reentered the living room, both men's faces were unusually somber. "What's the problem now?" Noah asked. "We got the crown back in mint condition."

"That's precisely the problem," Dan replied, his mouth set in a tight line.

"Problem?"

"It's in perfect condition," Carlisle agreed. "It's also a forgery. You two took the wrong crown."

Chapter Fifteen

"That's impossible!" Noah exclaimed. "It matches the description I was given."

"Not exactly," Carlisle said. "Take this cross, for example."

He pointed out the gold filigree cross on the top of the crown. It was engraved with the Christian monogram, which Constantine had commanded be painted on his soldiers' shields. Sara knew there were two versions of the origin of Constantine's decision.

One, from the Christian apologist Lactantius, was that Constantine had received the instructions from God in a dream. A slightly different version, given by the emperor himself to Eusebius, told of the sign appearing in the sky during a battle, with the legend "In this sign, conquer." Whatever its origin, Sara was not surprised the ruler had seen fit to include it when designing his crown.

"What about it?" Noah grumbled, obviously unmoved by the man's accusation.

"It's definitely not from the fourth century. They didn't use this method of soldering."

Sara leaned forward, suddenly interested. In her haste to remove the crown from the vault, she admittedly hadn't studied it closely. "You're right."

Noah was less than pleased with Sara's observation. "Whose side are you on, anyway?"

She ignored him for the moment. "It's nineteenth century, isn't it?" she asked Carlisle.

He nodded. "I'd say that what we have here, Ms Madison, is another Rospigliosi Cup."

She drew in a sharp breath. "But I thought he concentrated solely on Renaissance works."

"He obviously made an exception in this case," Carlisle insisted. "Look at that dragon; I've seen its twin on a bowl already proven to be a Vasters forgery."

"What the hell is a Rospigliosi Cup?" Noah demanded. "And who's this Vasters guy?"

Sara traced the flaming dragon with her fingertip. "The Rospigliosi Cup was one of the treasures of the Metropolitan Museum of Art for years. It dated back to the 1500s and was attributed to a mannerist sculptor and goldsmith, Benvenuto Cellini. After a while, there were doubts whether or not Cellini actually made the cup, but it was still considered a masterpiece of Renaissance art. In fact, a museum publication described it as revealing the pagan splendor of the Renaissance."

Noah studied the crown thoughtfully. "But it was a forgery?"

Sara's blond head bobbed in agreement. "About seven years ago, a curator for the Victoria and Albert Museum in London uncovered working drawings for the creation of new Renaissance projects. But they were all done in the nineteenth century by a German goldsmith named Reinhold Vasters. Museums all over the world began examining their Renaissance pieces, looking for Vasters forgeries. They discovered several hundred; the Rospigliosi Cup was one of them."

"And this guy made a copy of the crown?"

"It appears so," Carlisle responded firmly.

"Then it's worthless," Dan groaned.

Sara shook her head. "Oh, no," she insisted. "The gold and jewels are worth a fortune alone, not to mention the fact that Vasters has begun to fetch a very good price. One piece recently sold for a great deal of money."

"Sixty thousand," Carlisle offered helpfully.

Sara thanked him with a smile. "That's right. He's becoming quite popular," she assured Noah and Dan. "Actually, you should be quite pleased." Her eyes sparkled as she took in the delicate scrollwork on the cross. "I've always wanted to see one of Vasters' works," she murmured.

"You're forgetting just one thing," Noah pointed out.

"What is that?" she asked absently, her gaze moving to a gleaming emerald inlay. How she'd love to show this crown to her classes!

"The Turkish government is having a news conference tomorrow, and we're still short one crown."

She straightened, looking at him curiously. "Isn't this the one that was stolen from the palace?"

"I'm afraid not," Carlisle answered for Noah. "That piece had already been authenticated."

"Vasters has fooled the best experts," Sara argued.

"This isn't the crown, Ms Madison," the State Department official stated.

"But that doesn't make any sense," she murmured. "What are the chances of two crowns suddenly showing up in Phoenix all in the same week?"

"It's got to be Taylor," Noah stated abruptly. "He arranged the buy; he must have switched the crowns in transit."

"I don't know," Sara argued. "There's something missing. How did he even know there was a forged crown?"

Noah shrugged. "The guy's slippery. You stay here; we'll be back with the real crown before you know it."

"We?"

"Dan and I." He shot a glance toward the art expert the State Department had assigned to the case. "You'd better come, too, Carlisle. We don't want any last-minute mix-ups."

Sara moved in front of Noah as he headed toward the door. "What about me?"

Noah gave her a patient smile. "You're going to wait here. It could get dangerous, Sara. Taylor isn't going to be thrilled about handing over the crown. I don't want you to get in the way."

She rose to her full height, bristling furiously. "In the way? I suppose I was in the way earlier this evening?"

He moved her aside with ease. "You know I didn't mean it that way," he argued, pressing a quick, reassuring kiss against her lips. "Wish me luck."

"Always," she responded automatically. She said it to his back; Noah was already out the door.

"It isn't fair," she muttered, picking up the crown to study it in greater detail. "Just when I'm beginning to get into the swing of things, he clips my wings and grounds me."

She sat down in the big, comfortable chair. "Besides, it still doesn't make any sense. Why would Peter steal the crown, put this forgery in its place, then promise me that we would have the crown tomorrow morning?"

Sara's fingers rubbed at a sparkling diamond. "Perhaps he was only using it as an excuse to get me to stay the night," she considered aloud. She shook her head. "No, I'm sure he didn't have the crown this evening. I can't believe he would have stayed at the mansion. Especially once he discovered Malcolm's death."

Sara continued to dwell on the problem, going over everything that had happened this evening. Finally, the answer struck.

"Dumb," she muttered, jumping to her feet. "The answer was there all the time; we were all too dumb and blind to see it!"

She quickly changed into the black jump suit and scribbled a quick note to Noah to let him know where she had gone. Then, as she started out the door, Sara remembered the crown.

"You may not be priceless," she murmured, picking it up from the cushion, "but you're not exactly out of a box of crackerjacks, either." Her eyes skimmed over the apartment, searching for a place to hide the forged crown. As her gaze drifted to the kitchen, Sara knew just the place.

Seconds later, she was driving away from the apartment, secure in the knowledge that the Vasters crown was safely stashed away inside a stainless-steel stew pot.

Encouraged by her earlier success, it never entered Sara's mind that she might be biting off more than she could chew. Besides, this heist was going to be perfectly safe. The thief would be no more capable of hurting someone than Sara herself was. The house was dark as she pulled up in front of it. Sara smiled. Its owner was still at Malcolm's party. She had hoped that would be the case.

She closed the car door carefully, making her way to the front door. It was then she realized she should have remembered to bring along Noah's pick.

"Damn," she whispered under her breath. "There has to be another way into this place." She worked her way around the ground floor, trying every window but finding them bolted from the inside. It was then she spotted the tree. One branch extended past a second-floor balcony, and Sara decided it was her only choice.

She shimmied up the tree, stopping as she reached the large V in the trunk. She reached out, gingerly testing the weight of the branch. "Piece of cake," she quoted Noah. The words didn't sound quite as reassuring coming from her lips as they had his.

She inched her way out onto the branch, trying not to tremble as it began to sway. Suddenly, something dropped onto her back, sharp talons going through the thin jersey to dig into her skin.

"Damn!" she whispered harshly, looking back over her shoulder. "Get off me, you stupid cat!"

He began to mew, sniffing her with uncommon interest, his claws breaking her skin as he flexed his paws. Sara belatedly realized that the tomcat had been out for his nightly stroll when he'd come across her smelling like one gigantic mouse.

"Look, cat," she argued wearily, "I left the mouse home this trip. So why don't you go off and find some friendly lady kitty to serenade?"

In response, his claws dug in even deeper. Stifling her cry, Sara reached behind her, clutching at the cat's fur. There was a rustle of leaves, a ripping sound as her jersey gave way, and a loud howl shattered the stillness of the night as she yanked him from her back. He kicked furiously, wriggling for freedom, his frantic movements causing Sara to lose her grip.

Fortunately, she thought to drop the cat and grabbed for the limb from below. As she watched, the animal landed deftly on all fours. His eyes gleamed a tiger yellow as he glared up at her; then, spitting out a harsh sound, he strode off regally into the darkness, leaving her hanging from the tree limb like an ungainly opossum.

It took some effort, but she finally managed to pull herself back onto the branch. With a deep, steadying breath, she began to crawl toward the wrought-iron railing.

Once she had successfully climbed down onto the concrete balcony, Sara sighed in relief. So far, so good. She crossed her fingers as she tested the French doors, exhilarated when she found them unlocked.

Taking her penlight from her breast pocket, she entered Baroness Levinzski's house.

"Well, Sara," the deep voice drawled, "fancy meeting you here of all places."

Sara could only stare as Peter Taylor walked into the yellow beam of her flashlight, carrying the gleaming crown of Constantine in his hand. Something was terribly wrong. It was Gizella Sara had expected to be in possession of the crown, not Peter.

"What are *you* doing here?" she asked. "You're supposed to be back at the party."

He smiled as he turned on his own flashlight, capturing her in a circle of light. "The same party you're supposed to be attending, right?" His eyes skimmed over her. "I like that outfit. Is it new?"

"But Noah—" She shut her mouth a moment too late.

"But Noah is supposed to be arresting me at this very moment, right?"

"Something like that," Sara agreed bleakly. "You have to give the crown up, Peter."

He stared at her. "To your lover?" he asked acidly. "Really, Sara, you can try a man's patience. As disappointing a thought as it is, I'm willing to let the guy have you, but he can't have everything."

"Not to Noah," she stressed, not bothering to deny his accusation concerning her relationship with Noah. "You have to give it back to the government."

He shook his head. "Not on your life, little one. Brand owes me this one."

"But he's dead," she protested. "He won't even miss it."

"So, you ran across him, did you?"

Sara nodded.

"I should have realized something was wrong when that alarm sounded. I suppose you and that so-called reporter were responsible for that."

She nodded again, afraid to trust her voice. She didn't want Peter to know how frightened she was.

"But he was at the top of the stairs, standing right beside me when I turned the alarm off. Tell me how you did it," he instructed.

"I went in through the vent," Sara admitted.

Peter's eyes widened. "You? You're claustrophobic. I remember how you nearly fainted when Malcolm showed you his wine cellar."

"Noah came up with a cure."

Peter's answering laugh was harsh. "I'm not even going to ask.... I'm sorry you showed up tonight, Sara. You realize I can't allow you to go to the authorities."

Sara backed up a few inches. "Peter, you wouldn't kill me, would you? Just for some gold and jewels?"

He looked honestly stunned by her question. "Sara, I may be a thief, but I am not a murderer. Of course I'm not going to kill you. I'm simply going to take you a few miles out onto the desert. By the time you manage to walk back into the city, I'll be out of the country."

Her relief was almost overwhelming. "Why did you do it, Peter?"

"I worked for that tightfisted bastard for twenty years, doing all his dirty work, taking all the risks. When he knew he was about to die, he revised his will. Do you know what he left me?"

Sara shook her head.

"Nothing. Zero. Zip." His mouth was a cruel slash. "I probably would have been better off if he'd turned me in twenty years ago."

Those words jogged her memory. "You said I wasn't the only one Malcolm had blackmailed."

Peter scowled. "Twenty years ago, I was making a nice little living in Europe. One night I had the misfortune to be in the process of appropriating Andrew Mantegna's *Adoration of the Magi* from Brand's Monte Carlo villa when he arrived home early from the opera."

Sara drew in a surprised breath. That painting had sold a few years ago to the J. Paul Getty Museum for a record $10.4 million. A nice little living indeed, she considered.

"Of course he caught you," she guessed.

"Red-handed," Peter agreed.

"But why didn't he have you arrested?"

His eyes were shards of ice. "Surely you've realized Brand always acted in his own interests. It occurred to him that I was much more useful as an employee."

"Procuring stolen paintings in the art underground."

"Precisely. I should have realized that he never intended to reimburse me for all those risks I took. When I broke into the safe and discovered his will, I knew what I had to do. I took the crown shortly after it arrived last night and replaced it with Gizella's forgery."

"I don't understand why you bothered to make the switch. Surely it involved more risk than just stealing the crown and leaving the country."

"Malcolm Brand was not the kind of man to sit still for being duped," Peter explained. "He would have spent every last cent he had to track me down and take revenge. Believe me, Sara, that was a far greater risk than breaking into this place to take the forgery."

He shook his head. "Actually, as it turns out, that little manuever was unnecessary. Brand's heart attack would have kept him from ever knowing the crown was gone."

Something still didn't ring quite true. "But how did you find out about the forgery in the first place?"

Peter shrugged. "That was simply a stroke of luck."

Suddenly, the room was flooded with light. "Never trust in luck, darlink. On the contrary, I intended you to discover my little secret. Just as I planned for you to return my family's treasure to its rightful owner."

Baroness Levinzski appeared in the doorway, holding a small silver gun in her perfectly manicured hand.

"Sara," she murmured silkily, "what a surprise to find you here in my home." Her full red lips drooped in a feminine pout. "However, it is a shame," she continued regretfully. "It now looks as if I'm going to have to protect my home against two unwelcome intruders. I do hope you won't take it too personally, dear, but I have no other choice."

Peter reached out his hand. "Gizella, for God's sake, put that thing down!"

"And let you leave with the crown?" the baroness asked, arching a perfectly shaped blond brow. "Really, Peter, don't be absurd."

"You're not going to get away with this," Sara warned. "There are others who know you have the crown. They'll be here soon."

"You have watched far too much American television, Sara," the baroness stated with ill-concealed amusement. "Only in fiction does the hero ride up on his white charger to rescue the fair damsel in distress. As for the crown, what is that saying you have in this country? 'Possession is nine-tenths of the law'?" Her gaze moved to Peter. "It seems that I am back in possession. After more than four hundred years."

"That's when your family lost it?" Sara asked, stalling for time. Surely by now Noah would have returned home and discovered her note.

Gizella's green eyes narrowed. "You're really quite clever, dear. Far more astute than poor Peter; I had to let him see my crown before he even thought to steal Malcolm's and replace it with my forgery."

She granted Peter a cold smile. "I recognized the switch immediately. Honestly, Peter, I do think you've lost your touch; you should have been suspicious when you found my home so easy to break into last night. Of course, I was expecting you to return this evening for the original."

"Vasters did a good job," Sara admitted. "Whoever hired him got his money's worth."

"That forgery is a Vasters?" Peter asked incredulously. "Are you sure?"

The baroness laughed delightedly. "I should be. It cost my great-great-grandfather several thousand forints. Although, to be perfectly honest, he only had it recreated from the old drawings for his own pleasure. I'm sure he never realized how it would eventually serve as a tool in reclaiming the original."

"Which another relative brought back from the Crusades," Sara said, having put all the pieces together earlier in the apartment.

The baroness gave Sara a rewarding smile. "I forgot, your field is art history, isn't it? No wonder you caught on when so many others failed." Gizella nodded in confirmation of Sara's words. "When Pope Innocent the Third embarked on the fourth Crusades against Egypt, he enlisted Venetian aid."

"But the Venetian government had strong commercial ties with Egypt," Sara broke it, "which put the doge's policy directly in opposition with the pope."

"What does that have to do with the crown?" Peter asked impatiently.

"We're getting to that," the baroness replied calmly. She nodded toward Sara. "Since you have all the answers, dear, why don't you enlighten our friend?"

Sara had no desire to chat with either one of these individuals, but at this point she was willing to do anything that would give Noah time to arrive before the baroness made good her threat to shoot both Peter and herself. She drew a deep breath.

"You see, Peter, there wasn't enough money in the treasury to pay the Venetian crusaders, so a deal was struck that the Crusades would detour long enough to allow the army to capture Zara, a Venetian possession that had been granted protection by the Hungarian king." She glanced over at the baroness. "I believe you said he was a relative."

"Of course," Gizella remarked smoothly. "I told you I am descended from royal lineage."

"I suppose one of the crusaders became involved with a member of your family while in Zara?"

"You're quite astute," the baroness agreed.

Sara nodded, trying not to glance down at her watch as she continued the story. What was keeping Noah? "After returning Zara to the doge, the crusaders continued on to Constantinople. They sacked the city in 1204, and after a general massacre, the pillaging continued on for years.

"It was the city's worst period. The Venetians took control of the church; bronze statues were melted down for coin; sacred relics were stolen from the sanctuaries; everything was taken."

She glanced toward the baroness for confirmation. "I suppose that's when the crown ended up in your family."

"Precisely. It made an acceptable dowry, once the young crusader returned to Hungary." Her green eyes gleamed. "It stayed in my family for over three hundred years. Before those damnable Turks stole it from us.''

''During the Ottoman expansion in 1521?'' Sara asked, intrigued in spite of herself by the baroness's ability to trace not only her family tree but the crown over so many centuries.

''That damnable sultan Süleyman,'' the baroness muttered. ''The Ottomans called him the Lawgiver; the Europeans called him the Magnificent. I call him a thief,'' she spat out viciously.

''Not that this little tale of love and war isn't enchanting,'' Peter complained, ''but I still don't get it.''

Gizella expelled a weary sigh. ''Honestly, Peter, you have absolutely no sense of history. My family has been waiting for more than four hundred years to reclaim what was ours. And I'm finally going to be the one to accomplish the deed.''

''You are absolutely crazy,'' he said incredulously. ''Are you telling me that you have no intention of selling it?''

''Of course not.''

He stared at her. ''You're not even going to market the jewels?''

Gizella waved away that suggestion. ''Don't be foolish. If all I wanted was the jewels, the gems in the Vasters crown are equally as valuable,'' she pointed out. ''This is à question of honor.''

''I always knew you were a little cracked, Gizella,'' he muttered. ''But this takes the cake.''

''I was not too crazy to plant the seed to steal the crown in your mind,'' she retorted. ''I used your own avarice against you, Peter.'' She shook her head regretfully. ''We could have made a good team, you and I. But your greed makes you far too untrustworthy.''

Her brilliant green gaze moved to Sara. ''I am honestly sorry about your getting involved in this, my dear. But you understand that I can't let you go.'' Her teeth flashed in a reassuring smile. ''However, I promise to shoot you first so you won't have to watch Peter die.''

Sara couldn't believe this was happening to her. Her mind whirled as she tried to think of anything that would alter the outcome of her foolhardy plan to come here alone.

''May I at least hold the crown for just a moment?'' she asked with far more calm that she was feeling. ''All I've seen is the forgery. I'd like an opportunity to examine the real thing.''

The baroness considered that for a moment. ''I don't see why not,'' she agreed finally. ''Peter, give Sara the crown.''

His eyes were filled with apologies as he handed it over. Sara knew that Peter was certainly no happier than she by the way things had turned out.

''Thank you,'' she murmured, her fingers traveling over the gilt crown.

The stones flashed like fire in their gold settings. She wasn't going to die, Sara told herself firmly. She had too much to look forward to. She and Noah still had too many things left undone. Noah—if she had only listened to him. Despite her escalating fear, Sara clung to the thought that he would arrive in the nick of time, like something out of a Saturday matinee, to save her.

Her hopes were dashed when the baroness's bulky chauffeur suddenly appeared in the doorway, Noah in front of him. ''We've got company,'' the chauffeur announced grimly.

Sara's eyes widened as the two men entered the room, the barrel of a revolver pressed into Noah's back.

Chapter Sixteen

The baroness gave Noah a dazzling smile that was totally at odds with the mood of the moment. "I was wondering when you'd show up, Noah, darlink," she said sweetly. "Isn't this nice? It appears Malcolm's party has moved to my house."

"You'll never get away with this, Gizella," Noah warned gruffly.

"I will admit you make things a bit more difficult," she admitted. "But I have always been a resourceful person."

Noah's eyes slid to Sara. "Are you all right?"

She nodded, the lump in her throat disallowing words.

Noah's stony gaze returned to the baroness. "So help me God, if you hurt her, you'll spend the rest of your life regretting it."

She only laughed. "Don't be so melodramatic; there is nothing you can do to stop me." When his eyes moved down to the slender pistol the baroness held in her hand, Gizella shook her head.

"I wouldn't try it. Not while Hugo has his revolver directed at your back." Her red lips curved. "Hugo is a very loyal employee; he'll do anything I tell him to do. Won't you, Hugo?"

"Anything, baroness," the huge man agreed.

Sara stared bleakly at the chauffeur. While Noah was definitely not a small man, the baroness's henchman looked as though he could play on the defensive line of any NFL team in the country. When you included the weapons the pair held in their hands, Sara determined, the bad guys definitely had the upper hand. Peter appeared to have turned to stone. They would get no help from that quarter, she thought.

"You're a charming man, Noah," the baroness continued. "Unfortunately, you're going to meet with an accident." Her smooth brow furrowed. "Since it would be difficult to believe that I mistook all three of you for burglars, I think it will be necessary for Hugo to take you out into the desert. By the time they find your body, I will be far away from his place."

She waved the gun. "Hugo, I believe we have wasted enough time," she instructed.

"Yes, baroness," he said readily. "Come on," he instructed Noah. "You and I are going to take a little ride."

"What about her?" Noah asked, jerking his head in Sara's direction. "She doesn't have anything to do with this. Let her go."

"I'm afraid Ms Madison knows too much for her own good," the baroness stated apologetically. "I am sorry, Noah. I had no idea you were such a romantic."

"Let her go and I'll fix it so you can keep the crown," he suggested. "The authorities have no idea of your involvement, Gizella. Let Sara leave now and no one will ever be the wiser."

The baroness shook her head. "You know I can't do that," she protested. "If it weren't for you, she might remain silent. But I don't think she would be willing to forget you so easily, would you, dear?"

Noah could have cheerfully strangled Sara as she shook her head. "Never," she insisted.

When the baroness shot Noah a look that said, I told you so, he tried to come up with something else. Anything to buy time until he could make his move.

"Then let us all go," he said. "You've got the crown; you're only putting a noose around your neck if you kill us."

The baroness gave a coldly patient sigh. "You must think I'm incredibly foolish. Why should I trust you? Why should I trust any of you?"

"It's your only chance," Noah said calmly. "I'm not a reporter, baroness. I'm an army intelligence officer. If you think the government is going to simply shrug their shoulders when they find me missing, you're mistaken. They'll track you down, wherever you are."

"Baroness," Hugo protested, "if this guy is who he says he is, he's right. Remember what happened to my family?"

"Pooh—" The baroness dismissed his words. "That was a different government, Hugo, with entirely different tactics. As you well know."

She addressed her next words to the others. "Hugo's family was involved in the 1956 uprising. Several were executed; others were taken to the Soviet Union, where they were never heard from again."

Her attention turned back to her chauffeur. "Believe me, Hugo, the Americans do not use such storm-trooper tactics. They will bemoan their fallen comrade and make an attempt to find his killers. But this man is only a small cog in a very large machine. He's actually quite expendable."

Noah heard Sara's sharp intake of breath and sent her what he hoped was a reassuring look. He'd survived too many close calls to trade his life for a bit of gold. As he remembered the senseless stabbing in Ankara, his anger flared even higher. Despite the baroness's uncaring attitude, Noah could sense Hugo's hesitation. He decided to play on it.

"That's a pretty little scenario, baroness," he began amiably. "But why don't you tell Hugo the rest of the story? Why don't you tell him that I'm here representing the joint effort of two countries to locate the crown?"

"Shut up!" Gizella instructed sharply, shifting her attention from Sara and Peter to point her own gun at Noah.

Noah ignored her, glancing back over his shoulder at the attentive Hungarian. "She may be right about America not resorting to violent means," he agreed, "but I'm afraid I can't say the same about Turkey. They're bound and determined to find the people who stole their national heirloom, Hugo. And I wouldn't want to be in your shoes when they do."

Hugo appeared decidedly apprehensive as his gaze shifted back and forth between Noah and Gizella. "Baroness—"

"Don't listen to him," Gizella snapped. "He's only trying to frighten you."

Sensing Hugo's vacillation, Noah made his move, spinning around to knock the revolver to the floor.

"No!" Sara cried out as the baroness began to pull the trigger on her own handgun.

She lunged toward Gizella, hurling the crown with all her might. The woman turned toward Sara just as the crown hit her arm, deflecting the shot.

Peter was finally jolted into action. He charged forward, his fist connecting solidly with the baroness's jaw. The gun fell from her hand as she crumpled to the floor. Noah, who had managed to knock out the massive Hugo during the flurry of fists, scooped up the man's revolver. He and Peter faced each other, guns in hand.

Sara had slumped into a chair, her head spinning dizzily. Through her dazed senses, she realized it wasn't yet over. There was still Peter to contend with.

Peter surprised her by saying to Noah, holding the gun gingerly by the handle, "You'd better take this. I've never liked these things myself."

Noah's relief was visible as he reached out his hand. "I know what you mean," he agreed. "The damn things are far too dangerous." He glanced around the room. "Why don't you see if you can find something to tie these two up with while we wait for the police to arrive."

Peter nodded, leaving the room. Noah glanced over at Sara. "Thank you."

She managed a weak smile. "Anytime. Just don't make it too soon, okay?"

He winked. "You've got yourself a deal. How are you?" he asked, concerned by the pallor of her complexion.

"I've been better," she admitted. "And I've got a killer of a headache."

She put her hand to her temple, puzzled by the warm stickiness against her palm. When she lowered her hand, she could only stare blankly at the red stain.

"Damn," Noah muttered, "you've been shot."

"Shot?" Sara echoed blankly.

As Peter returned, carrying a length of nylon clothesline, Noah shoved the guns into his hands. "Take care of these two," he ordered brusquely. "And call a damned ambulance!"

He crossed the room in two long strides, squatting down beside Sara. "You idiot. You could have been killed!"

Sara blinked, fighting against the swirling blackness behind her eyes. "So could you have," she managed to point out. "And is that any way to talk to a woman who just saved your life?"

"You had no business doing that. You had no business being here in the first place, dammit!" He brushed the sticky hair away from her forehead.

Sara felt her tongue thickening. "I wanted to help," she said weakly.

"Just shut up," he instructed gruffly. "Dan should be here in a minute; I called him when I found your note." Noah yanked a handkerchief from his pocket, pressing it against the angry wound. Ice ran through his veins as he watched the spreading red stain.

Sara struggled to focus on him. "I found the crown, Noah. I figured it out after you left."

"I know you did," he agreed. "And you were a damn fool to try to take it by yourself. I swear, lady, if you ever pull a stunt like that again, I'll beat you black and blue."

Sara shook her head slowly, feeling as if she were floating. Her eyes drifted shut, her lashes resting against her cheeks. "You wouldn't do that."

"Don't bet on it," he ground out. "I've half a mind to do precisely that right now. Fortunately for you, I've always had a rule about decking women after they take a bullet meant for me."

She reached up blindly to pat his harshly set face. "You don't fool me with that gritty old Jake Hawke impression," she whispered.

He swore. "Would you just shut up? You're wasting precious energy."

Bright lights swirled on a background of black velvet. Sara's hand fluttered to her lap. "Noah?"

"What is it now?"

Her complexion was the color of driven snow, her words thick and slurred, her skin ice cold. Why couldn't she just rest until the ambulance got here? There would be plenty of time for conversation. Later.

"Am I going to die?"

Noah's answer was an incoherent buzz in her ear, and Sara discovered she lacked the strength to lift her lids to look at him. As he gathered Sara into his arms, the swirling blackness enveloped her.

SEVERAL HOURS LATER, Sara opened her eyes, disoriented by her strange surroundings. The sea of white first led her to believe that she had stumbled into a snowstorm. *But that's ridiculous,* she reminded herself. *It never snows in Phoenix.* She blinked in an attempt to clear her blurry vision. Her puzzled gaze took in the white walls, the white ceiling, the white tile floor. Even the stiff sheet covering her was white. Where was she?

A deep voice broke into her puzzled musings. "You're awake."

At the wonderfully familiar voice, Sara tried to focus on Noah, seated a few feet away. "I think I am."

He extricated himself from the too-small vinyl chair and stood beside the bed. "Here," he said, holding out a glass of water, "you probably need this."

She gratefully accepted Noah's help to sit up. As Sara sipped thirstily, she discovered that even drinking required a major effort.

"Thanks," she whispered as he laid her back on the pillow. "My mouth feels all fuzzy," she complained, licking her dry lips with her tongue.

"That's the shot they gave you when they stitched you up," he explained.

"My head feels as if it's filled with cotton, too."

He brushed her hair back from the thick bandage wrapped around her head. "Just think of it as a cheap drunk," he suggested.

She pressed her fingers against her temple. "I have stitches?"

"A few. They'll never show under your hair," he hurried to assure her.

"Was I in an accident?" she asked blankly.

He took her hand in his. "You don't remember?"

Sara wrinkled her brow. "I'm trying. I remember going to Malcolm's party." Her eyes shadowed. "Is he dead, or did I dream it?"

"He's dead."

"I thought so. And I remember stealing the crown." Her teeth worried her bottom lip. "But it was a forgery," she recalled. "And you left me to go to Malcolm's. But I figured out that Gizella had the real crown." She looked up at him. "Did I tell you about that?"

"I heard you explaining it to Peter," he said with a smile. "By the way, it was a brilliant bit of detective work."

"Thank you," she responded absently, her mind still focused on her problem. Sara sighed. "I can remember driving to Gizella's. But that's all."

He bent down, brushing a soft kiss against her dry lips. "Get some sleep," he suggested. "We'll talk about everything later."

Sara gratefully closed her eyes. "Later," she agreed in a whisper.

Noah remained by her side all night, glowering at one charge nurse who suggested he might go home and let the staff take care of Sara. When Sara awoke the next morning, the first thing she saw was Noah's tawny eyes studying her intently.

"You look awful," she murmured, her gaze taking in his stubbled jaw, his rumpled clothing, his uncombed hair. Deep lines she'd never noticed before creased his face.

"Thanks a bunch," he drawled. "I'm glad to see you're back to normal."

She hitched herself up in the bed, cringing a little as rocks tumbled around in her head. "I didn't mean it that way," she argued weakly. "It's just that you look tired. How long have you been here."

"Since you came in. About eighteen hours ago."

"Have I been sleeping all that time?" she asked incredulously.

"You woke for a few minutes, but the rest of the time you were out like a light. Not that it was any surprise; that shot they gave you down in the emergency room was strong enough to fell a bull moose."

She lifted her fingers experimentally to her head. "I was shot, wasn't I?"

"The bullet grazed your head."

"I remember. I was shot, and you were yelling at me."

He flinched inwardly at that one. Of all the damned things for her to remember, it had to be that. "I was worried about you. You had no business risking your life like that."

"I couldn't let Gizella kill you," she countered. She closed her eyes. "Are we going to fight?"

He took her hand in his. "No."

Sara didn't open her eyes, but she did smile. "I'm glad."

They both remained silent for a time. "Did you get the crown back in time for the press conference?"

"Yes."

"And everything went well?"

"Yes."

Again, that slight smile. "I'm happy for you, Noah. I know how much it meant to you."

It took all Noah's willpower not to shout at Sara. Not to tell her that the crown didn't mean a damn thing when compared with her life. But she'd been through enough already. He remained silent.

"Your sister was here most of the night," he told her after a while. "She went home to fix Kevin's breakfast and let him know that you were going to be all right."

"Jennifer was here?"

He nodded. "With that guy, what's his name."

"Brian," she murmured.

"Yeah. I think she's got something to tell you about that."

Sara's lips curved into a small, satisfied smile. "I thought she would.... What happened to Peter?" she asked.

"He's in a lot of trouble, but the authorities are taking into account the way he came through in the end. I think he'll probably get off with a light enough sentence."

"Good. He wasn't really all that bad. Did you hear what Malcolm did to him?"

"He told us."

"I forgot to ask—who did Malcolm leave all that money to?"

"The Metropolitan Museum of Art," Noah answered casually.

Sara's eyes flew open. "You're kidding! The man didn't have a philanthropic bone in his body."

A light twinkled in Noah's eyes. "His motives were far from altruistic, sweetheart. The stipulation is that part of all those millions go toward building the Malcolm Brand memorial wing."

She sighed. "He's still trying to buy respect. As smart as he was, Malcolm never did figure out he had to earn it."

Noah heard the depression in Sara's voice and sought for something to make her smile. "I brought you a present."

She glanced over at him warily. "Last time you brought me something, it was a risqué burglar's outfit. I shudder to think what you have up your sleeve this time."

He picked up a book from the chair and dropped it in her lap. "I figured you might want something to read until we could get you sprung from here," he suggested.

Sara picked up the book. "That's very nice of you, Noah," she said blankly. Her eyes widened as she took in the cover. "It's the new Jake Hawke book! And an advance copy, no less." She looked at him suspiciously. "How did you get your hands on this?"

He shrugged. "Don't worry; I didn't steal it. I happen to know the author."

"You know Max Ryder? Why didn't you tell me before?"

"It's a little complicated."

"You know Jake Hawke's creator." Sara sighed happily. Her eyes brightened, banishing the shadow of pain that had resided in them earlier. "Noah, do you think I could meet Mr. Ryder?"

He rubbed his chin as he considered the idea. "I'd say that could be arranged." Deciding that it was now or never, he took a deep breath before continuing. "In fact, you already have."

Sara stared at him as she attempted to understand. As she watched the flush darken his neck above his shirt collar, comprehension slowly dawned.

"It's you, isn't it?" she asked softly. "You're Max Ryder." She frowned. "But you told me Noah Winfield was your real name."

"It is. I had to use a pseudonym for professional reasons."

"I don't understand."

He sat down on the edge of the bed, covering her hands with his. "I had signed an agreement that I wouldn't write about my experiences after I left the army. While the Jake Hawke books are fiction, I'll admit they were loosely based on actual incidents. Keeping my own name off the cover helps keep me out of trouble."

Sara considered that for a moment. "You *are* Jake Hawke, aren't you, Noah?"

His jaw tensed. "Would it matter if Jake and I possessed a few of the same qualities?"

She rubbed her palm along the rough line of his cheek. "I always thought the two of you had a great deal in common. I suppose that's why I could never see you as a common thief." She smiled. "No wonder everything happened so fast between us. You had a head start."

He arched a dark brow. "A head start?"

She laughed lightly, pressing her lips against his, punctuating her answer with kisses. "I was fascinated with Jake long before I met you, Noah. It's as if you sent in your alter ego to pave the way."

He braced his hands on either side of her, observing her intently. "I remember you once saying that no woman would ever be able to live with the guy."

"Jake does have a few rough edges," she admitted. "But I imagine he could be domesticated, given enough time."

Noah grinned down at her. "Know anyone brave enough to take on the job?"

Sara's blue eyes danced as she considered the matter. "I just may. Depends on what you're offering."

His fingers spread around her waist, and his thumbs rubbed sensually against her midriff. "How about a lifetime with an admittedly jaded ex-army intelligence officer turned writer who plans to scandalize our children by carrying their mother off to bed every chance he gets?"

"That's not bad for a beginning," she replied, her thumbnail tracing his smiling lips. "Did you say children?"

"I want it all, Sara," Noah said huskily. "You, a houseful of kids. . . . Hell, even a dog. I want us to be a family."

"I like children; I always pictured having a big family someday. Maybe one of them could turn out to be an artist. Or a writer." Sara smiled. "Of course, we could always end up with a family full of little bankers."

"If they look like you, I won't even care," he promised. "Then you'll marry me?"

"If we're going to have all those children, I suppose marriage would be in order."

Relief swept over him, and he kissed her hungrily, unable to believe his luck.

When the blissful kiss finally ended, Sara tilted her head back to look up at him. "Noah, are you going to write about all this?"

"Probably. It'll make one helluva story. Although my agent will probably scream bloody murder when he gets the manuscript."

"Really?" she asked curiously. "Why is that?"

He grinned down at her. "What would you say about the next Jake Hawke adventure having a happy ending?"

Her blue eyes drank in the rugged features of this man she loved—a man who had spent far too many years with danger and intrigue as his only companions.

A dazzling smile lit Sara's face as she twined her arms about Noah's neck. "I'd say it's about time."

Take 4 books & a surprise gift FREE

SPECIAL LIMITED-TIME OFFER

Mail to **Harlequin Reader Service®**

In the U.S.
901 Fuhrmann Blvd.
P.O. Box 1394
Buffalo, N.Y. 14240-1394

In Canada
P.O. Box 2800, Station "A"
5170 Yonge Street
Willowdale, Ontario M2N 6J3

YES! Please send me 4 free Harlequin Superromance® novels and my free surprise gift. Then send me 4 brand-new novels every month as they come off the presses. Bill me at the low price of $2.50 each—a 10% saving off the retail price. There are no shipping, handling or other hidden costs. There is no minimum number of books I must purchase. I can always return a shipment and cancel at any time. Even if I never buy another book from Harlequin, the 4 free novels and the surprise gift are mine to keep forever.

Name	(PLEASE PRINT)

Address	Apt. No.

City	State/Prov.	Zip/Postal Code

This offer is limited to one order per household and not valid to present subscribers. Price is subject to change.   DOSR-SUB-1R

WHAT READERS SAY ABOUT
HARLEQUIN INTRIGUE . . .

Fantastic! I am looking forward to reading other Intrigue books.

> *P.W.O., Anderson, SC

This is the first Harlequin Intrigue I have read . . . I'm hooked.

> *C.M., Toledo, OH

I really like the suspense . . . the twists and turns of the plot.

> *L.E.L., Minneapolis, MN

I'm really enjoying your Harlequin Intrigue line . . . mystery and suspense mixed with a good love story.

> *B.M., Denton, TX

*Names available on request.